PRAIS

"Storytelling in a different league ... perfectly
poised to capture children's imaginations."

THE CHIME SEEKERS

ROSS MONTGOMERY

WALKER
BOOKS

First published 2021 by Walker Books Ltd
87 Vauxhall Walk, London SE11 5HJ

2 4 6 8 10 9 7 5 3

Text © 2021 Ross Montgomery
Cover and interior illustrations © 2021 David Dean

The right of Ross Montgomery to be identified as author
of this work has been asserted in accordance with the
Copyright, Designs and Patents Act 1988

This book has been typeset in Adobe Garamond Pro and Matrix

Printed and bound by CPI Group (UK) Ltd, Croydon CR0 4YY

British Library Cataloguing in Publication Data:
a catalogue record for this book is available from the British Library

ISBN 978-1-4063-9119-0

www.walker.co.uk

For Jules

Come away, O human child!
To the waters and the wild
With a faerie, hand in hand,
For the world's more full of weeping
than you can understand.

– W. B. Yeats, "The Stolen Child"

THE NEW HOUSE

YANNI HATED THE HOUSE THE MOMENT HE SAW IT. It was nothing like their old house. Their old house was a ground-floor flat on a terraced street, tucked between homes on every side. It had a blue front door with gold numbers that led right from the street to the living room. There was just enough room for Yanni and Mum and Dad to live together. Being inside it felt like being hugged.

This house sat alone in an empty field, framed by cold October sky. It stuck out from the earth like it wasn't meant to be there. The front door was the colour of a rotten tooth.

"Our own driveway," said Mum, shaking her head. "I still can't believe it. It's going to change everything."

"And listen – do you hear that?" asked Dad.

Yanni listened, but the only sound he could hear was the rain prickling on the car roof and the *slack, slack, slack* of wipers on the windscreen.

"Silence," said Dad blissfully. "You could make all the noise you wanted out here, and no one would ever notice."

Yanni wasn't sure why this was a good thing. Places were *supposed* to be noisy: it meant people were close. He peered out of the rain-streaked car windows and searched the fields surrounding them. He had never been anywhere so empty, so flat, so close to the ground before. It made the sky look enormous, pressing down like a vast set of hands. There were no other houses.

"You said it was a village," muttered Yanni.

Mum pointed down the road. "Fallow Hall's ten minutes that way. You're going to love it, Yanni! There's a little square and a church – and the bus stop, of course. You'll be using that every day after half-term's over!"

Yanni's hairs stood on end. *Riddleton.* His new school. He'd be joining halfway through the first term, weeks behind everyone else. The move was supposed to have been finished months ago, but it had been delayed so many times that Yanni had been forced to start at another secondary back home, before leaving after a few weeks. The teachers hadn't even bothered to learn his name.

He stared at the ugly house, the grey sky, the barren fields. This was where he lived now. He'd left behind his friends and everything he had ever known for … *this*?

"Right!" said Dad. "The movers will be here soon. Let's see how the decorators have got on!"

He reached for the ignition. Mum shot out a hand to stop him, her eyes wide and desperate.

"No! She needs at least another—"

It was too late. Dad had turned the key. The car fell silent – and then filled with a blood-curdling scream that sang off the windows and shook the air.

"I'm sorry," Dad whispered. "I'm so, so sorry."

Mum slumped weakly in her seat. "Oh God. That's it. That's it for the rest of the afternoon."

Yanni glared at the screaming lump beside him. There – squirming away in her car seat like the Queen of all Maggots – was the reason they had moved to this horrible place.

Ari.

Yanni's baby sister had arrived one year ago, screaming, and she'd hardly paused for breath since. She screamed when she woke up; she screamed when you held her; she screamed when you put her down. The slightest thing would set her off – loud noises, quiet noises, medium-sized noises – and it had got even worse since she'd started teething. Now she kept Mum and Dad up until dawn, bleeding out their energy drop by drop, transforming them into zombies. They slept when they could; they ate when they remembered. Sometimes Dad fell asleep while talking to Yanni, mid-sentence.

"Give her to me," said Dad wearily. "I'll put her in the sling for a bit."

"No, no, it's her teeth," said Mum. "Give her the ring."

"I don't have the ring, she threw it out the window."

"Oh God."

"Just get her a biscuit."

"Where are the biscuits?"

"In the bag."

"They're not here."

"No, the *bag* bag."

"This *is* the bag bag!"

Yanni sighed. Mum and Dad bickered all the time now. The house move had only made things worse.

No one made you move house, Yanni wanted to say. *No one made you have another baby.*

But he didn't; instead he let the words sink back down his throat and curdle in his stomach, and stepped outside into the hammering rain.

The house looked even worse than it did from the car: a hulking grim brick box, tired and ugly. The driveway turned into a cracked lane that led to the village. Yanni could see an old faded sign announcing that you were now entering Fallow Hall. Someone had put a statue at the base, a stone frog slumped over a toadstool with a broken fishing rod. It looked sad, like everything else around here. One of its eyes was missing; the other one scowled at Yanni like it was annoyed to see him.

"Well, I don't want to be here, either," Yanni muttered.

It was true: Yanni had never wanted to leave his life behind. But now that Ari was here, their old house – their old, perfect little hug of a house – was too small. Mum and Dad couldn't afford a bigger place in town. That was when they started talking about moving to the countryside: they could have more space for less money; Dad could take a break from his job and look after Ari for a few years; Mum could start working again. His parents had been so excited that they made the decision without telling Yanni first.

They hadn't once asked him what he wanted. And now here he was, miles away from anything he'd ever known. He gazed down at his phone … and, sure enough, there was no reception. He couldn't even call his friends.

"So! What do you think, mate?"

Dad was standing by the car, trying to wrestle Ari into a baby sling. She was struggling against the straps for all she was worth, howling and flailing her chubby arms.

"I hate it," said Yanni.

"*Pfft!* Stop exaggerating," said Dad. "Think of how much space you'll have out here! And we've got family just around the corner in Riddleton, too. How good is that?"

Yanni bit his lip in frustration. "Dad – I don't know anything about Amy. I've told you a hundred times!"

Dad scoffed, narrowly avoiding Ari's flailing fists. "What do you mean, you don't know her? She's your cousin."

"Second cousin," said Yanni. "And she never even talks to me at those family things. She just ... stands around, being weird."

Dad didn't reply. He'd finally got Ari in the sling, but she was writhing like a trapped salmon and booting him repeatedly in the groin. Dad sagged against the car, just letting it happen, like a cliff edge surviving a storm. He wasn't even listening any more.

Yanni sighed and walked into the house by himself. It never used to be like this. There was a time, before Ari was born, where *everything* had centred on what he wanted. Yanni had only to ask for something – a film night, a sleepover – and Mum or Dad would make it happen. Things hadn't been like that for a while now. These days, he felt like he had to fight just to be noticed.

The inside was, somehow, worse than the outside. The decorators had been here for weeks, painting the walls and pulling out the old carpets, but it still looked like a set of barren rooms. Mum was standing by herself in a cavernous living room, grinning from ear to ear.

"Massive, isn't it?" she said.

"Freezing," said Yanni, with a shiver.

"It's these lovely big windows," said Mum happily. "They let the cold in. That's why we got the decorators to fix this up!"

She patted a huge stone fireplace beside her. It clearly hadn't been used in years: the inside was caked with cobwebs and dry leaves. A heavy iron panel had been ripped off the front, and now rested against the wall on one side. It made the fireplace look like a gaping mouth.

"Can you believe it?" she said. "They had a beautiful working fireplace, and they just blocked it up!"

Yanni shuddered. The fireplace wasn't beautiful at all: it was horrible. He wasn't surprised that the last owners had blocked it up. The bricks inside were all scorched black, and covered in...

"What are those?" he asked.

Someone had carved symbols into the bricks. Rings, circles, spirals – dozens of them, clustered together in the dark like watching eyes. Mum caught sight of Yanni's face, and squeezed him into a hug.

"We'll sand those off tomorrow. Want to see your new bedroom?"

Yanni glowed. Usually he would have squirmed away from a hug – he was nearly twelve, and felt too old for stuff like that now. But he didn't get many times like this any more – him and Mum, just the two of them. He couldn't explain how much he missed them: simple, thoughtless kisses as she walked past, or being bear-hugged from behind. There were some people who could always say how they were feeling, whether they were angry or lonely or sad, but Yanni wasn't one of them.

They went upstairs and found his new bedroom. Yanni's heart sank: it was the worst one of all. The rest of the house had been stripped and painted, but this room had been forgotten. Stained curtains still hung at the window. There was a moth-eaten carpet on the floor, with faded shapes where furniture had stood.

"Oh, for heaven's sake!" Mum cried. "They were supposed to do this room, too…"

In the centre of the room was an old wooden bed frame, stood like a waiting guest. Yanni gulped. "I'm not going to have to sleep in that, am I?"

"Absolutely not," said Mum. "It could be infested."

"Infested?"

"Bedbugs." She shuddered. "They hide in the cracks."

Yanni recoiled. The bed frame was riddled from top to bottom with hairline fractures. There could be *things* living inside them, waiting to scuttle out and bite him while he slept. The thought made him want to jump in a hot shower and never stop washing.

There was a scream from downstairs – Ari had arrived.

Mum sighed. "I'm sorry, darling. We'll see if the movers can help fix it. Can you take down those old curtains while I feed Ari?"

She left, and that was their moment together gone. Yanni pushed down the words bubbling up inside him. That was all he got now: half a hug, and the worst room in the house.

He gazed out of the window: a single sheet of glass, ringed with mildew. His old bedroom had looked out over his neighbours' back gardens; this one looked out over the bare blank fields of Fallow Hall. Yanni's heart sank even further. He had never seen anywhere so cold, so bleak, so unwelcoming in all his life. There was nothing for him out here, *nothing*...

He stopped. He was wrong: the fields weren't completely empty. In the far distance, the grass suddenly bulged into a mound. It was too small to be a hill, too big to be nothing; but the moment Yanni saw it, he felt the shrivel of skin against his bones.

He knew, deep in his gut, that there was something wrong with it. It was like a monster crouched beneath the earth: a boil in the grass. Yanni could swear that his ears even started ringing when he looked at it – like high-pitched bells, echoing in a distant empty room.

Don't ever go near that thing, whispered a voice at the back of his head. *It's bad.*

Yanni shook himself, and quickly turned away from the window. Of course the mound was bad: everything in Fallow Hall was bad. He was stuck in a horrible house with a horrible baby and a horrible family that didn't even care about him.

How could things possibly get any worse?

THE GIFT

YANNI WOKE UP EARLY THE NEXT MORNING. HE didn't have a choice – without the tatty curtains the room was flooded with daylight.

His bedroom – if you could call it that – looked even worse than it had the day before. The movers had taken the old bed and carpet, so now it was just bare, splintered floorboards covered in cardboard boxes. Yanni had begun unpacking them yesterday, but after he started he realized he had nowhere to put anything.

He got up, trying to work out which box had his clothes in it. After a while, he lost patience and started emptying boxes onto the floor. It was only when he'd found a top and trousers that he noticed the framed photo lying beside them.

It was a family portrait, taken last year. Mum and Dad sat in the centre with newborn Ari between them, glowing with shell-shocked happiness. Yanni stood to one side, his hair gelled and combed, scowling in a suit jacket that was far too big. He looked like an undertaker. Behind him were two other adults, also dressed in smart clothes. They stood with their arms circling the family, gazing proudly at the camera as if to say: *Yes, that's right; they're all ours.*

Yiayia and Pappou.

Yanni felt a tug on his heart. Normally his family went to visit his grandparents every summer – but this year, the annual trip to Greece had been cancelled because of the problems with the house move. It was the first summer in Yanni's life that he hadn't spent lounging in a sunlit courtyard, being dragged into the kitchen ten times a day so Yiayia could squeeze his cheek and stuff him full of dripping *loukoumades* or great wobbling slices of *galatopita*. Or being summoned to Pappou's study, rich with the scent of coffee and cigarettes, so he could tell Yanni family stories and secretly give him crisp banknotes and promise that he'd get even more next time if he was a good boy and learned to speak Greek. Yanni had missed it all so much. The late warm outdoor dinners that stretched long into the night, where he could stay up as late as he wanted, lost in a haze of chatter and food in the afterglow of a summer's day…

It all felt so far away now. Whenever Yanni did see his grandparents again, he knew it wouldn't be the same. He was no longer the precious only grandchild of the family; he was another man of the house. When he spoke to Yiayia and Pappou on the phone, on name days and at Easter, they just asked if he was being a good brother and then Pappou would tell him off for not speaking more Greek. Yanni felt like he had crossed over a threshold into a place where summer was gone and hugs didn't exist any more, and there was no way of ever turning back. It had all changed so fast...

That was when he saw it: a shimmer of blue glass, buried in the clothes on the floor.

It was a necklace on a leather thread. A blue stone that had a white circle in the middle, and then a pale blue circle with a dark blue dot inside that. Yanni recognized it at once: it had been a gift from Yiayia on their last trip to Greece, when Mum was still pregnant with Ari. Yiayia was always buying him little presents.

"This is for you," she had said, holding up the necklace. "A *mati*. You like, yes?"

Yanni wasn't sure if he did like it – the blue stones were everywhere in tourist shops, on keyrings and wall hangings and jewellery, but they'd always creeped him out a bit. They looked too much like eyes.

Yiayia tied it carefully around his neck.

"I remember when you were a baby, *mátia mou* – so beautiful, but so sick! Many nights you were in the hospital. Pappou and me, we pray night and day for you to be safe."

She placed her hand on the stone that now hung at his chest, just above his heart.

"Is always to protect you. And when your sister is here, you protect her, yes?" She cupped his face, and her hands were as soft as tissue paper. "Good luck for nice boy."

Yanni had promised that he would, and then he had put the necklace in a drawer when he had come home and forgotten about it. And now, here it was in this horrible place: the very last thing Yiayia had given him, back when he was her precious only grandchild. It even smelled like her perfume.

Yanni glanced up to make sure he was alone. Then he quickly kissed the necklace, hung it around his neck so no one could see it, and left his bedroom.

Mum and Dad had been busy: the hallway was lined with framed family photos. Yanni found Dad downstairs on his knees in the living room, silently sanding the carvings off the back wall of the fireplace. He was so tired he didn't even look up when Yanni walked by. Ari was suspended from the kitchen door frame in her bouncer, wailing forlornly while Mum unpacked boxes with grim determination.

"She was up all night," said Mum, her voice frazzled. "Can you take her for a bit, Yanni? I think she wants you."

Mum was right: the moment Ari saw him, she held out her arms and whined. Yanni sighed. Ari *always* wanted him – it was the only thing that stopped her crying sometimes. Everyone told him how lucky he was to have a sister who loved him so much, but Yanni didn't feel lucky. It just meant he got his hair pulled and his face drooled on or savaged by her one and only razor-sharp tooth. He lifted her out of the bouncer and, sure enough, she dug it straight into his nose.

"Ow!" he muttered. "Stop, that hurts – wait, why are you squirming?"

Yanni knew why – she didn't want to be held; she wanted to stand up, even though she'd just made him pick her up. He tried to put her back in the bouncer but she cried, so he let her stand on the floor instead while he held her hands; but she still kept crying – she wanted to stand up by herself, even though she didn't know how to yet.

"Yanni, can you not get her so worked up, please?" Mum sighed.

He kept trying to hold her, but Ari wouldn't take no for an answer. Eventually he decided to let her try standing by herself; but the moment he let go of her hands, she keeled over sideways and hit the floor. Her scream filled the room like a flare.

Mum snapped round. "Yanni! What did I just say?"

25

Yanni burned with the injustice of it all. "It's not my fault! She wouldn't let me hold her!"

But Mum wasn't listening. She picked up Ari and made comforting sounds to soothe her. Yanni watched as his sister burrowed greedily into his mother's shoulder and felt his insides blacken like burning paper. It seemed like all he did was disappoint people nowadays.

Dad walked into the kitchen, dusting off his hands. "Right! That's the fireplace done – next stop, Ari's bedroom!"

Mum slumped against the kitchen counter, cradling Ari listlessly. "What about tonight? Did you get everything sorted?"

Dad looked blank. "What's tonight?"

Mum stared at him. The room went still. When she next spoke, her voice was very calm and very level, like a tray of glasses balanced on the tip of a pin.

"The thing I mentioned yesterday," she said. "And last week. And the week before that. The thing that you promised – *promised* – you wouldn't forget."

Dad slapped his head.

"Oh, *that*! Ha ha ha. Of course I haven't forgotten!" He dragged Yanni out of the kitchen. "Yiannaki, come and help me with these boxes!"

Yiannaki was Dad's pet name for him – he always used it when he wanted something. Yanni waited until

Dad closed the kitchen door before he spoke.

"What's Mum talking about? What's happening tonight?"

"No idea," said Dad nervously. "I was going to ask you. I think she's confused – it's not like me to forget something important."

This was the biggest lie in the history of the world. Dad forgot everything – and it'd become even worse now that Ari kept him awake half the night. He hastily scrolled through his phone calendar and his eyes lit up.

"Ah – of course! All Hallows' Eve!"

Yanni frowned. "What's All Hallows' Eve?"

"Halloween, you muppet! Didn't they teach you anything at that school?"

Yanni felt a little needle of sadness. *Halloween.* His friends back home would be having a party tonight, like they always did. They'd told him that they weren't, but Yanni knew they were only saying that so they didn't hurt his feelings.

"That must be it," said Dad, sighing with relief. "Your mum wants to make a good impression on the village. We can't let trick-or-treaters leave empty-handed on our first Halloween here, can we?" He reached into his pocket and handed Yanni some coins. "Here – pop to the village shop and get some sweets. And a pumpkin – and some decorations, too. We'll have a proper Halloween party to celebrate the move! Maybe after Ari's gone to bed, you and I can stay up late and watch a scary film together. How about it?"

Yanni felt a flicker inside him. He couldn't remember the last time they'd had a film night. Part of him felt stupid for being so excited about hanging out with his parents, but another part of him wanted it more than anything in the whole entire world.

"Yeah, sure, maybe."

"*Maybe!* Such a poser. I can see right..." He looked down, and stopped. "Hey – your *mati!*"

Yanni blushed. Ari had drooled on his T-shirt, so the glass eye was visible through the damp cotton. Dad beamed.

"Yiayia would love that you're wearing it, you know. It's supposed to protect you from the evil eye."

He crossed himself, just like Yiayia did in church.

"She's so superstitious! You had to keep out of her way on Halloween when I was a kid – she spent the whole day spitting on the floor to scare off the Devil. *F'tou!*"

He mimed spitting on the floor. Yanni snorted, despite himself. It was nice, joking around with Dad like this – that didn't happen very often now. Before he could enjoy it too much, Dad shooed him out of the front door.

"Quick! It's supposed to rain later. You can take in the sights of Fallow Hall on the way!"

"What sights?" muttered Yanni sarcastically.

"Enough of that," Dad shot back. "There's loads of things to see. The village square, and the church – they've even got a dolmen!"

Yanni blinked – all at once, he felt like he could see the strange grass mound right in front of him, and hear the ringing in the back of his head. Without meaning to, he found himself reaching up and holding the necklace for comfort.

"Wh-what's a dolmen?" he asked nervously, dreading the answer.

Dad just smiled – and when he spoke, the voice that came out was a spot-on impression of Yiayia.

"See for yourself, *mátia mou*."

FALLOW HALL

YANNI MADE HIS WAY DOWN THE DIRT LANE towards the village. It was another overcast and dreary day outside, with clouds the colour of bleach. He couldn't help but glance at the one-eyed frog statue as he walked past – it really did look like it was glaring at him.

After what felt like for ever, he reached a crossroads that split the lane into four directions. Each one looked equally unpromising. In one corner was an old, weathered signpost, all rotten wood and peeling paint. Someone had stuck an old hat on top of it for a joke.

"Ha ha ha," said Yanni.

He didn't know why he was talking out loud – it wasn't like the signpost could hear him. He sighed, and read the faded words on the wooden arms.

"VILLAGE SHOP, CHURCH, PLAYING FIELD..." Yanni paused. "DOLMEN."

He gulped. He might as well get it over with. He made his way down the first path and, after a few minutes, a wooden plank crossed a ditch and became a worn track leading to the middle of a field.

There, brooding like a blister in the earth, was the mound of grass he'd seen from his bedroom window. The dolmen.

He could see now that it wasn't really a mound. It was a ring of ancient stones, covered over with grass so it formed a kind of bunker. Three huge rocks made an entrance at the front, leading to a crawl space of wet darkness. A wooden placard stuck in the ground explained that the dolmen was a Neolithic burial mound. In olden days, people used to call them faerie mounds, and believed that if you tried to plough the field around them, the faeries would come and get you.

Don't go near it, said the voice in his head. *It's evil.*

Yanni stood and stared at the dolmen. He could hear the ringing in his ears again. Now that he was closer, he realized the ringing sounded more like bells: thousands of tiny bells, a half-step out of tune with one another, coming from somewhere far away. Yanni glanced around uneasily. It had to be the wind rattling through the electricity pylons.

He snorted. He was too old to scare himself like this. His friends back home would have laughed to see him now. He scurried away back to the crossroads and followed the second turning, which led to the village square.

After a few minutes, the path became a cluster of grey houses surrounding a patch of grass. Yanni was wondering how much further he'd have to walk before he came to the village square … when he spotted the bus stop. He looked around – and then it all clicked. This *was* the village square; this dismal ring of houses was Fallow Hall.

"They said it was nice," he said out loud in sheer shock.

Stop doing that, said the voice in his head.

He found the village shop in a corner of the square. It was the least welcoming shop he'd ever seen in his life: the windows were dark and barred, and the doorway was surrounded by old burglar alarms. Inside, the sagging shelves of ancient stock were lit by the glare of a single bulb.

"Yes? What do you want?"

It wasn't a friendly question – but the man behind the counter didn't look friendly, either. He was hunched in a stained vest, scowling at Yanni over a set of smeared glasses. The tip of a snaggle-tooth poked from his bottom lip like a little tusk.

Yanni looked around helplessly. This shop didn't look like it sold pumpkins or decorations. "Er … do you have any sweets?"

The man harrumphed. "Might have some mint imperials in the back. Wait here."

He started the lengthy process of manoeuvring from behind the counter, clearly annoyed at having to move. Yanni was amazed. He'd never been inside a shop that was so determined not to sell anything. He picked up a magazine from the rack beside him and saw, to his amazement, that it was almost two years old.

"Oi!"

Yanni jumped. The shopkeeper was stood by the back door, glaring at him.

"I wouldn't do that if I were you," he snapped. "Put it back."

It took Yanni a moment to realize what the shopkeeper was suggesting. He shoved the magazine back in the rack, mortified. He hadn't even considered reading it, let alone stealing it. He stared at his feet, burning with anger as the shopkeeper shuffled into the back room. He hated this place, *hated* it...

His eye caught on something – a fifty-pence piece that had rolled under the rack. Normally Yanni would have handed it over, but he didn't want to give anything to this horrible man. Instead he pretended to tie his laces and slipped the coin into his pocket before the shopkeeper came back with the mints. It wasn't much of a rebellion, but it still felt good.

Yanni wasn't ready to go home yet. He made his way back to the crossroads, followed the signpost down a third path, and came to a small church with a neatly trimmed graveyard. It was painfully obvious to Yanni that there would be nothing interesting inside, and sure enough he was proved right. This wasn't like the great golden churches that they visited with Yiayia and Pappou in Greece, with their glowing candles and gleaming stone; this was a set of dull pews facing a plain dirty window. There was a stone font at the back; a small sign explained that it had been damaged in a big storm in 1703 and rebuilt the following year.

Yanni searched for anything else that might kill more time, but there wasn't anything. He turned to go home … and realized he wasn't alone.

There was a woman beside the door. She was sat bolt upright on a wooden chair, both knees pressed together and her hands folded in her lap. Her head had fallen so far forward that her face was obscured. She was so completely still, so silent, that Yanni hadn't noticed her when he came in. She might as well have been a statue. Yanni realized, with alarm, that he couldn't see her breathing.

"H-hello?" he asked. "Are you…?"

The woman's head snapped up, fast as a bear trap.

"Goodness! You gave me a shock. Are you here for the font?"

Yanni almost leaped a foot in the air. He was so startled that he forgot how to form sentences. "I – no! Sorry, I didn't… What?"

The woman glanced him up and down. "You're not from around here, are you?"

Yanni wasn't sure what that meant. "We moved here yesterday. The big house just outside the village."

The woman looked surprised. "Well! I can't remember the last time a family came to Fallow Hall. There were dozens of children living here when I was a girl, but they all left after that boy went missing."

Yanni felt a shudder up his spine. "M-missing?"

The old woman laughed. "Oh, don't worry – it would have been long before your parents were even born! Some poor boy disappeared one night and never came back – no trace of him. John, his name was. All the other families left after that." She sighed. "It's not the first tragedy to afflict Fallow Hall, you know – the village has quite a history! It was once a thriving market town, but then the church spire collapsed and crushed the mayor in the storm of 1703, and then the crops failed, and the next mayor fell down a well and broke both his legs, and then the horses went lame, and the farmers got smallpox…"

Yanni had a feeling that she wasn't going to stop. "Is there … anything nice to do around here?"

The woman looked puzzled. "What do you mean?"

Yanni waved his arms around. "You know. Activities."

She frowned. "There's always the playing field," she said, as if suggesting that Yanni consider cutting off both his legs.

The playing field was the worst of all. The goalposts were cracked and green with mould, their nets slung from rusted hooks. A drain must have become blocked somewhere and the pitch was covered in an inch of stagnant water. It made a dark mirror of the field and Yanni could see himself, small and scared and alone, standing beneath a rolling sheet of grey clouds. A dead branch stuck up from the water like a piece of twisted bone. It looked like something out of a horror film.

Yanni gazed around in despair. It had taken him less than half an hour to see everything Fallow Hall had to offer, and it was even worse than he'd expected. There weren't even any other children. A vision of his life in Fallow Hall stretched out before him – long, endless, lonely days like this. He checked his phone to see if any of his friends had texted him yet, but he still didn't have any reception.

And suddenly it all came boiling up at once: a surge of anger, greater than he'd ever felt in his life. The move, the new school, Mum and Dad, Yiayia and Pappou, and Ari, Ari, *Ari…*

"I hate this place," he said.

There was a flash: a sudden, almost imperceptible flicker of light that lit up the field around him like a stage set. In that instant, Yanni felt as if he'd caught sight of another village, lurking just beneath the surface of this one. A village that had been there the whole time, lying in wait, like a man leering behind a curtain.

The image faded as fast as it came; Yanni was left dazzled, trying to remember what he had just seen, but there was nothing except black spots in his eyes and the faint sound of bells at the back of his head. There was a sudden crash of thunder, and when Yanni blinked, he saw that the clouds on the horizon were smearing black. The storm was here. If he didn't run home fast, he was going to get soaked.

He turned to take one final look at the football pitch … and stopped.

There was a raven perched on the rotten goalposts, staring right at him with eyes like beads of black glass. It had appeared silently, as if from nowhere, like a predator.

The downpour came, and Yanni's nerves finally gave in – he turned and fled the field, racing back towards home and safety, leaping over every crack in the lane without knowing why. He pushed down the thought that he was somehow leading the bird back to his house: it was just a bird, just a field, just a storm. But even so, he was sure he could feel the raven watching him the entire way home, a feeling that scuttled over the surface of his skin like bedbugs.

ALL HALLOWS' EVE

BY THE TIME YANNI RACED THROUGH THE FRONT door, he was completely soaked. Mum was with Ari in the living room, feeding her.

"Where have you been?" She glanced out of the windows at the hammering rain. "You weren't outside in *that*, were you?"

Yanni tried to hide his annoyance that she hadn't even noticed he was gone. He held up a sodden bag. "I had to get mint imperials."

Mum was confused. "Er ... why?"

Dad strolled in, looking triumphant. "For the trick-or-treaters!" He gave Mum a quick kiss. "I thought we could have a Halloween party tonight. Scary films, apple-bobbing, the lot!"

Mum stared at him, baffled. "We don't have time for that. What about the babysitter?"

Dad blinked. "Babysitter?"

Mum stopped feeding Ari. She froze. The temperature in the room plummeted.

"The babysitter," she said quietly. "The one you arranged for tonight. For our anniversary dinner."

Dad's face turned the colour of stale bread. Mum kept talking, her voice slowly sharpening to an edge.

"The dinner that we couldn't do last year because Ari had just been born. The dinner we had to cancel last month because of the move. The dinner you promised you'd sort for tonight because it's the last evening, *the only evening*, that we can do before my job starts."

Yanni glanced between Mum and Dad. This was going to be bad. Mum hadn't blinked in almost ten seconds. Dad looked like a man who'd accidentally locked himself in a petrol silo while holding a lighted match.

"I – I thought you wouldn't want to do it any more," he said quietly. "We've only just got here, and Ari didn't sleep and—"

Mum finally exploded. "Of course! Why would I still want to do it? It's only something I've been talking about for *months*!" She was crying now. "I don't believe it: I asked for one night off – *one night* where I'm not stuck at home looking after the kids – and you *still* forgot!"

Dad panicked. "I'll sort it! I'll find a babysitter and—"

"How?" she cried. "It's Friday night! It's *Halloween*!

No one's going to be free now, with just a few hours' notice!"

"I don't need a babysitter," said Yanni.

But no one was listening to him – Yanni might as well have not been there. Ari was crying again, harder than ever, flailing her limbs and trying to wriggle free from Mum.

"Oh, Yanni, take her, please…"

Mum dumped Ari into Yanni's arms, and suddenly he found himself standing in the centre of the living room with a screaming baby while Mum stormed into the kitchen and Dad ran after her, fumbling with his phone and swearing under his breath in Greek. The house was filled with the sound of slamming cupboard doors and recriminations, and the rain hissing against the glass like something trying to get inside, and Ari crying, and crying, and crying.

"So … are we still doing the film night?" he asked.

Later on – when the argument was over, and Ari had been put to bed, and all was dark – Yanni sat alone at the dining table.

The weather had only become worse as the day wore on. Yanni could barely hear the car pulling into the driveway over the sound of the pouring rain. There was a howl of wind as the front door was flung open and then Dad's cheerful voice bouncing around the hallway like a bright red balloon on a string.

"*Whoo!* Some weather, eh? Thanks again. Honestly, you're a real lifesaver… Just through here… He can't wait to see you!"

Dad strolled into the dining room, beaming from ear to ear. He had shaved and was wearing trousers that weren't tracksuit bottoms for the first time in months.

"Yiannaki – look who it is! It's your cousin, Amy!"

Yanni stared at the girl shuffling through the door. She had changed in the two years since he'd last seen her: now she had a bright pink streak in her hair, and wore bright pink glasses that were currently steamed up with rain. But just like always, she kept her head ducked low, like she was permanently avoiding a low branch. A backpack was slung over her shoulder.

"It turns out Amy was free tonight!" exclaimed Dad. "Isn't that great? You two, together again!"

"I wasn't doing anything," she mumbled.

Yanni glared at Dad in fury. He understood exactly what was going on: Dad had messed up, so now he was setting Yanni up with his weird cousin – his weird *second* cousin – like they were two toddlers on a play date. Amy looked just as uncomfortable with the situation as he did. She kept her gaze fixed on the ground, water dropping off her wet hair onto the floor in a loud, steady stream.

Dad clapped his hands, determined to ignore the awkward silence. "So! That's quite a T-shirt you're wearing, Amy. MONSTERS AND MAGIC... Is that a game?"

Amy blinked. "It's an MMORPG."

Dad looked blank. "Is that ... a type of game?"

Amy thought about it, then shrugged helplessly. The silence was now making itself at home, putting its feet up on the table with no intention of going anywhere. Dad opened his mouth to ask Amy another question, then decided that excruciating silence was preferable and shut it again. The three of them waited like furniture until Mum came downstairs. She was dressed smart, too – like how she used to look, before Ari was born. For some reason, this made Yanni want to smash up the table.

"I finally got her to sleep," she sighed. "She'll be good for a couple of hours. What time are Paula and Steve..."

She saw Amy and trailed off. "Amy!" she said, clearly surprised. "It's ... you!"

Dad grinned widely. "Isn't that great? Her parents are out tonight, but Amy was completely free!"

"I wasn't doing anything," Amy repeated.

Mum gave her a warm smile. "How ... *lovely!*"

Mum turned to Dad and managed to give him a look that communicated the following with just her eyes: *You stupid man, do you honestly think I am going to leave two children alone with a one-year-old baby? Pass me the phone so that I can hire a solicitor and immediately commence divorce proceedings.*

Dad quickly grabbed her hand.

"Listen. The restaurant's only in the next village. We'll be a few hours, tops. Ari's going to be exhausted after crying all day. Yanni and Amy are old enough to keep an eye on everything until we get back."

Mum's eyes flashed with concern. "They're only *eleven…*"

"I'm twelve," murmured Amy.

"See?" said Dad. "Practically a grown-up! Yanni knows how to look after his sister, doesn't he? I've even spoken to Mr and Mrs Edwards – remember that nice old couple down the road? They said if there's any trouble, Yanni can call them and they'll be here in minutes. I've left their number by the phone."

Mum looked at Dad, then at Yanni and Amy, weighing them all up – and gave a deep sigh.

"Fine. Did you hear that, Yanni? This is a lot of responsibility. I'm going to lock all the doors. You're not to answer them to anyone, understand? No trick-or-treaters, nothing!"

Yanni felt a tug in his guts. So that was it. Mum and Dad really were leaving him behind. The film night had been dropped like it was nothing. Yanni felt like he'd been offered a present, and then had it snatched out of his hands. He wanted to scream, to shout, to throw things … but instead he pushed down all the words and let them bubble inside him.

Mum turned to Amy. "How about you, Amy? Is there anything you need before we go?"

Amy shook her head. "No thanks, Mrs Kastellanos. I'll bless the house right after you leave."

Mum blinked. "You will?"

Amy finally looked up, suddenly animated.

"It's All Hallows' Eve. Tonight the boundaries between our world and the Land of Fae are at their very thinnest, and Fallow Hall is well known for its levels of spiritual activity. I'm going to read a few protective incantations to ward off any roaming faeries, and I made a rowan garland for the front door."

She pulled a ring of branches out of her backpack and beamed. Yanni stared at Mum and Dad in disbelief. Surely, after hearing all that, they weren't going to leave him alone with someone who talked about *faeries* just so they could have a nice dinner?

"A garland! How lovely," said Mum. "Now – keys!"

Yanni sat in shocked silence as his parents listed off the last few instructions, kissed him on the head, and locked the front door behind them. The sound of their car faded down the driveway, and then it was just the three of them: Yanni, Amy and the silence.

Yanni sat in shock. They were forgetting him. Everyone was forgetting him. His parents, his grandparents, his friends…

"Wow," Amy mumbled. "This is awkward, isn't it?"

She stood at the end of the table, shifting from foot to foot like a nervous horse. The thunder growled; the wind bristled at the windowpanes. Yanni didn't reply. He felt like if he opened his mouth, all the words he'd forced down would suddenly come out at once. Amy gave him a hopeful smile.

"So … your dad said you like playing games. Do you know ORC'S QUEST?"

Yanni shook his head.

"Omigod, omigod – *how*? It's, like, the best game *ever*!"

The change was instantaneous. Amy's face lit up. Her voice was suddenly light and animated again; her hands twitched with excitement. It was like she'd become a different person, comfortable in her own skin at last. She whipped out a box from her backpack and held it up. On the front was a lurid drawing of an orc beating the absolute stuffing out of a minotaur.

"It's a board game?" asked Yanni. He couldn't remember the last time he'd played a board game.

"The expanded edition!" said Amy. "It's not like a normal board game; you go on quests and build up your character over campaigns. You can be whatever you want: a knight, a tracker, a goblin, *anything*! I'm a level ten mage-chancellor already, but it's OK – you can still play if you're a beginner."

She started eagerly unpacking the box and arranging the figurines, so excited that she hadn't noticed Yanni hadn't actually agreed to play.

"It's best with three players," Amy explained, "but you can still make it work with two – me and my best friend, Chloe, play all the time." She snorted. "It's really funny, actually. She does the silliest voices for all the characters! I'd do them myself, but I'm rubbish at voices. You're going to Riddleton, right? That's where I go. Chloe, too. I can show you around on your first day, if you'd like."

Yanni felt his fingers grip the table. The new school was the last thing he wanted to think about now. The feeling in his stomach was getting worse, like a drawstring being pulled tighter.

"Right!" she said. "The rules take a few hours to explain, but you can learn as we play! You go first, as it's your first game. Which die do you want?"

She held out two dice for him, carved with runes – and Yanni finally snapped. He didn't want to play some stupid board game. He didn't want Amy to be here. He didn't want Mum and Dad to be here, either. He didn't know what he wanted.

"I'm going to check on Ari," he said, pushing away from the table.

Amy blinked, all excitement gone in a puff of smoke. "Do … do you want to play something else, or—"

Yanni didn't reply – he didn't even let her finish the sentence. He stormed out of the room and up the stairs, leaving her alone. He knew he was being rude, but he couldn't help it. He felt angrier than he'd ever felt in his life. He seethed past the row of family photos that Mum and Dad had hung in the hallway, his blood raging in his head, the drawstring inside his stomach pulling tighter and tighter, like it was attached to the pin of a grenade.

He came to Ari's bedroom door. Mum and Dad had spent all afternoon sorting it out: the curtains were up now, and the mirrored wardrobe, and her night light was on. Dad had even built a set of shelves for all her toys. Yanni's room was still a cold, carpetless box.

Ari was fast asleep in her cot, tucked up like a bun in her baby sleeping bag. She looked so warm, so peaceful, so happy. Yanni stood beside the cot and gazed down at her.

"This is all your fault," he whispered.

Ari shifted in her sleep. Nothing that Yanni could say mattered to her. She didn't even know he was talking.

"We were happy before you came along," he said. "Everything was perfect. Now it's ruined and it's all because of you."

Ari slept on. Yanni could have stopped there, but he didn't. The words that he had pushed down were itching at the back of his throat. He had a stomachful of anger and he wanted it out.

"I never wanted to come here," he said. "I never even wanted a sister. I never wanted any of this."

The words were rising now, demanding to be spoken. Yanni gripped the edge of the cot and found, to his surprise, that his hands were shaking. He suddenly caught sight of himself in the mirrored wardrobe – a nasty, angry little boy, unloved and unwanted – and it was all too much. The words he'd held inside him for months came tumbling out.

"I hate you," said Yanni. "I hate you and I wish you'd never been born."

And that was when everything changed.

THE VISITOR

Yanni felt the shift in the room first — as if the whole house had flipped to face a different direction. The light flashed, almost imperceptibly. There was a faint sound of chimes from somewhere in the distance, a half-step out of tune with one another. He had a sudden sense that he was no longer alone.

"Well, well! What do we have here?"

Yanni swung round in shock. He *wasn't* alone. There was someone standing in the bedroom doorway. The light in the corridor was too dim to make out their face. All Yanni could see was that the stranger was very thin, and very tall, and stood ramrod straight with their arms behind their back.

"Wh-who are you?" asked Yanni.

The stranger leaned back and gave a high trill of laughter. "What a question! Who do you *think* I am, young man?"

Yanni was stumped. It wasn't the answer he'd expected. "Um … Mr Edwards, from down the road?"

"Right first time!" said the man cheerfully. "Now, aren't you going to invite me in?"

Yanni's head was spinning. Why had Amy let Mr Edwards in without telling him? Why had he come upstairs on his own? Yanni hadn't even heard the front door open. "Er … sure, but—"

With the simple grace of a fox, the man slipped through the doorway and into the room. Yanni was suddenly filled with a certainty that he had been tricked – that a threshold had just been crossed and could not be uncrossed. The man stood in the light of the bedroom, angling his neck like a bird.

"*Hmph!* This is a strange room for a young boy, isn't it?"

Yanni stared at the man standing in front of him. He had never seen anyone who looked quite like him before. He was … well, he was *beautiful*, for one thing. His face was sleek and chiselled, his teeth were like polished marble and his hair hung down in folds of grey silk. He was dressed in the clothes of a dandy, with a jacket the colour of wine and white ruffled breeches, and high, polished wingtip boots that creaked with his every movement.

But something about the man's beauty was *wrong*, somehow. His skin was as white as sheep's bone. He

51

must have been almost seven feet tall: the top of his head practically brushed the ceiling. But that wasn't the strangest thing about him. It was his eyes: Yanni had never seen eyes so dark before. He couldn't even tell where the pupils began.

Yanni shook himself awake. He'd been so captivated by the man's appearance that he'd forgotten he'd just been asked a question. "Sorry – what?"

The man held out his stick-thin arms. "This bedroom! All these cuddly toys and fluffy things... Surely a young lad like yourself is more interested in weapons, and fighting, and laughing at the misfortunes of your enemies?"

Yanni frowned. What a weird thing to say. "It's not my room; it's..."

He froze. The voice at the back of his head was suddenly there again, high and urgent.

Don't talk to him. He shouldn't be here. He's a stranger.

Yanni swallowed. The voice was right: he was alone in his sister's bedroom with a man he had never met before. Yanni suddenly understood, deep down in his gut, that he could not let this man find out Ari was here. He stole a glance over his shoulder. Luckily she was still fast asleep in her cot. He stepped in front of her, blocking her from view.

"Um ... excuse me, Mr Edwards? I don't mean to be rude, but what are you doing here?"

The man smiled, his teeth gleaming in the night light. "What a question! Is it *wrong* for a man to visit his neighbours on a cold and inhospitable night like this?"

Yanni blinked. He supposed the man had a point. "Sorry. It's just that Mum and Dad didn't say you were coming, and…"

"Mum and Dad!" cried the man, flinging up his hands. "Of course! How foolish of me! What ever must you think of me? A thousand apologies, dear boy! How wise of your parents to place such a brilliant young man like yourself in charge of the household!"

Yanni snorted – the way the man spoke was so ridiculous, so over the top, that he couldn't help but laugh. "Right."

The man's eyes widened. "I'm being perfectly serious, young man! Surely your parents realize what a gift they have? *Surely* they tell you a thousand times a day how wise and wonderful and precious you are?"

Yanni felt a prickle of resentment – he couldn't think of the last time Mum or Dad had said anything nice to him like that. The man seemed to read his thoughts; he gave a sorry shake of his head.

"It's a crime, I tell you – a crime! A child like you should be cherished! Why, if you were my son, I'd place a crown atop your head! I would shower you with gold!"

Yanni glowed. The man might be a stranger, but it had been so long since anyone had spoken to him like that; so long since he had felt like anything other than a disappointment. The man held out his hands imploringly.

"Let us not be strangers any more, child. I've told you my name, haven't I? Now you must tell me yours."

Yanni nodded – that *did* seem fair. He didn't want to be unfriendly. Besides, Mr Edwards was so nice, so kind, so generous, so handsome and brave and clever, it would be *wrong* not to give him whatever he asked for. Yanni felt like all of his problems had drifted away – like he was floating above the room somehow. He could barely even think straight over the sound of tiny bells that blocked out everything else. He opened his mouth to answer…

And suddenly the voice at the back of his head was screaming, bursting up through the layers of compliments that had been piled on top of it.

Get him out get him out get him out!

Yanni snapped awake. It was the strangest thing – for a second, he'd completely lost track of what was happening. Suddenly he was back in the room, his head spinning. Everything was exactly as before.

But the man had moved closer.

Yanni froze. Mr Edwards had taken a step forward. He was reaching out towards him with a gloved hand.

"What are you doing?" asked Yanni.

The man startled, like a rug had suddenly been pulled from under him. He glanced at Yanni in shock.

"How did you do that?" the man muttered.

Yanni swallowed. Something was wrong here, deeply wrong. He had to get the man out of here, now. If he could just get him back downstairs, back with Amy, he knew that he would be safe.

"Mr Edwards, I … I think we should go downstairs. I don't think my parents would be happy if they knew you were up here."

The man stayed where he was, still smiling widely … but Yanni felt as if he saw something flash beneath his face. Like an eel, rippling under the surface of a pond. He drew back his hand and stood up straight again, all charm and friendliness.

"Of course! I understand completely. Your parents have taught you well, boy – how sensible of you! How wise and clever!"

The man kept praising him, but now the compliments all felt hollow. Yanni tried to steer him out of the door. "I don't mean to be rude – it's just that my sister's trying to sleep and—"

He shouldn't have said it – he shouldn't have said it. The moment Yanni mentioned her, the man's eyes snapped onto Ari's cot. It was like he was suddenly able to see her, for the very first time. His teeth flashed.

"Aha! A baby! A tiny little *baby*!"

Before Yanni could react, the man had pushed past him and was leaning over Ari's cot, low enough for his hair to brush against her sleeping face. Yanni was filled with deep-down, unspeakable horror. It was like the man was trying to smell her; he looked like a bird of prey gazing at a piece of meat. All at once, his face became a sneer.

"*Hmph*. Are you *sure* this is your sister? No no, I don't like the look of her at all! She seems awfully *dull*, doesn't she? Awfully dull and awfully spoiled!"

Yanni's heart pounded. This was wrong, all wrong. He knew that something terrible – something indescribable – would happen if Ari woke up and saw the man. "M-Mr Edwards, we need to go…"

But the man ignored him. "I don't understand it! Weren't your parents happy with you? Why would they want such a horrid, smelly little child, when they had *you* to begin with?"

It caught Yanni off guard. He felt like the man was voicing his most hidden, private thoughts – the secrets he would never tell anyone.

"I bet she's *awful*!" said the man. "I bet she screams and begs for more, more, more, until you're sick of it!"

Yanni found himself nodding. "Y-yes. She does."

The man kept going. "I bet you were much happier

before she came along. I bet you wish things would go back to the way they were!"

Yanni's heart ached. He *did* feel like that. He felt himself floating again, soft and warm and glowing. It was like golden oil was being poured between his ears, flooding his brain and making his own voice murmur, "Yes."

"I bet you really *hate* her, don't you?"

"Yes."

"I bet sometimes you wish she would go away and leave you alone!"

"I do."

"Why don't you give her to me?"

The voice in Yanni's head burst out like a klaxon:

GET HIM OUT GET HIM OUT GET HIM OUT!

Yanni snapped awake again, his head spinning; the room swung back, reeling and awful.

"Wh-what did you just say?" he gasped.

The man didn't move. He stayed bending over Ari's cot, so that Yanni couldn't see his face. When he spoke, his voice was calm and steady and reasonable.

"I heard everything you said to her. How you hate her. How you wish she had never been born. So let me take her away. I'll make it so that it's just you and your mother and father and you never have to think about her, ever again."

The man turned around to face him and Yanni saw that he had changed. His eyes were no longer kind or sparkling. There was another pair hidden behind them: his real eyes.

And that wasn't all that had changed. There was now a raven on his shoulder – the one from the playing field.

"Y-you're not Mr Edwards," said Yanni faintly.

"Just say the word," ordered the man, "and I'll take her."

The voice inside Yanni was screaming now, a long, low moan of terror. He shut his eyes; he had to get the man out of here. He had to get him away from Ari. He fumbled for the *mati* at his chest, gripped it tight, and found his courage.

"N-no," he said. "You can't have her. Get out of my house, please."

The words froze the room. The man didn't move. His face darkened for a second, his imposter eyes burning, hateful and vicious…

And then the charming, friendly demeanour swung back instantly, like a piece of stage scenery. His eyes sparkled once more. It was as if none of the last few minutes had happened.

"Of course! A thousand apologies, my dear boy. There is nothing ruder than outstaying one's welcome.

I shall impinge on your time no longer! You shall

not see me again. Are you sure I can't take the baby?"

Yanni pointed a trembling hand at the door. "I - I'm sure. Get out."

The man nodded, all smiles and politeness. "I understand completely! I shall leave at once. No need to show me out. Perhaps you could just give me a piece of her instead? I'd be perfectly happy with a fingernail or some hair."

Yanni shut his eyes. This was like a nightmare. "Go now, please."

"You drive a hard bargain! How about a tooth, then? A single tooth. Removing it would take a matter of seconds. No one would miss a single tooth!"

"I'm going to call the police now."

"Absolutely! Which way shall I leave? The back door, the front door? Out of a window, perhaps? The choice is yours, dear boy. Say the word and I shall go!"

"I don't care; just go."

"Yes! Of course! Shall I go? Right now? With the baby?"

"Yes, go, and—"

It happened so quickly that Yanni could barely follow it. The man gave a demonic shriek of triumph so shrill and loud that it seemed to split the room in two. His eyes bulged wide and white, his hair and fingertips stretched out until they reached the walls, and his arms became a great smothering shadow that filled the room like wings. He sprang through the air with a howl of delight, bearing over Ari's cot like a vulture…

CRACK!

And then he was gone. The sound of his scream rang off the walls like a struck bell, echoing into silence. Yanni stood, frozen to the spot, his heart racing. The man was gone; so was the raven. The room was back to normal, as if he had never been there.

Except for one thing.

Every piece of glass in the room had cracked. Every mirror, every window and every framed picture was split down the middle, from top to bottom. Yanni gazed around the room, trying to see where the man had gone, but all he could see was a room full of small, scared boys, his own reflection staring back at him, over and over and over and over.

A Turn of Events

Yanni stood in Ari's bedroom, trembling with shock. He had no idea what had just happened. Everything looked perfectly normal ... but those cracked reflections told another story. Something had just happened here: something terrible. But what?

"*Yanni!*"

Amy charged through the doorway, breathless and pale. One of the lenses of her glasses had cracked, too, split in half from top to bottom.

"I heard a scream!" she cried. "And then all the mirrors and windows broke downstairs and..." She gazed around the bedroom in horror and trailed off. "Omigod – Yanni, what happened?"

Yanni tried to get his thoughts straight, but it was impossible. It was as if the memories were already muddling themselves into nonsense in his head.

"Th-there was a man. A tall man. With a raven!

He came inside and he wanted … he wanted…"

He had to fight to remember it. What had the man wanted? He had been asking for something; he kept demanding it and wouldn't take no for an answer and—

The memory slammed back into him at once: the man leaping onto Ari's cot. He gasped.

"Ari – he wanted Ari! He's taken her and…"

Amy blinked. "Ari's right there."

She pointed. Sure enough, Ari was still in her cot, safe and sound. She was wide awake, standing up and looking at him with a faint smile on her lips. Yanni could have cried with relief.

But there was something odd about Ari – something different. It took him a moment to realize what it was.

"Hang on – she's standing up," he said.

It was true. Ari wasn't even holding the edge of the cot for support. She'd never done that before. Amy didn't seem to think this was as interesting as Yanni did.

"Wait – there was a *man* in the house?" she said. "Are you serious?"

Yanni didn't reply. He was too busy staring at Ari. She was now gazing up at the ceiling, where a moth had landed next to the light. She calmly unbuttoned the straps on her sleeping bag and strolled to the other side of the cot as if she'd been doing it for years.

"She's … walking now," said Yanni. "By herself."

Amy was fully panicking now. "Yanni – the man? Where did he go?"

Yanni watched as his baby sister heaved herself up onto the edge of the cot and balanced on it like an acrobat.

"Yanni, the man could still be in the house! We have to phone the police!"

"Amy."

"And what if the police can't get here in time? We'll have to overpower him and tie him up ourselves. I'm rubbish at knots!"

"Amy."

"I had to wear Velcro shoes until I was ten—"

"*Amy!*"

"Yes?"

"Ari's climbing the walls."

"I *bet* she is! I haven't felt this stressed in months."

"No, I mean she's *actually* climbing the actual walls."

Yanni pointed. Ari was clambering up the shelves that Dad had built for her, hand over hand, scattering books and toys to the floor. She was already halfway to the ceiling.

Amy's mouth fell open. "H-how's she doing that?"

"I don't know," said Yanni, stunned. "She's never done it before."

Ari had reached the top shelf and was stretching

out a hand, trying to reach the moth on the ceiling. Yanni suddenly snapped awake – what was he doing? She was going to fall! The moment he thought it, Ari's foot slipped from the shelf and she fell backwards, arms pinwheeling. Yanni leaped forward, arms outstretched to catch her…

But he didn't need to worry. Ari wasn't falling.

She was standing on the ceiling.

Yanni and Amy stared up in speechless shock. Ari stared back at them, suspended from the ceiling like a bat.

"What about that?" Amy whispered. "Has she done *that* before?"

"Er – no," said Yanni.

Ari calmly walked across the ceiling, crouched down beside the moth, and ate it. Then she looked at Yanni, gave a final giggle and shot from the room faster than Yanni had seen a baby move in his entire life.

The stunned silence lasted only a moment – then Yanni and Amy tore out of the door at the same time, scrambling to the stairs. Just as Amy had said, every mirror in the house had cracked; every window was broken. The glass in the photo frames that hung along the hallway had split. Ari was waiting for them at the bottom of the stairs – or, more precisely, just above the stairs, hanging by her legs from the ceiling fan.

"How is she *doing* this?" Amy cried.

Yanni gulped. He had no idea what had come over his sister, but he had a horrible feeling he knew who was responsible. "L-let's just get her down before she—"

Too late. Ari had found the cord on the fan and yanked it. The fan started spinning like a propeller. Ari made several high-speed rotations before she lost her grip and was sent spiralling through the hall like a Catherine wheel and into the living room, straight into the flat-screen TV. Yanni cried out in horror … but right before his very eyes, Ari sprang off the TV, somersaulted over the sofa and landed expertly on her feet, before charging into the kitchen without a moment's pause.

Yanni didn't have time to be impressed. He could already hear Ari ransacking the cupboards. By the time he made it through the kitchen door, Ari was flinging mugs and plates to the floor in a frenzy.

"Ari – stop!" he cried. "What's got into you?"

He ran forward to pick her up – but as he came close, Ari turned around … and hissed at him.

Yanni was taken aback. Ari didn't even look like a baby any more – she looked like some kind of wild animal. He felt dread building in his stomach.

"What are you doing? It's me, Yanni! Your brother!"

Ari hesitated for an instant, glancing him up and down, and then flung herself towards him, mouth agape and nails flailing. Yanni had just a moment to notice that his sister now had a full set of razor-sharp teeth…

"GOT YOU!"

Amy snatched Ari out of thin air at the very last second, her hands swaddled in a pair of oven gloves. Her timing was spot on – any later, and Yanni would have been wearing his sister like a face mask. Amy held the struggling baby above her head as Ari shrieked and writhed to escape. Her strength was incredible – it was all Amy could do to keep hold of her.

"She's too strong!" Amy cried. "Help!"

Yanni looked around for something – *anything* – that could hold her, and spotted the baby bouncer hanging from the door frame. Quick as a flash, he grabbed Ari and shoved her inside the harness, tightening the straps and jumping back before she could try to bite him again. Ari spat and screamed, seething like a cobra, but it was no use – the straps were too tight. There was nothing she could do except bounce on the spot furiously.

Yanni stood, gasping for breath. He'd seen Ari angry before, but never like *this*. She'd never tried to attack him. She'd never been able to climb walls. She'd never grown a full set of teeth, either. She was staring at him like he was a complete stranger. Yanni searched her eyes, but he couldn't find a single shred of recognition in them.

And that wasn't the only thing that was different about her eyes.

Yanni swallowed. It seemed almost mad to say it – but it was no madder than anything else that had happened in the last ten minutes.

"Amy?"

"Yes?"

"I think there's something wrong with Ari."

Amy stared at him. "You *think*?"

Yanni shook his head. "No – I mean I don't think this is her." He gulped. "It's her eyes. They've changed colour."

It was true. The thing in the bouncer might look like his sister, and sound like his sister, but her eyes weren't brown any more. They were black.

So black that Yanni couldn't even tell where the pupils began.

Amy swallowed. "Yanni – what happened upstairs, exactly?"

Yanni closed his eyes and spoke carefully, straining to remember every detail, trying to piece it into an order that made sense.

"There was a man. He asked to come into Ari's bedroom. I thought he was Mr Edwards. I kept trying to make him leave, but he always stopped me somehow. He asked for my name, and then he asked to take Ari away … and there was a raven, and then I accidentally said yes, and he screamed and…"

He trailed off. The story was utterly ridiculous –

there was no way Amy would believe a word of it. No wonder she had such a shocked look on her face.

"Let me get this right," she said quietly. "This man asked for permission to enter the room. He asked for your name. Then he asked to take Ari … and you said yes?"

Yanni felt a twist of guilt – he hadn't meant to say it. He hadn't meant to say *any* of the terrible things he'd said, not really. "It was an accident! He sort of asked me three questions at the same time, and I got confused and…"

He trailed off again. Amy's face was transforming, right in front of him. Her eyes were alight; her mouth fell open. It felt weird to say it, but it almost looked like he had just given her the most exciting news of her life.

"All Hallows' Eve," she whispered, her voice crackling at the edges with electricity. "When faeries come roaming. When the borders 'twixt here and the Land of Fae are at their very thinnest."

Yanni frowned. "What are you talking about?"

Amy turned to him. Behind her broken glasses, her eyes were blazing like fireworks.

"Yanni," she said, "I know this might sound strange, but I think your little sister's been stolen by a faerie."

THE CHANGELING

Yanni stared at Amy. His cousin was completely serious.

"A *faerie*," he repeated.

"I mean it! All the signs are there – look!"

She ran into the dining room and returned with her backpack, emptying it onto the floor. A set of wizard pyjamas and a toothbrush shaped like a wand fell out, quickly followed by a book the size of a paving slab. She picked it up and started frantically flicking through its pages. It was filled with pictures of magical creatures: centaurs, selkies, trolls, dwarves, elves, hobgoblins…

"Here!" she said breathlessly. "Is *this* what the man looked like?"

She held out the book and jabbed a finger at one of the illustrations. It was a drawing of a creature in a forest glade, with high cheekbones and long hair. Yanni frowned. The drawing wasn't right – this creature was wearing moss for clothes and playing some sort of flute – but he had to admit, it sort of looked like the man from upstairs.

"Er … a bit, maybe?"

Amy practically squealed. "*I knew it!* It was a faerie! Omigod, omigod, I *knew* I should have said those incantations…"

Yanni looked back down at the book – and suddenly realized what Amy was holding. It was the instruction manual for ORC'S QUEST.

He put his head in his hands. For a brief moment, he'd been prepared to listen to Amy – but now he could see that she was confusing reality with one of her stupid board games.

"We – we don't have time for this," he said. His sister – his *actual*, real sister – was in trouble. "We need to get a doctor to look at Ari before—"

"A doctor can't help us now, Yanni!" Amy cried. "Your sister's gone. The faerie's spirited her back to his realm."

Yanni finally lost his patience. "For heaven's sake, there's no such thing as faeries!"

Amy glared. "Oh, right – and Ari's just going through a growth spurt, is she?"

Yanni opened his mouth to argue – but he had nothing to say. He only had to take one look at the thing writing and snapping in the bouncer to know that it wasn't Ari any more. Its teeth, its strength, the way it moved, those raven eyes...

"But ... if that's *not* Ari," he said nervously, "then what is it?"

Amy gulped. Her voice was barely a whisper. "A *changeling*. A faerie child. It's been swapped for Ari so that the faerie could take your sister away."

Yanni shook his head. "Sorry – *faeries*? Like ... Tinker Bell?"

"No, no, nothing like that!" said Amy. "*Some* faeries are good, but some are powerful, dangerous, magical creatures. And on certain days of the year – St John's Eve, Midsummer's Day, Halloween – the boundaries between their world and ours are thin enough for them to cross over. The good ones come over and help, but the bad ones come over and steal human children."

Yanni blinked. "Why?"

"Lots of reasons. In some legends, they take humans and keep them as pets, or as servants. In others, they sell their souls to hell as a tax."

Yanni was filled with horror. The thought of his sister being kept as a pet – or, worse, being sent to hell – was too awful even to consider. But Amy kept going.

"Think about it," she said. "The man *asked* to come into her room, right?"

Yanni nodded. "Yeah, but—"

"That's because faeries live by strict rules. They can't walk through a door unless they're invited. That's why he asked for your name, too. Once you tell a faerie your name, they have power over you. Don't you see? The faerie was trying to steal *you* away first! And when he couldn't take you, he took Ari instead. You gave him permission!"

Yanni's mind raced. He hated to admit it, but everything that Amy just said made sense. The way the man had talked to him, like he was getting inside his thoughts. The strange things he'd said. The way he had disappeared…

"So … can we get her back?"

He turned to Amy hopefully, but he only had to take one look at her face to know the answer. His sister was gone for ever – and it was all his fault.

The guilt hit him like a stomach ache. He'd lost Ari. How could he ever explain what had happened to Mum and Dad? They'd never forgive him – they wouldn't even believe him. They'd think he was making it all up. The thought was too terrible to contemplate. Yanni stared at the screaming creature in the bouncer, and made up his mind right then and there.

"No. I won't let this happen. I have to find that faerie and get Ari back!"

Amy's eyes widened. "Yanni – you can't. He's gone! He's taken her back to the Land of Fae!"

"So?" He grabbed Amy's shoulders. "You said that tonight, faeries can cross over – so let's cross over, too! Let's find Ari and bring her back!"

Amy spluttered. "Yanni, if it was that easy to go into the Land of Fae, *everyone* would be doing it! No one knows how to get there – it's a magical world!"

Yanni shook his head. "He can't have disappeared into thin air; there must be some way he got into the house. If we can just follow his footsteps…"

He stopped. There was a sound just beneath the surface of the house – one that had been there the entire time, but Yanni had barely noticed it in all the excitement.

"Wait – can you hear that?"

It was the distant ring of tiny bells, high and discordant. It was the exact same sound he had heard at the dolmen, and in Ari's bedroom … and now it was coming from the living room.

He flew from the kitchen, searching for the sound, and found it straight away. It was coming from the fireplace.

"There!" he exclaimed. "That sound was playing when the man appeared. If we follow it, we'll be able to find him!"

Amy stared at the fireplace, her eyes widening.

"The hearth. Of course! Faeries *always* came through the fireplace in old stories! People even used to protect them with…" She trailed off. Her eyes had suddenly alighted on the old metal panel, still leaning against the nearby wall. "Hang on – did that use to be over the front?"

Yanni nodded. "Mum and Dad made the decorators take it out when we…"

Before he could finish, Amy raced into the kitchen, and came back with a googly-eyed fridge magnet. She held it to the metal panel – and it stuck.

"It's made of iron!" she cried. "Faeries *hate* iron! People even used to put old horseshoes over their doorways to ward them off." She peered inside the fireplace and frowned. "Did someone change the inside, too?"

Yanni nodded. "There were these weird carvings at the back, so Dad—"

"Witch's marks!" Amy screamed, making Yanni jump. "To protect the house… Oh, Yanni, can't you see what this means? Whoever put in that panel and carved those markings did it to protect the house from faeries! *That's* how he got inside – he came through the fireplace!"

Yanni frowned. "What, like … crawled down the chimney?"

He stuck his head into the fireplace and peered up. He shuddered. The thought of the man slithering down the chimney to get inside made him feel sick … but sure enough, the sound of badly tuned bells was even louder here.

"So do we climb up it or…"

He reached out a hand to the back wall of the fireplace to steady himself – and fell straight through.

The next thing he knew, he was lying on a cold stone floor. He looked up, heart pounding. He had fallen through the wall of the fireplace as if it were made of nothing more than smoke. He had landed in another room – a room that lay *behind* the fireplace. Or at least, his top half had. His legs were still in the house behind him.

He knew, right away, that this room wasn't part of his house. It belonged to somewhere else entirely. The floor was made of ancient, weathered stone. The windows stretched from floor to ceiling, strung with cobwebs so thick that they looked like curtains shifting silently in an unseen breeze. The air was cold and dark.

"Omigod – *it's a faerie gateway!*"

Amy's head poked through the fireplace wall beside him – *just* her head, like she'd been stuffed and mounted.

"Don't you see? This is how the faerie entered the house! Normally the iron panel and the witch's marks would have stopped him, but when your parents took them off…"

Yanni didn't reply. He was too busy looking through the windows. "Amy."

"Yes?"

Yanni reached up and tilted Amy's head, so that she could see what was outside. Her mouth fell open.

The view out of the windows was different on this side of the fireplace, too. Back in Yanni's house, the weather was wild and stormy; here, the sky was calm and clear and peaceful.

It was also purple.

Yanni blinked. His eyes weren't deceiving him: the sky was purple, stained like a neon bruise as far as the eye could see. It was dominated by a vast and swollen moon, bigger and brighter than any moon Yanni had seen in his life, lighting up the world beneath it like a stage set.

And as for the world beneath it...

The bare blank fields of Fallow Hall were gone. Stretching from the windows was a dark and boundless forest, filled with towering ancient trees so broad that ten men couldn't reach their arms around them. The ground beneath them was thick with mist, covered in a twisting tangle of briars and filled with unseen things that twitched and tittered.

And it wasn't silent. From somewhere beyond the trees came the sound of tiny broken bells, closer and louder than ever before. Yanni could taste the magic in the air like paraffin, feel the very hum of it vibrating against his skin. There was no doubt where they were.

"It's the faerie realm," Amy whispered, her voice faint with wonder. "We're in the Land of Fae."

CROSSING OVER

YANNI AND AMY STAYED HALF IN AND HALF OUT OF the fireplace, gawping at the scene before them.

It couldn't be real – it wasn't possible. But there was a whole other world, right in front of them. Yanni could see faint lights drifting between the trees like embers, and hear the rattle of wind in the brambles, and feel the chill of the ancient stone beneath his arms…

He froze. There was something pressed into the dust on the floor before him: a set of fresh footprints, leading straight to an open door and outside. The shape of the wingtip boots was unmistakable: there was no doubt whose footsteps they were.

"That's the faerie," said Yanni nervously. "It … it looks like he went that way."

He couldn't believe the words coming out of his mouth. Was he *really* going to follow those footprints into the forest? All this was like something from a nightmare – but the thought of facing his parents without Ari was even more frightening.

"C-come on," he said, hoping he sounded braver than he felt. "If we're fast, we can rescue Ari before Mum and Dad get home."

Amy's face turned pale. "Sorry – *we*?"

"You're coming with me," said Yanni.

Amy stared at him for a moment longer – then her head snapped back through the fireplace wall.

"Hey – wait!" he yelled.

He clambered back through the fireplace, and his own living room reappeared in an instant – the light, the warmth, the driving rain against the cracked windows. Yanni shuddered: passing between the two worlds felt even weirder than it sounded. The air seemed thicker on this side of the fireplace, almost heavier. It felt like being flung off a cliff into a freezing sea, backwards.

Amy was pacing the carpet, wringing her hands.

"What are you doing?" asked Yanni.

"Don't you understand?" she cried. "The Land of Fae is the most dangerous place there is! If we go in there, we might never come back." She shrugged. "Maybe you were right. Maybe we should phone the police."

Yanni shook his head. "No! Mum and Dad can *never* find out about this. We have to get Ari back from that faerie ourselves!"

Amy looked at him. "How?"

Yanni opened his mouth to answer, but nothing came out. He hadn't thought that far ahead.

"Ask him nicely?" he suggested.

Amy threw up her hands. "See? You haven't got a clue what you're doing!"

Yanni grabbed her, stopping her mid-pace. He hated to admit it, but the thought of going into that world by himself was terrifying. Amy – his weird, awkward cousin – was his only hope.

"Exactly – I *don't* have a clue. If you let me go in there by myself and I don't come back, it'll be all your fault!"

It was a mean trick – but it worked. Amy stared at him in horror. "N-no!"

Yanni racked his brains. He had to convince her to join him. "What's the character you play in that board game, ORC's LAIR?"

Amy frowned. "It's ORC's QUEST. And it's not just a board game; it's an immersive—"

"Right, yes," interrupted Yanni. "Your character, the level twelve … mason-batchelor, or something? Would he…?"

"Mage-chancellor," corrected Amy. "And I'm only level ten. I still haven't properly powered up yet."

"Yes, very good," said Yanni impatiently. "What would *he* do? Would *he* let—"

"She."

"What?"

"She. Her name's Saphiana. Mage-chancellors can be girls, too. It's not the Stone Age."

Yanni's eye began to twitch. "Right, yes, absolutely. What would Saphiana do? Would *she* let a faerie steal Ari?"

Amy's own eyes flickered behind her broken glasses. "No. Of course she wouldn't. She's sworn to defend the weak and the helpless."

Yanni nodded. "So let's be like Saphiana! Let's march right in there and take back Ari!"

Amy gave him a pitying look. "Yanni, you *can't* take your sister back now. Faeries live by strict rules, remember? When you said he could take her, you entered into a magical contract with him. Ari belongs to him now."

Yanni spluttered. "But I never meant to!"

"I know you didn't," said Amy. "But that doesn't matter. You have to play by his rules. If you want to get your sister back from him…"

Yanni's face lit up – so there *was* a way. "Tell me!"

Amy sighed with resignation, and pointed to the kitchen doorway.

"Well, for a start, you'll have to return his changeling. As long as it's here, the contract stands."

Yanni gulped. The changeling was trying to gnaw

through the straps of the bouncer and doing a pretty good job of it. Handing *that* over wasn't going to be simple.

"Then," said Amy, "you have to tell the faerie that you reject his deal and demand your sister back. He'll refuse – he'll give you every reason under the sun why the deal can't be broken – but you have to be insistent. No matter what he says, no matter what he does, no matter how much he tries to scare you, you have to stand your ground until he gives in."

Yanni turned pale. The faerie had wormed his way into his mind and controlled his thoughts without even trying. The idea of standing up to him made his insides turn to water.

"He'll probably use magic to stop you," Amy sighed. "And his powers are going to be stronger when he's back on his own territory. You'll need some kind of amulet or charm to block his magic."

Yanni felt the last of his bravery wither. "Like what?"

Amy sighed. "Iron would be good, but we can't carry around the great big panel; it's far too heavy. Unless…" She gasped. "Of course!"

She rooted around in her backpack and found the rowan garland. "Here! Faeries hate rowan. That's why I was going to hang it on the front door." She snapped off a twig. "Put that in your belt, and he won't be able to hurt you."

"I'm not wearing a belt."

"Your pocket, then."

Yanni took the twig. It didn't look like something that would block the magic of an evil faerie. "How exactly is *this* supposed to protect me?"

"Faeries are powerful creatures, but they still have weaknesses," said Amy. "If you have rowan on you, even a tiny amount, then their magic won't work."

"That doesn't make any sense."

"I said the rules were *strict*. I didn't say they had to make any sense."

Yanni sighed. He still didn't understand, but he had a feeling that faeries didn't care much whether you understood or not. He stuffed the twig into his pocket and grabbed Ari's baby sling from the sofa.

"Right. We can carry around the changeling in this," he said, strapping the sling over his shoulder. "We carry Ari around in it all the time…"

He turned to the changeling – and it hissed at him. Yanni gulped.

"Er … maybe it'll be easier if we both do it."

It took ten minutes to wrestle the changeling into the sling but felt much longer. By the time it was securely strapped in place – facing away so it couldn't bite Yanni in the face – he and Amy were both exhausted and covered in scratches. The changeling, meanwhile, was just as energetic as before, kicking and thrashing with rage.

"Wow," gasped Amy. "Are all babies like this?"

"There's usually more poo," said Yanni weakly. "Come on – we're running out of time! Mum and Dad could arrive home any minute…"

Turning back to the fireplace, his courage faltered. He was trying to sound brave, but the truth was he didn't want to go into the Land of Fae and confront a faerie any more than Amy did. Back home in his group of friends, it was easy to pretend to be brave – someone else always went first, so you just tagged along behind. But now it was all up to him. He was completely, utterly petrified. Was he really about to do this?

He gripped the *mati* around his neck – and heard Yiayia's voice in his head.

And when your sister is here, you protect her, yes?

Yanni's heart sank – he couldn't turn back now. He had to save his sister. For Mum, for Dad, for Pappou and Yiayia.

He got on his hands and knees, crawled through the fireplace, and crossed over the threshold into the Land of Fae.

HALLOW FALL

THE SHIFT BETWEEN WORLDS DIDN'T FEEL ANY more pleasant the second time around. Yanni felt the buzz of magic against his skin, the cold chill of the stone beneath his hands, and within moments he found himself standing in the room beyond the fireplace.

He glanced about him. The room was cavernous and dark as a crypt, lit by pale blades of moonlight that cut through the windows. It was eerily quiet, too: except for the wind in the trees and the incessant chime of distant bells, there wasn't a sound to be heard. Amy followed moments later, gazing around in wonder.

"So this is it – the Land of Fae," she said breathlessly.

"It kind of looks like my house," he pointed out.

It was true – the house on this side was bigger and colder and darker, but the layout was exactly the same as his house. The footprints led to the front door; the windows were all in the same places. It was like Yanni's house had an evil twin.

The changeling growled and swung its hands viciously at Yanni's face.

"Let's just get going," muttered Yanni. "The quicker we find that faerie and get this thing off me, the better."

They followed the dusty footprints out of the door. Up close, the forest looked even more frightening, thrumming with dark power. The trees were as tall as monuments, their twisted branches clawing at the moon. The undergrowth teemed with malevolent life; Yanni caught glimpses of small winged creatures flitting between the brambles, things that slithered in the dark beneath them, sets of yellow eyes that flashed briefly before disappearing. He felt his nerves wither – how on earth were they going to find the faerie among all *that*?

He looked at the ground – and saw, to his relief, that the footprints followed a cobbled road that twisted through the forest. It was in the exact same place as the lane that led to Fallow Hall back home, but the similarities ended there. Up ahead the lane became a bridge, made from the trunks of two gnarled and twisted trees. The bridge didn't cross over a river – it crossed a fathomless black gorge, so deep and dark that Yanni couldn't see the bottom. Before it stood the village sign, but this had changed, too. It was now a crumbling headstone that looked as if it had been standing there for hundreds of years. And carved into the surface were the words…

"Hallow Fall?" Yanni read, baffled.

Amy nodded, piecing it all together. "Don't you see? Everything in the Land of Fae is like *our* world, but different. That must be how faeries can find their way around when they cross over." She pointed to the bridge. "That massive gorge is one of the cracks in the lane outside your house. I mean – everything's bigger on this side, isn't it?"

Yanni gulped. Amy was right – but if everything on this side of the fireplace was bigger and darker and scarier, then what was the faerie going to look like?

"Oi!"

He leaped a foot in the air. The shout had come from the shadows beside them – but there was nothing there.

"What are you doing? Get away from my bridge!"

A small squat shadow flew from beneath the headstone, waving a tiny stone fist. The fist had a fishing rod in it.

Yanni was speechless – it was the frog statue from Fallow Hall. It had the exact same head, the exact same fishing rod, the exact same scowling amber eye … but now it was alive, and extremely angry. It jumped up and down, stamping its stone feet on the road like little hammers.

"Oi! Are you stupid? I said, get away from my bridge!"

Yanni steeled himself. He had to stay brave; he couldn't let fear get the better of him now.

"We're ... we're looking for someone who came this way a while ago." He pointed at the changeling, whipping his finger away before it could bite it off. "He'd have been holding a baby that looked like this. Have you seen anything?"

The frog stopped. It slowly turned to face Yanni, rigid with anger. "What did you just say to me?"

Its voice was low and dangerous. Yanni was certain he heard all the creatures in the nearby brambles squeak and run away at the same time. "Er ... pardon?"

"You're *looking* for someone?" the frog growled. "Did I *see* anything? I know what you're up to! You're after my eye, aren't you?" It jabbed a finger at its one remaining eye. "Everyone's always after my eye! I bet you're the ones who stole my other one, aren't you? Admit it! It was you!"

Yanni was baffled. "But we only just got here..."

The frog wasn't listening, it had already started foaming at the mouth. "I knew it! You toerags! Give me back my eye!"

Amy whimpered behind him. "Um ... Yanni, I think we should go before—"

Yanni squawked in pain as something twanged off his head. It was the frog's fishing rod, quickly followed by several handfuls of gravel.

"I'll kill you!" the frog screamed. "I'll kill all of you!"

"Run!" Yanni yelled.

He and Amy tore across the warped wooden bridge as fast as they could, the frog screaming and chasing behind and kicking Yanni's ankles every step of the way. Yanni wailed with agony – the frog might have been small, but its feet were still made of stone and hurt like hell. Yanni glanced at the haunted forest flying past him – the twisted trees, the flashing eyes, the murderous brambles. How on earth were they ever going to find Ari in this terrible place?

Then, all of a sudden, the road simply stopped. Yanni skidded to a halt; he and Amy were now standing at a crossroads, just like the one in Fallow Hall. For some reason, the frog couldn't take another step further. It hung back in the darkness at the exact point where the lane ended, throwing stones and shaking its fist.

"Ha! You'll be back – you've *got* to come back sometime! And I'll be waiting for you when you do!"

Yanni's heart sank like a well stone. They'd been in the Land of Fae for barely two minutes and they'd already made an enemy. He gazed around hopelessly. The crossroads split into four paths, just like the one in Fallow Hall, but he had no idea which path the faerie had taken. There were no more dusty footprints left to follow.

"What do we do now?" he groaned.

"Ah! Might I be of service?"

Yanni jumped, for the second time in two minutes. There was someone hiding in the shadows by the crossroads. This person was far bigger than the frog – nearly three metres tall, in fact. Yanni leaped back.

"G-go away! Leave us alone!"

Amy glared at him. "Yanni! Don't be rude – they just offered to help us!"

"I'm not being rude," Yanni protested. "I'm trying to make sure we don't get killed!"

Amy rolled her eyes and turned back to the person in the shadows. "Sorry, sir – it's our first time in the Land of Fae, and we're a little lost. We're trying to find…"

Amy trailed off as the person leaned out of the shadows. Only … it wasn't a person.

It was a signpost. In fact, it was the exact same signpost from the crossroads in Fallow Hall. Its paint was still peeling; its wood was still worn and cracked – but now, just like the frog, it was alive, its whole body tilting from the ground like a sunflower. Yanni noticed, somewhat dazed, that it was still wearing a hat.

"Well," said the signpost, "it's been a long time since anyone called me *sir*."

Yanni shook his head – he had to pull himself together. They couldn't afford to lose any more time.

"I – I'm looking for someone who came this way

a little while ago," he said. "He's tall and thin, with long hair and old-fashioned clothes…"

The signpost creaked forward and backwards. It took Yanni a moment to realize that it was nodding.

"I know *exactly* who that is," said the signpost cheerfully. "If that's not Lorde Renwin, then I'm not a signpost. He came this way just a few moments ago."

Yanni gasped. So now they had a name. "Lorde Renwin? Is he a faerie?"

"He certainly is!" said the post. "And the most powerful one there is, too. He's the lord of the manor around these parts – everything you can see here belongs to him, and more besides."

Yanni's heart raced. They were finally getting some answers. "Did he have anything with him? A baby that looked like this one?"

He pointed at the changeling on his front, who gave another hiss. The post recoiled. "*Oof!* That's a nasty little changeling you've got there. Let me guess – Lorde Renwin took your baby, and left this one behind?"

"My sister," Yanni explained.

"We're going to find Lorde Renwin and reject his deal," said Amy.

The post sagged – Yanni could have sworn that this time, the creak of the wood sounded like a sigh.

"I see. Well, children, if you want my advice – and

you should take it, because I'm a signpost – forget about your sister. Forget about Lorde Renwin and Hallow Fall. Go home and pretend none of this ever happened."

Yanni felt a chill up his spine. "Wh-why?"

The post straightened, and gestured with its wooden arms to the darkness around them.

"Look at this place. Hallow Fall wasn't always so ... *desolate*, you know. So poisoned and broken and sad. There was once a time when the village was *full* of magic. Thousands of faeries lived here – the good kind, too."

Its voice darkened.

"And then Lorde Renwin appeared. He's not one of the good ones. He's nothing but sneer and bile and hatred. He imprisoned every faerie in the land and stole every drop of magic from Hallow Fall. Listen – do you hear that?"

At first, Yanni wasn't certain what he was supposed to hear – but then he realized that the signpost was talking about the sound of tiny bells, ringing through the trees. Out here, they sounded even more jarring and out of tune.

"That's the sound of broken magic," explained the signpost. "It's all out of kilter. And that's all thanks to Lorde Renwin. He's spent the last three hundred years making Hallow Fall as sick and twisted as he is ... and he'll do whatever it takes to keep your sister." The post leaned closer to Yanni. "So follow my advice, young man – don't try to fight him. Head back, before it's too late."

Yanni felt his stomach drop. He wanted to do what the signpost said, more than anything. He wanted to go back through the fireplace and hide in his room and put his head under the covers that still smelled a little like his old house and forget that any of this had ever happened. But it *had* happened. And if he went back home now, without Ari, then nothing would ever be the same again. His parents would never forgive him. This was his one and only chance to fix it. He gripped the *mati* tight beneath his shirt, and found his courage.

"Th-thank you for the advice," said Yanni, his voice thin and frightened. "But I can't go home now. I have to save my sister."

The post shook from side to side sadly.

"Humans – you can't tell them anything." It sighed. "Well, suit yourself, young man. Lorde Renwin's tower is that way." It pointed down the first road. "Left at the toadstools. Follow the chimes and you can't miss it."

Yanni peered into the distance. He couldn't see any sign of a tower down the path, but he wasn't about to argue with a magical signpost. Besides, if that was where the chimes were coming from, then the faerie was bound to be there. The signpost angled in closer, almost conspiratorially.

"And before you go, let me give you one final word of advice. No offence, but you're going to need all the help you can get."

Yanni and Amy leaned in as the post cupped a wooden arm to where they assumed its mouth must be.

"Don't let Lorde Renwin keep you inside his tower. Get in and get out, as fast as you can."

Yanni frowned. "Why?"

The signpost would have winked, if it had had eyes. "Faerie magic is a dangerous thing, young man. The less time you spend here, the better. And don't forget – there are only a few hours left before All Hallows' Day." It raised an arm to the point where the vast moon hung beyond the trees. "Once midnight comes, the paths between our worlds will be closed once more. You'll be trapped here until the gateway opens again, on—"

"St John's Eve," said Amy, her voice blank with horror. "In June. Nearly eight months away."

Yanni gulped. The prospect of being stuck in Hallow Fall for eight months didn't even bear thinking about. They'd barely survived ten minutes so far. "It's fine – we'll have left long before then. We have to get Ari home before Mum and Dad come back, anyway."

"That's the spirit!" said the signpost, in a tone that sounded an awful lot like pity. "Now, remember: be swift! Be smart! And come and find me if you need any more advice. I am, after all, a signpost." It doffed its hat. "Best of luck to the both of you!"

THE DARK TOWER

Yanni and Amy walked down the path in silence, both too frightened to speak. The sound of broken chimes rose and fell through the forest around them. The only other sound was the changeling, seething as it tried to escape the sling. The path seemed to go on for ever.

"This is taking too long," muttered Yanni. "Surely we'd have seen a tower by now?"

"Faeries follow different rules from us, remember?" said Amy. "We'll have to follow them, too, now we're in their realm. That's going to be even more important when you're with Lorde Renwin."

Yanni swallowed. "How – how do you mean?"

Amy perked up, pulling the enormous ORC'S QUEST manual out of her backpack. "Good thing I brought this!"

Yanni gawked at her. "You brought that with you?"

"Of course! It'll tell us everything we need to know about faeries. Let's see…"

She flicked through until she came to the right page.

"Here we go. First rule – never accept their food. If Lorde Renwin offers you anything to eat or drink, turn it down. If you taste faerie food, you'll become a faerie, too."

Yanni snorted. That was easy. The last thing he wanted to do was eat. He was so stressed that his stomach felt like a clenched fist.

"Secondly – don't tell him your name, ever," said Amy. "If he knows your name, he'll have power over you. Don't tell him mine, either."

Yanni's hairs stood on end as he remembered how, with one word, he had nearly condemned himself for ever. He hoped he was going to be able to remember all this.

"And lastly," said Amy gravely, "the most important thing of all, whatever you do: never, ever, *ever* enter into any deals with him. Faeries love wagers – they'll never turn one down if you offer it. But they're *experts* at trickery. No matter how clever you think you are, no matter how good the deal might seem, they'll always fix it so that you can't win. OK?"

Yanni nodded. "O-OK."

It wasn't OK at all. Their task suddenly seemed even more difficult and frightening than before. How on earth was Yanni supposed to find this tower and stand against a magical faerie?

He stopped. There was a patch of bright red toadstools beside the road, glowing like night lights in the gloom. They were alive, too, glancing at Yanni and Amy suspiciously and muttering in mushroom language.

"Here are the toadstools," said Yanni. "But where's the tower? The signpost said it would be right…"

He turned around – and jumped, for the hundredth time that day.

The forest beside the path had completely disappeared. In its place stood a tall and crumbling archway, its surface choked with ivy. A thin walkway lined with stone ravens ran beneath it, just wide enough for a single person to walk across. It stretched hundreds of metres across a vast crater of endless darkness, until it reached a rock in the very centre.

Standing on the stone island was Lorde Renwin's tower.

Yanni gazed up … and up … and up. The tower was the single tallest thing he had ever seen in his life. It split the sky in two like a crack in a mirror, so tall it almost seemed to pierce the moon. Every square inch of its bricks was deepest, most desolate black. Yanni had no idea how he hadn't seen it – but he knew that nothing in the faerie realm worked the way it should. He could feel it at once – the magic coming off it, pulsing into the land around it like radiation … and with it came the sound of broken chimes, brighter and clearer than ever before.

And suddenly it all clicked into place. Yanni realized exactly where they were. "It's the dolmen!"

Amy frowned. "What do you mean?"

Yanni's heart pounded. It all seemed so obvious now. "Everything on this side of the fireplace is linked to Fallow Hall, right? The tower must be the dolmen. That's where I first heard that chime sound! I knew there was something weird about it."

He looked up to the very top of the tower. Right at the highest point stood a single flickering square of light.

"That's where he is," said Yanni. "I – I guess Ari will be there, too. You wait here."

Amy glanced at the dark forest around her. She didn't look thrilled about being left on her own with a bunch of muttering toadstools for company. "Why do I have to wait here?"

"You heard what the signpost said. We have to spend as little time in that tower as possible. I need you out here in case something goes wrong. If I'm not back in twenty minutes, come and find me."

Amy looked unconvinced. "You really think it's only going to take that long?"

Yanni nodded. "It has to. We have to get back before Mum and Dad."

His stomach flipped. The thought of his parents coming home to find the house empty, the windows cracked and all three children gone… It didn't even bear thinking about.

Amy nodded reluctantly.

"OK – I'll wait here. But remember what I told you. Whatever he says, whatever he does, no matter how much he tries to scare you, you have to stand your ground. Tell him you've come to return his changeling and demand your sister back, and don't give up."

Yanni nodded again, but inside he was trembling. Was he really about to demand an evil faerie give back his sister? He clutched the rowan twig in his pocket – the one and only protection he had. How on earth was this supposed to work? But what other choice did he have?

After all, said the voice at the back of his head, *this is all your fault, isn't it?*

Yanni gritted his teeth and pushed down the voice. He couldn't think like that – he had to keep a clear head. His only hope now was to be brave.

He took a deep breath and walked through the crumbling archway towards the black tower, the changeling hissing and shrieking every step of the way.

LORDE RENWIN

YANNI STEPPED ACROSS THE FOOTBRIDGE, TRYING to hold his nerve as best he could. The raven statues lining the walkway seemed to follow his every move; Yanni tried to convince himself that it was a trick of the moonlight, and that they weren't really turning their polished beaks towards him as he passed.

The walkway finally ended, and he stood at the base of the tower. There was no sign of any entrance: every inch of the tower was deepest black. But when he stepped closer, a section of the wall simply opened by itself without warning.

The changeling whimpered. Yanni glanced down. For the very first time, the changeling wasn't angry; it was petrified. Yanni gulped. What was it so afraid of?

He crept inside. A grand hallway stood before him, the ceiling hung with ornate chandeliers that bloomed in the dark like glowing bouquets. Yanni had never seen anywhere so lavish and decadent before. The floor was decked with luxurious rugs and lined with antiques – weapons, vases, tapestries, a suit of armour with two helmets and six arms. The walls were gleaming with gold-framed paintings. Yanni turned to the nearest one … and started. It was the man from Ari's bedroom. Yanni would recognize those piercing black eyes anywhere. The plaque at the bottom read:

LORDE RENWIN

EVERLASTING OVERLORDE
OF HALLOW FALL

THE MOST POWERFUL
FAERIE IN EXISTENCE

BETTER AT MAGIC
THAN YOU, BOY

Yanni felt what little courage he had leave him. He looked at the next painting along – and blinked. Lorde Renwin was in this picture, too. It showed him shaking hands with another man – who was *also* Lorde Renwin.

Yanni looked at the next painting along, and the next one, and the next. Sure enough, every person in every single painting was Lorde Renwin. The faerie's alabaster face and raven eyes gazed out of every frame in the hallway, a hundred times over. In one picture, a hunting party of thirty Lorde Renwins stood triumphantly over the dead body of a giant, hog-tied Lorde Renwin. In another, two love-struck Lorde Renwins frolicked on a flowery swing together – one in a boater, the other in a billowing white ball gown.

At the end of the hall was a grand spiral staircase. A polished banister snaked into the darkness, leading to a glowing pool of light at the very top of the tower. The sound of chimes echoed from above.

Yanni gritted his teeth, clenched the rowan twig in his fist and began to climb. He climbed until his legs throbbed and his knees sang and his shoulders burned from the weight of the changeling. Slowly, step by step, the glow at the top grew closer, as if Yanni were emerging from the bottom of a dark well. Finally – just as he began to feel like he might never stop climbing – the stairs ended at a set of double doors. From inside came the sound of broken bells, louder than ever... And that wasn't the only noise he could hear. There was laughter, too – Ari's laughter. And with it, the high-pitched, tittering laugh of a man.

"That's right, my little one! My very precious little baby girl!"

Yanni summoned all his courage, and pushed open

the doors. The room inside made the hallway downstairs look like a broom cupboard. It was a ballroom – and, judging by the state of things, the ball had only just finished. The floor was strewn with scattered food; the chandeliers were hung with paper streamers. On the furthest wall stood the biggest fireplace Yanni had ever seen in his life, stuffed with an inferno of branches; the mantelpiece was tall enough for a man to ride a horse beneath.

There were no portraits of Lorde Renwin here. Instead, every inch of the walls was covered in cracked mirrors, reflecting the candlelight and bathing the room in a glorious golden light. A thousand Yannis gazed back at him from every single angle: it felt like standing in the gaze of some giant insect.

"Ah! Look who's finally come to join us!"

In the centre of the room was a high-backed throne. On it, smiling widely, sat Lorde Renwin. Like everything else in Hallow Fall, the faerie had changed, too. He was somehow even more beautiful here in his own domain. His frame was taller, his clothing finer, his raven eyes wider and brighter. He no longer wore a glove on his left hand: Yanni could now see that the spindle-thin fingers beneath it were thick with rings. The first was made of finest gold; the second a cluster of diamonds; the third a knot of wood, tied with a blade of grass; and the fourth was bone, a single chunk of spinal column looped around his finger.

"Sit down, dear boy! We've been waiting for you. You must be *starving* after all those stairs!"

He gestured to a vast dining table beside him. Yanni gasped – he had never seen so much food. There was enough to feed an army, steaming hot, sticky sweet and bubbling, and every colour under the sun. There was food that bristled, food that was only half there, food that crept along the table.

"Have as much as you like!" said Lorde Renwin. "Why not invite your friend outside to join us, too?"

Yanni glanced up. "How do you know about A—"

He stopped himself, just in time. Lorde Renwin flashed a smile.

"Gustiver saw you both approaching from the window," he said. "*Nothing* gets past Gustiver!"

He gestured to the top of the throne – there, gazing silently at Yanni, was the raven. Yanni's blood froze – the raven had changed, too. It now had a tiny set of stag antlers growing out of the top of its head.

"Look at your face!" sniggered Lorde Renwin. "Doesn't he look silly, my little dumpling? Doesn't he, my sweet?"

Yanni looked down – and his heart lurched. There in Lorde Renwin's lap, bouncing up and down, was

Ari. The faerie had dressed her in so many bonnets and frilly nightgowns that Yanni had mistaken her for a decorative cushion. She looked utterly ridiculous – but she looked happy, too. She reached out for Yanni with a great greedy cry.

"*Uh-uh-uh!*" Lorde Renwin chided, waggling his finger. "Remember what I said? You're going to stay here with me, for ever and ever and ever! You're *my* child now!"

Yanni closed his eyes. This was it – this was when his test began. He stepped forward and unbuckled the sling.

"I – I've brought back your changeling," he said, trying to hide the tremble in his voice.

The changeling leaped free of the sling and landed with a smash on the table. It gave Yanni one final angry hiss, then turned away to wolf down the food in messy handfuls.

"I'm rejecting your deal," said Yanni, pointing at Ari. "That child isn't yours. Give her back."

Lorde Renwin raised an eyebrow. "*Give her back?* Oh no, no, no, I'm afraid I can't do that. The child is mine, fair and square. I want her, so I should have her. Don't you think that's reasonable?"

Yanni nodded – that *did* sound reasonable. He opened his mouth to agree…

And stopped. The faerie had crept into his thoughts again, hypnotizing him into agreeing. He gritted his teeth – he had to concentrate. "No. It's not reasonable. Give her back, please."

Lorde Renwin laughed fondly. "Quite impossible! You see, I get bored *ever* so easily. Ever since I imprisoned all the other faeries in Hallow Fall and stole their magic, there's been nothing to do around here! There's only so much cavorting in the moonlight you can do on your own before it starts to feel silly." He sighed. "Besides, it's been years since I last brought a child back from Fallow Hall! That gateway's been blocked up for decades. I did once find some adults who had stumbled into the Land of Fae by mistake, but they were hopeless – just moped around and cried until they perished clean away. Do you know, the last one died *right* where you're standing!"

Yanni looked down at the floor – and yelped. At his feet was a large dark stain in the shape of a person in the floorboards. He leaped back in terror, heart pounding…

He closed his eyes and focused. The faerie was just trying to scare him. It was all as Amy had said. He had to stay firm, no matter what.

"N-no. She's not yours. You tricked me. Give her back."

Lorde Renwin looked scandalized. "*Tricked you? I did no such thing!* You're the one who said you hated her and wished she'd never been born! Didn't he, my little dumpling?"

He tickled Ari under the chin, and she giggled. Yanni felt a stab of guilt — he had said that, every word. But he hadn't meant any of it, not really.

"She's much happier here with me," said Lorde Renwin. "Your parents won't even notice she's gone. I gave you a perfectly good replacement, didn't I?"

He gestured at the changeling, who was neck-deep in something that looked like a cross between a ham and a kiwi. Yanni fumed, forcing his thoughts to stay clear.

"Of course they'll notice. You can't replace one baby with another!" He pointed. "It doesn't even have the same colour eyes!"

Lorde Renwin frowned. "Well — of course it doesn't. Why would I give it horrible, nasty *human* eyes, when it could have lovely, beautiful eyes like mine? Still, if that's what you want, I suppose…"

He raised the hand that was thick with rings and casually flicked it in the changeling's direction.

"There! All fixed. You can go now."

Yanni glanced at the changeling. Sure enough, its raven eyes were staining from black to brown right in front of him. Yanni felt his courage slip, but he had to stay strong. He couldn't take no for an answer.

"No. I don't want your changeling," Yanni snapped. "I'm taking my sister home. Now, for the last time — give her back!"

Lorde Renwin was still for a moment – and then the room changed. The lights dimmed and flickered; the walls closed in. The very air fizzed like gunpowder. The faerie towered over Yanni like a column of smoke, his eyes burning like twin fires. His face was slowly darkening into something unspeakable. Yanni had never seen anything so mean, so vindictive, so cruel, in all his life.

"Give her back?" he spat. "How dare you! She's mine! You can't have her, *no, no, no!*"

Yanni was terrified, but he closed his eyes and tightened his fingers around the rowan twig in his pocket. He *had* to stay strong. "N-no. You can't frighten me with your magic. I'm taking her back."

Lorde Renwin gave a high bark of laughter. "How fascinating! And how will you – a stupid, weak little boy – stand against *me*, the most brilliant and powerful faerie in all existence?"

He leaned closer; the sound of chimes was suddenly louder than it had ever been before, as if Yanni were trapped inside a thousand glass bells at once. When Lorde Renwin spoke, his voice was as deep as darkness and as sparse as starlight.

"Look upon me, boy. I defeated every single faerie in Hallow Fall and I wasn't even trying. I hold ten thousand names inside me. I have more magic in a speck of dust on my finger than you possess in your entire body. I can turn water to stone and make flowers out of fire. With one flick of my wrist, I could bury you in the bowels of the earth and curse you with grave-scab until the end of your days. What do you possibly have that could stand against me?"

Yanni summoned all the strength he had, grabbed the rowan twig from his pocket and held it high.

"This...!"

He trailed off. It wasn't a rowan twig any more – it was a set of jester's bells, jangling feebly in his hand.

The room shrank back to normal; the clamour of chimes faded. Lorde Renwin cackled with delight, clapping his thin white hands with glee.

"Ha ha ha! That was a most excellent joke, wasn't it? I *did* think about making both your arms fall off, but that was *so* much better!" He wiped away a tear. "Oh, you foolish boy – don't you understand who you're dealing with? Rowan might work on lesser faeries, but not on me!"

The last of Yanni's courage failed. He tried to stand firm, but the voice that came out was weak and frightened. "G-give me back my sister!"

Lorde Renwin didn't even bother to shake his head. He just smiled.

"Boy – look at her hands. She's mine already."

Yanni looked at Ari's hands ... and his heart froze. They

were stained with a thick blue paste – she was scooping it from a silver platter and stuffing it into her mouth.

"That's right – she's eaten faerie food," said Lorde Renwin, his voice low and malicious. "She hasn't *stopped* eating since I brought her here! And you know what that means, don't you? In a matter of hours, she'll become a faerie. She'll forget all about her old life – her ugly little house, her stupid boring parents, her selfish, mean, ungrateful brother... You couldn't take her back now, even if I wanted you to!"

Yanni felt himself fill with despair. "No – no, please, change her back!"

Lorde Renwin snorted. "*Change her back?* Why, only the most powerful faerie in existence would be able to do that! Which is me, I suppose. And I don't want to." He waved a hand at him. "Go, please. We grow bored of you. We faeries get bored *ever* so easily, don't we, my dear?"

Lorde Renwin turned away, cooing and giggling at the baby in his lap. Yanni fell to his knees in desperation. His one and only plan was in pieces. He couldn't let this happen. He couldn't go home without Ari. "Please! I'll give you anything you want, anything!"

Lorde Renwin snorted. "What could you *possibly* offer me that I might be interested in, boy?"

Yanni's heart sank – he was right. What on earth

did he have that Lorde Renwin didn't already have a hundred times over? He searched his mind for *anything* that might convince him to agree, anything at all that could sway his mind, anything that might persuade the faerie to change Ari back to normal…

And the answer hit him head-on, like a shaft of light in a tunnel. Yanni looked up, dreading the words even as he said them.

"How about a wager?"

THE WAGER

Yanni's words echoed through the cavernous ballroom. The raven on the back of the throne startled in shock. Every light in the room winked at the same time; the paper streamers that hung from the chandeliers shuddered and trembled like snakes, as if a gust of wind had blown inside. Even though he was facing away, Yanni knew he had Lorde Renwin's full attention.

"A *wager*, you say?"

Yanni swallowed. He was breaking the most important rule that Amy had warned him about: never, ever enter into a deal with a faerie. But what other choice did he have left?

"That's right," said Yanni. "I don't know much about faeries, but I know you can't turn down a wager if it's offered. So set me one – a challenge to win back my sister. If I win, you stop her from becoming a faerie and let me take her home."

"And if you lose?" Lorde Renwin shot back, his voice trembling with barely contained excitement. "What's in it for me?"

Yanni gulped. There was only one thing Lorde Renwin wanted that he didn't have.

"Her name. That's what I'll give you. If you have her name, you'll have total power over her."

Lorde Renwin snorted derisively. "Oh, *please*! I'll be able to find out her name the moment she starts talking. She's practically mine already."

Yanni laughed back at him. "You don't know much about babies, do you? It'll be *months* until she can talk – let alone tell you what her name is! And you don't like waiting, do you?" A thought suddenly occurred to him. "Besides, you said that when she becomes a faerie, she'll forget everything from her old life. That includes her name!"

A muscle twitched in Lorde Renwin's neck. The faerie turned around and fixed Yanni with his raven eyes.

"An excellent point, boy. But tell me – why don't you just give me her name *now*?"

He raised his left hand, and the change was instantaneous. Yanni's legs turned to jelly; his brain was cut adrift from his body and sent swimming in his skull. The ballroom floated in a pool of shifting golden light, warm and inviting, trembling with the clang of discordant chimes…

"I know – you're very tired," said Lorde Renwin kindly. "Why don't you just tell me your sister's name right now? You could even tell me yours while you're at it!"

Yanni smiled; that sounded like a great idea. He opened his mouth to—

NO NO NO NO NO…

The scream at the back of his head woke him with a jolt; the ballroom slammed back into place. Yanni stood, gasping like he'd been flung into ice water.

"Stop it!" he cried. "I mean it – try that once more, and I'll leave. Then your one and only chance to get her name is gone for ever!"

Once again, Lorde Renwin was shocked – even the raven on the throne looked surprised.

"*Hmph,*" the faerie muttered. "I don't know *how* you keep doing that, but it really is most displeasing." He sat bolt upright, drumming his hands and tapping his feet with impatience. "A wager it is! I'll set you a challenge, and if you complete it, you get your sister back. Shall we shake on it?"

He held out a hand. Yanni rolled his eyes. "Please – I'm not stupid. I'm not going to shake on *anything* until I know what the challenge is."

Lorde Renwin nodded. "Of course! How about a simple treasure hunt? I'll give you a list of objects to bring back here. Once you've collected them all, you win the challenge. Simple!"

Yanni frowned. Did he have time to do that before Mum and Dad got back?

"What kind of objects? You're not allowed to trick me with something impossible, like … bring back the inside of a bubble, or something. It has to be something I can actually do. And they have to be in Hallow Fall – I'm not having you send me to the other side of the world to bring back a single grain of sand."

Lorde Renwin held out his hands innocently. "I wouldn't dream of it! Shall we say … ten objects?"

Yanni shook his head. "Ten's too many   one object."

Lorde Renwin bristled. "*Five* objects. And take all the time you need, dear boy!"

Yanni snorted. "Don't lie to me. I know the truth – the gateway back home closes at midnight. If I don't leave Hallow Fall before then, I'll be stuck here. *Three* objects."

Lorde Renwin clenched his fists with impatience. "Fine! Three objects, all from Hallow Fall. If you succeed, I'll fix your sister and let you take her home, if you fail, you reveal her real name to me!" He held out his hand. "Now – do we have a deal?"

Yanni gulped. There was no way he'd be able to find three objects and get home before Mum and Dad –

but that didn't matter any more. All that mattered was saving Ari.

Yanni glanced down at Lorde Renwin's outstretched hand – and saw the ring of bone on his last finger, glinting in the firelight. There was no way Yanni could trust him. The faerie was arched in his seat like a cobra, fixing him with the steady gaze of a predator. What was Yanni *doing*? He was going against everything Amy had told him. "I … I'm not sure…"

Lorde Renwin snapped his hand back with fury, his raven eyes suddenly wild and hateful.

"*Blah, blah, blah!* Are you *trying* to bore me? All you do is argue and complain! After I've sat here and listened to your stupid, whingeing little voice, and been the model of kindness and patience!"

Every candle in the room started roaring like a gas lamp, sending cascades of wax gushing from the chandeliers. Lorde Renwin leaped to his feet, his whole body shaking with rage; he was suddenly twice the size. Yanni stumbled backwards; the changeling squealed and hid beneath the table. The faerie bore down on him, and Yanni caught a flash of the real eyes again, the ones he kept hidden behind his false ones, burning out from their centres…

Then, in an instant, it all stopped. Lorde Renwin calmed himself and sat back down with a sigh. The room returned to normal.

"Fine! If you're still not sure, I'll sweeten the deal. How about it?"

Yanni was reeling; the change had happened so fast that he was still locked to the spot, trembling. "Wh-what?"

"I'll let you take someone else with you on the challenge," offered Lorde Renwin. "Does that sound fair?"

Yanni hadn't even thought about that. Amy was still waiting for him outside: with her knowledge of faeries, he'd have a much better chance of finding his way around this place. "S-sure. That sounds fair."

"So we're agreed, then?" said Lorde Renwin, eagerly sticking out his hand. "Shake on it?"

Yanni looked up at the faerie's smiling face. The raven was staring down at him, too; it felt like every candle in the room was bending and twisting to face him, waiting to see what he would do next. Was he *really* about to do this?

Then he saw Ari in her ridiculous clothes, her face plastered with faerie food. He couldn't leave her here; he had to get her home, no matter what it took. He stepped across the ballroom, his feet echoing loudly on the polished floorboards, and shook Lorde Renwin's hand.

"There," he said. "I—"

He never finished the sentence. Lorde Renwin leaped from his throne and clasped him by the wrist with a shriek, his double eyes suddenly huge and wild and bright with glee. Yanni cried out – the faerie was holding him so tight that his rings dug into the flesh of his arm, almost drawing blood.

"I tricked you!" screamed Lorde Renwin. *"I tricked you, I tricked you, I tricked you!"*

Yanni screamed – something was happening beneath the faerie's grip, writhing against the surface of his skin. He tore his hand away – and saw that there was now a twisted golden shackle fastened around his wrist. He tried to wrench it off, but it was no use – the shackle was stuck tight. He watched in horror as a gold chain grew out of it, uncoiling like a snake across the floor, shooting towards the changeling beneath the table…

"Tricked you, tricked you, tricked you!"

The end of the chain snapped around the changeling's wrist like a crack of lightning, locking it fast to Yanni. Yanni tried to pull free, but it was hopeless – he and the changeling were stuck together. He suddenly realized what had happened.

"No! I didn't mean the changeling!" he cried. "I thought I could choose who I took…"

It was no use. The changeling screamed with fear … and in front of Yanni's eyes, it began to transform, flicking and flashing between a hundred different animals one after another. First it was a hawk, flapping madly to escape; then a stoat, squirming and seething between the chairs; then a cat and a hare and an adder and a bristling beetle, fighting with all their might to get free…

"Tricked you, tricked you, tricked you, tricked you!"

Yanni swung round, his blood wild with terror. Lorde Renwin was standing over him, his thin white hands clasped high above his head. The air between his palms was smouldering and darkening, forming into a solid shape: a black log, long as a spear and as dead as a stone. With a final shriek of delight, Lorde Renwin spun round and flung it straight into the fireplace.

The log erupted into bright green flames; the room swelled like a furnace – and the world was sent wheeling. Suddenly Yanni found himself tumbling through darkness, as if flying backwards down a well that rang with discordant chimes, down and down and down as Lorde Renwin's demonic cackle echoed after him…

GUSTIVER

AND WITH A SNAP THE BALLROOM DISAPPEARED, AND the purple sky took its place, and Yanni was plummeting down through a nest of branches, hitting every single one on the way before landing on the ground with a sickening *thump*.

He looked up blearily. Lorde Renwin had magicked him out of the tower. He was lying on the path beside the archway, gazing through a Yanni-shaped hole in the canopy above him. It was quickly replaced by a shocked, familiar face in broken glasses.

"Yanni?" gasped Amy. "Are you OK?"

He sat up, dazed. His head was spinning and his back throbbed, but otherwise he was fine – luckily his fall had been softened by the family of toadstools, who were squawking angrily beneath him.

"Where's Ari?" she asked. "Did the plan work?"

Yanni swallowed. "Um … not *quite…*"

He was cut off by a screech, and their heads shot up. There was something tangled in the branches above them.

It took Yanni a moment to understand what he was looking at. It was a baby – but this was no human baby. Its skin was white as bone, its eyes were raven black and its hair was a mass of grey tufts. It was wearing some sort of nappy made from moss and leaves. It was dangling from a branch by a golden chain … and it was very, very, *very* angry.

It was the changeling, returned to its real faerie form. It glared at Yanni with hate in its eyes, baring a full row of razor-sharp teeth. Amy's eyes followed the golden chain from its wrist down to the shackle on Yanni's own.

"Um … Yanni?" she whispered. "What is that, and why is it attached to you?"

"It's the changeling," said Yanni. "I, er … I might have made a wager with Lorde Renwin."

Amy's face fell. "You did *what*?"

The branch snapped, and the changeling landed on the road with a thump, flattening the last of the toadstools. It didn't stay still for long: it leaped to its feet and bolted down the road, managing only a few metres before the chain ran out and it was sent sprawling. Yanni howled with pain as his arm was almost yanked out of its socket – the changeling was only the size of a baby, but its strength was unbelievable. Within seconds, it was back on its feet and trying to run away again, dragging Yanni down the road after it. He only just managed to stop it by grabbing hold of a tree root.

"What did I tell you?" Amy cried. "I said to never, *ever* make a deal with a faerie!"

"I didn't have a choice!" Yanni wailed, holding on to the root for all he was worth. "Lorde Renwin had already given Ari some of his food – she was going to turn into a faerie, no matter what! My only chance to turn her back to normal and get her home was to make a deal with him. He said I could take someone with me on the challenge, and I thought he meant you, so—"

Amy froze. "Wait … what challenge?"

"Ahem."

Yanni spun round – and saw that they were no longer alone. There was something standing on the path behind them.

It was Lorde Renwin's raven, the tips of his antlers flashing in the moonlight, staring at him with its cold eyes. Yanni's blood froze. There was a moment of silence, and then the raven spoke.

"Right! Best get greetings out of the way, then."

He bowed with an elegant swoop of his wing.

"I'm Gustiver – Lorde Renwin's envoy, personal secretary and legal adviser." He ruffled his feathers importantly. "As per faerie law, I've been sent to explain the full details of the wager which you have just entered into with my master. Is now a good time?"

Yanni and Amy stared at the raven in stunned amazement.

"You can talk," said Yanni.

"Ravens are highly intelligent birds," said Amy, on factual autopilot. "They can copy human voices."

"Yeah, but it's got a Yorkshire accent," said Yanni.

The raven gave a deep sigh, and glanced at the changeling, which was still tugging at the end of the chain.

"Right – I suggest you get *him* calm before we proceed any further," he muttered. "I'm only allowed to explain these rules once, you know."

He hopped onto Amy's shoulder, making her screech in surprise, and poked his beak inside her backpack.

"*Hmm* – yes, this should do nicely. He'll calm down once he's somewhere dark – faeries like hiding in gaps. Shouldn't be too hard, between the two of you: one gets his arms, one gets his legs, job done!"

Thirty-four intense seconds and three hospital-grade bites later, the changeling was zipped inside the backpack. Just as Gustiver said, it calmed down the second it was somewhere dark, grumbling and occasionally kicking inside the bag but otherwise fine. Amy and Yanni, on the other hand, were much the worse for wear. They stood on the road in front of Gustiver, badly shaken.

"Grand!" said the raven. "Now that matter's dealt with, I can explain the terms and conditions of the wager. Any questions before I begin?"

Amy put her hand up. "Why do you have antlers?"

The raven gave her a look that could chill a freshly made cup of tea.

"I suggest," he said primly, "that we keep the questions to matters that are relevant to the challenge. Time's marching on."

Yanni shot Amy an annoyed look. Gustiver was right – from now on, every second counted. They'd made enough mistakes for one evening. The raven put his wings grandly behind his back and cleared his throat.

"You have now entered into a wager with my master, Lorde Renwin. As per faerie law, this arrangement has been signified by placing a log of deepest blackthorn into my master's fireplace, thus setting its terms in motion. The log will burn until midnight – you have up to then to complete the challenge."

Yanni gulped. Midnight had sounded like plenty of time in the tower, but now it seemed like hardly any at all. How was he going to complete the challenge, save his sister *and* escape from the Land of Fae before the gateway closed at midnight?

"Your challenge," Gustiver continued, "is to locate

three objects hidden in Hallow Fall. I will provide you with the details of each object at the beginning of every task. When you have found an object, you will bring it back here for my master to inspect and verify. If you successfully return all three objects before the log burns through, your sister will be returned to you in human form, and you may return home. If you do not, you will hand over your sister's full name and relinquish all ties with her, as agreed."

Amy gasped. "Yanni, you didn't…"

Yanni didn't look at her – he didn't need reminding of what he'd done. He felt sick to his stomach. The raven turned back to Yanni, and continued.

"All tasks must be completed by yourself and the changeling. The shackles binding you together are made of eldritch magic and cannot be broken. If you attempt to break the shackles before the challenge is completed, the wager will be forfeited, and you will hand over your sister's full name in recompense. Any other infraction of the rules will likewise result in penalties." He glanced around. "Any questions?"

Amy put her hand up again. Gustiver sighed.

"You don't have to put your hand up every time; you can just—"

"You say that the shackles are made of *eldritch* magic," said Amy. "Does that mean there are different kinds of magic in the Land of Fae? Like, one magic for good and another for evil? Or do different faerie clans have their own strands of magic, so they have to swear allegiance to an allocated deity in order to channel their divine powers?"

Yanni finally lost patience. "We don't have time for this!"

"I'm just interested in the specifics of the magic system," muttered Amy.

Gustiver gave her a weary look, and turned back to Yanni.

"The first object for you to locate is the Toadstone: a sacred and precious jewel hidden in Hallow Fall. You are to find it and bring it, undamaged, to my master."

Yanni looked blank. "Where's it hidden?"

Gustiver looked at him for a moment – and then tossed back his antlers and gave a bitter caw of laughter. Yanni had never been laughed at by a raven before, but it turned out they were really good at it.

"That, lad, is the entire point of the challenge!" He arranged his feathers. "Good luck to you both – I suspect you'll need it!"

With that, he launched himself from the ground and flapped up through the branches, still laughing as he flew to the top of the tower. Yanni ran after him. "Wait – can't you at least tell me where to begin, or…"

It was no use – within just a few seconds the raven had disappeared inside the tower. Yanni's stomach clenched. There was a silhouette at the window: a man, standing with a baby in his arms. It was Lorde Renwin and Ari. Yanni could swear he could even hear the faerie laughing at him, too, over the endless ringing of bells.

Yanni burned with humiliation. He'd been so easily tricked: he'd ignored Amy's advice and tried to fix everything himself, but had only made it worse. He'd never felt more stupid or small in his life. He turned back round – and saw Amy flicking through the ORC'S QUEST instruction manual.

"What are you doing?" he muttered.

"Looking to see if there's anything in here about a Toadstone," she said. "Maybe we can use it to find—"

Yanni's anger suddenly boiled over. He grabbed the manual and threw it into the forest.

"Hey!" protested Amy. "What are you—"

"For heaven's sake – don't you understand?" he cried. "None of that stupid fantasy nerd stuff works here! This isn't a game! The rowan didn't make a blind bit of difference. Magic systems, mage-chancellors … none of that's going to help me save my sister. So unless you're going to actually help me, don't say anything!"

Amy flinched like she'd been burned. Yanni turned away, guilt churning in his stomach. He hadn't meant to throw the book away; he hadn't meant to be so mean. But he couldn't help it. He was in more trouble than he had ever been in his life – and there was no way of turning back now. All he wanted was to go home, and it was the one thing he couldn't do.

He grabbed the backpack and swung it over his shoulders. The weight of the changeling hung even heavier on his shoulders than before as he stormed down the path, through the prison of trees and on towards the first task.

THE FIRST TASK

YANNI AND AMY WALKED IN SILENCE BACK TO THE crossroads. The signpost was still there when they arrived, waving cheerfully.

"Back so soon? Any luck rescuing your sister?"

"No," grumbled Yanni. "I got tricked into entering a wager with Lorde Renwin."

He held up the chain. The signpost reeled. "Oh *my*. That *is* bad news! To enter a wager with a faerie…"

The last thing Yanni needed was further details about the mistake he'd made. "Listen – I'm looking for something called a Toadstone. Have you heard of it?"

"Of course!" said the post. "I know everything. I'm a signpost."

"And … can you tell me where it is?"

"Absolutely!" said the post. "I'd only be happy to help. It's been a long time since I had the pleasure of meeting two such polite young children!"

Yanni began to perk up. This was easier than he'd expected. Maybe finding the Toadstone wasn't going to be so tough after all. He glanced at Amy, but she just stood in silence, her gaze fixed on the ground. Yanni felt another surge of shame, but he pushed it down – he didn't have time to worry about that.

The signpost scratched its head.

"Hmm, now let me see. Toadstone, Toadstone... Ah yes, I remember! It's with the Goblin Queen."

Yanni thought he'd misheard. "There are goblins in Hallow Fall, too?"

"Of course there are!" said the post. "Thousands of them. But they all hid underground when Lorde Renwin appeared. Goblins and faeries are sworn enemies, you know. If you want the Toadstone, it'll be inside the Goblin Queen's keep."

"And where's that?" asked Yanni.

"Inside the Goblin Fortress, of course!" said the post. "Which is found beyond the endless twisting tunnels of the Goblin Maze, which is hidden in the darkest heart of Goblin Mountain, which is defended by the Goblin Queen's loyal army of goblin soldiers."

Yanni's face fell. So much for the task being simple. "Are you *sure* that's where it is?"

The post fell quiet. Yanni had never been given such a reproachful look by a piece of wood before.

"You're right," said the post calmly. "Maybe you *do* know better than me. After all, I'm just a magical signpost."

"Don't mind him," said Amy quietly. "He forgets his manners sometimes."

Yanni shot her a glance. Amy still wasn't looking at him.

"No offence taken!" said the post, cheerful as always. It pointed down one of the roads. "Walk down there until your fingers start tingling, and then look over your left shoulder. The entrance to Goblin Mountain will be straight ahead."

Yanni frowned. The directions made no sense. How were you supposed to walk until your fingers tingled? But the signpost was already doffing its hat.

"Good luck!" it said. "And be careful around the Goblin Queen – she's got a hell of a temper on her!"

Yanni stood on the path, gazing over his left shoulder and holding up his tingling fingers.

"I guess that's Goblin Mountain," he said.

Once more, the forest beside the path had disappeared; in its place stood a towering peak of desolate rock, belching bursts of smoke into the sky. Rivulets of red-hot lava poured down it, scoring its face into blades and forming pools on either side. The air reeked of fire and singed iron.

A vast stone entranceway lay before them, flanked by two enormous stone statues. Yanni could only assume they were goblin soldiers: they had arms like tree trunks and necks like bags of oranges. They wore heavy armour that looked like it was made from anvils and helmets covered in spikes; the faces beneath their visors were mean and ugly and vicious, all squat piggy eyes and tusks.

Yanni squinted. He had a feeling that he recognized them somehow. In fact, looking around, he felt like he recognized *all* of this...

He finally got it. "It's the village square!"

It all made sense. The broiling pool of molten lava was the village green. The bat-infested caves of blackened rock were the houses. The remains of a charred tree stump beside them was the bus stop. Yanni pointed at the stone doors ahead.

"I guess that makes Goblin Mountain the village shop," he said. "Weird, huh?"

Amy didn't reply; she was still staring at the ground, refusing to meet his gaze. Yanni squirmed with guilt. The sooner he finished the challenge and got everything back to normal, the better...

Yanni paused. Did he *want* things to go back to normal? *Normal* meant being stuck alone in Fallow Hall. *Normal* meant that Mum and Dad would still be exhausted. Yanni had been so concerned with fixing everything, he'd forgotten how miserable he'd been in the first place.

He shook away the thought and adjusted the changeling on his back – at least the faerie creature was being easier now. It had hardly made a peep since they put it inside the backpack.

"Well – let's go," said Yanni, walking towards the stone entrance. "The Toadstone's somewhere inside that mountain…"

"Sure," said Amy, not moving. "Best of luck."

Yanni stopped dead. "You're … you're not coming?"

Amy finally looked at him. Her face was very calm and very blank.

"Me? Oh no, I don't think so. It's probably best if I stay here, where I won't bother you."

Yanni opened his mouth – and closed it again. He glanced at the entrance to Goblin Mountain. He really didn't want to go in by himself.

"Um … maybe it's better if you come, too," he said, trying to hide his nervousness. "We'll cover more ground if we—"

"You know, you haven't once thanked me?"

Yanni was thrown off balance. "What?"

Amy was staring right at him now. "You haven't thanked me. Not once. I didn't have to come with you,

you know. When Ari got stolen, I could have run home and let you sort this out by yourself. But I didn't. I stayed and helped. If it weren't for me, you'd never have even thought about faeries. But not once have you said, 'Thanks, Amy, I really appreciate it.' You haven't even been *polite* to me!"

Yanni frowned. He hated to admit it, but she sort of had a point. "Er ... we don't really have time for—"

But Amy wasn't planning on stopping any time soon. "You know what your problem is, Yanni? You think that just because *you* have issues, no one else's thoughts or feelings matter. You're *spoiled.* You've always been spoiled!"

Yanni was stumped. "I'm not spoiled."

"Yes, you are!" said Amy, hitting her stride. "Even when we were little kids, you used to boss me around like I was your servant. And now you never even bother to talk to me at those family gatherings." She fumed. "You know the funniest part? Tonight, I didn't want to come to your house. But I told myself to give you another chance. I thought, *Hey, maybe Yanni's not so bad now.* And look how wrong I was! Here we are, transported to another world and about to fight our way inside Goblin Mountain, and you're *still* ungrateful, you're *still* bossy, and you're *still being rude to me!*"

Yanni was speechless. No one had ever spoken to

him like this – not Mum and Dad, not his grandparents, not his friends, not anyone.

Amy glared at him. "*Well?* Are you going to thank me now? You could say, 'Thanks, Amy, for helping me save my sister, even though I've been really rude to you all evening and called you a nerd for no reason whatsoever.'"

Yanni's eyes widened. "Wait … do you *actually* want me to say that, or…?"

Amy just folded her arms and stared at him. Yanni groaned, looked at his feet and took a deep breath.

"ThanksAmyforhelpingmesavemysister."

"Even though…?"

"EventhoughI'vebeenreallyrudetoyoualleveningand calledyouanerdfornoreasonwhatsoever."

"Great. And how about an apology, too, while we're at it?"

Yanni blinked. "For … for what, exactly?"

"I'll take anything at this point! Sorry for being rude? Sorry for calling me names? Sorry for throwing my manual into the forest? Sorry for storming upstairs and leaving me on my own when I offered to help you on your first day of school? Take your pick!"

Yanni turned bright red – when you put it like that, he really had been completely awful. He tried to work out which answer was least likely to get him shouted at again.

"Er … sorry for everything you just said. And sorry for being rude when we were kids, too. Basically, sorry for everything I've said and done to you up until this point."

Amy weighed this up, nodded with approval and finally unfolded her arms. "Thank you, Yanni. Apology accepted. Shall we get going?"

With that, she marched off towards the mountain entrance. Yanni watched her go, dazed. Once, at his last school, all the fire alarms and school bells had suddenly gone off for five ear-splitting seconds, and then stopped at the same time. Being shouted at by Amy had felt a bit like that.

He followed her to the great stone doors at the base of the mountain – and found, to his surprise, that they'd been left ajar.

"They're not even locked," said Yanni. "It doesn't seem very fortified, for a fortress."

Amy shrugged. "Maybe they don't need to lock anyone out, if there's a maze inside?"

Yanni nodded. The doors weren't quite open enough to slip through, and looked like they weighed a ton. "Come on, let's open them together and—"

He caught himself just in time.

"I mean – Amy, would you mind helping me open the doors, please?"

Amy looked impressed. "Thank you, Yanni! I'd be happy to help."

"No," he replied. "Thank *you*. I appreciate your help very much."

"All right, all right, don't lay it on."

They heaved the doors open together, just enough for them to squeeze through. Inside lay a long, low tunnel, stretching deep into the mountain. It was almost pitch-black, except for a few flickering torches lining the walls. Yanni could *feel* it already – the beating red-hot heart of the mountain, breathing out from inside a mile of rock. From somewhere deep, deep, deep within came the dull and steady sound of hammering.

"It sounds like they're making something," said Yanni nervously. "Maybe we can follow that sound to get through the maze?"

Amy shook her head. "We could still get lost. We should leave a trail of something so we can retrace our footsteps – some string, or breadcrumbs, or something. Let's check our inventory."

"Inventory?"

"Look in your pockets."

Yanni emptied his pockets, but all he had was the coin he'd taken from the shop floor earlier. "I've got fifty pence."

Amy sighed. "That's better than me. Since you chucked away my manual, I've just got these."

She held out the two eight-sided dice from ORC's QUEST.

"I must have put them in my pocket when you stormed upstairs." She gave him a hurt look. "You know, I was really looking forward to playing it with you tonight. I haven't played in months."

Yanni winced – he wasn't sure he could handle any more shouting. "I thought you played it with your friend, Chloe."

Amy bit her lip.

"I haven't seen Chloe in a while. We used to see each other all the time – every day. We were best friends at primary school. We were even going to set up an ORC's QUEST club when we started at Riddleton this year." Her voice fell quiet. "Then when term began, Chloe started hanging out with another girl called Cecile. She's really popular. I kept inviting Chloe over to mine, but suddenly she was busy all the time. Then she stopped talking to me during breaks. She doesn't even answer my texts now." She shuffled her feet. "So, for what it's worth, I was really looking forward to hanging out with someone tonight. My Friday nights have been kind of boring recently."

Yanni felt a stab of guilt. He'd known Amy was quiet, but he had no idea that she was so lonely. He suddenly felt very sorry, *extremely* sorry, for throwing her manual away. She sighed, and quickly changed the subject.

"Right! Well, we'll just have to hope we don't get lost looking for this fortress. More importantly, we need to come up with a plan for what we're going to do when we get inside it." Her eyes lit up. "Like DISGUISES!"

Yanni frowned. "Disguises?"

"We'll dress up like goblins, so no one recognizes us!" she said excitedly. "I've always wanted to do that!"

Yanni smiled. It was nice to see Amy excited again. "Where are we going to find disguises? You saw those statues outside – they all wear goblin armour."

Amy shrugged. "We're bound to find *something* inside this maze – come on, let's get going!"

She scampered down the tunnel without looking back. Yanni squirmed – the tunnel was so dark that he could barely make out the wall beside him.

"Wait!" he cried out. "Let's take a torch at least…"

He grabbed a torch from the wall and tried to wrench it free, but it didn't budge from the torch-holder. He tried again with both hands: nothing. Yanni gritted his teeth, placed his foot against the wall, heaved with all his might…

"I wouldn't do that if I were you," said a voice in the dark.

Yanni fell back in fright. What he had mistaken for a torch-holder was, in fact, a hand: the biggest, beefiest hand Yanni had ever seen in his life. It was attached to an arm that looked like a tree trunk, which led to a neck like a bag of oranges, which held up a big mean scowling head with piggy eyes and little tusks…

Yanni finally realized who the goblins reminded him of.

"It's the shopkeeper!" he cried. "That's it! The goblins all look exactly like the—"

Yanni didn't finish his sentence. The goblin guard stepped out of the dark, whacked him on the head with the torch, and that was that.

GOBBROX

Yanni opened his eyes. He wished he hadn't. His head felt like a smashed egg.

It took him a moment to understand what he was looking at: a stone floor, racing beneath a giant goblin bottom. He was slung over the goblin's back, being carried through winding stone tunnels while the goblin talked to himself excitedly.

"*Two* intruders! TWO! I can't wait to see the look on their faces…"

"Y-Yanni?"

Yanni glanced groggily to one side; Amy was slung over the goblin's other shoulder, looking very much like someone who'd also just been knocked unconscious by a massive torch.

"H-how long have we been out?" she slurred.

Yanni had no idea – it could have been one minute; it could have been twenty. He panicked. Every second was another second closer to midnight and losing the challenge – how much time had they lost already? He knocked politely on the goblin's back.

"Um ... excuse me, sir? Could you put us down, please?"

The goblin snorted. "Put you down? Very funny! There's only one place I'm putting you down, chum, and that's the Goblin Dungeon!"

Yanni's stomach dropped. Being locked in a dungeon, with time ticking on, was the worst thing that could happen to them. He had to stop it. He hammered his fists on the goblin's armour.

"Put us down! Right now!" he demanded.

The goblin stopped. Then he picked Yanni up by the scruff of the neck and dangled him in front of his face like a wet rag. Up close, the goblin's resemblance to the Fallow Hall shopkeeper was uncanny. If the shopkeeper grew four feet taller and put on about fifty stone, they'd be identical twins.

"I said *no*," snapped the goblin curtly. "Now, if you don't mind, you're ruining my special moment. I've just caught the first-*ever* intruders into Goblin Mountain. This is a big day for me!"

He slung Yanni back over his shoulder and kept on running, weaving through the tunnels as if by instinct.

"That's right – you two are going to make me

famous!" the goblin chuckled. "Everyone laughed when I got allocated Cave Entrance Duty – well, who's laughing now? That's right! Me! Gobbrox!" He giggled. "When the Goblin Queen hears about this, I'll be promoted! I'll finally get my own helmet. And armour. She might even let me have a weapon again!"

Yanni's face fell. His plan hadn't worked at all. He turned to Amy sheepishly. "Um … any better ideas?"

Amy shook her head. Yanni knew she was right; even if they did manage to escape Gobbrox, they'd never find their way out of the Goblin Maze. It was like a tangle of jumbled wires. The only sign of life was the red-hot glow that seemed to be getting brighter and brighter with every step, and the blistering heat getting hotter and hotter, and the relentless hammering growing louder and louder, like a clock grinding down the seconds…

The tunnel suddenly ended, and Gobbrox raced into a vast stone cavern, lit by roaring red fire. Yanni gasped: the cavern floor was filled with a great glowing lake of lava, surrounded by columns of black smoke and steaming fissures. The ceiling was as high as a cathedral, teeming with shadows and stalactites. The heat inside was demonic, making Yanni's eyes water and his nose hairs char and shrivel.

Gobbrox ran to the lake's edge and, without a moment's pause, flung himself into the centre. Yanni didn't even have time to scream before Gobbrox landed on a blackened boulder floating halfway across, then leaped through the air again and slammed onto the furthest shore.

"*INTRUDEEEEERRRRSS!*" he bellowed.

Yanni looked up, heart pounding. There was another great set of double doors before them, lined with more goblin statues. A goblin guard stood in front of them – or rather, stood leaning against the doors and snoring loudly. Unlike Gobbrox, he wore a heavy metal breastplate and spiked helmet, and carried a giant club studded with nails. He woke with a start, raised his visor and scowled. Yanni blinked. The guard had the exact same grumpy face of the shopkeeper.

"Oh – you again, Gobbrox," the guard muttered. "What do you want?"

Gobbrox was dancing up and down with excitement. "I've done it, Grunta! I've finally found some intruders!"

Grunta sighed. "Course you have. What is it this time – a squirrel? A spider? Another one of those *suspicious*-looking pigeons you spotted last week?"

"They're real this time!" Gobbrox insisted. "Look!"

He held out Yanni and Amy in front of him, waving them like a pair of handkerchiefs.

"I caught them sneaking through the cave entrance, talking about how they were going to break into the fortress!" said Gobbrox. "I'm taking them straight to the Goblin Queen!"

He tried to step past, but Grunta stopped him. His eyes had narrowed.

"Maybe *I* should take them," he suggested, carefully lifting Yanni out of Gobbrox's hands. "After all, I'm on Door Duty, aren't I? You can get back to your post and—"

Gobbrox tried to grab Yanni back. "No! *I'm* getting the credit for this, not you! I'm sick of being stuck on Cave Entrance Duty – I want to get back in the fortress. I want my own armour and helmet – and a weapon, too! A big one!"

Grunta gave him a pitying look. "Gobbrox, they're *never* going to let you have a weapon again. Not after what happened last time."

"That was years ago, no one remembers," muttered Gobbrox. "Now stop stalling! Let me past!"

Yanni watched in horror as the two guards fought and squabbled. What on earth could he and Amy do now? They'd *never* be able to get back across the lava lake by themselves, let alone escape a locked dungeon. And that wasn't the only problem. The changeling wasn't asleep in the backpack any more – for some reason, it had started kicking and thrashing to escape. Something was driving it crazy – but what?

"Fine!" Grunta snapped. "Final offer – we split the intruders, fifty–fifty."

"No!" Gobbrox shouted.

"You won't be allowed anywhere near the Goblin Queen, you idiot," said Grunta. "Not after … that *thing* you did. If you're with *me*, you've at least got a chance of being granted permission to speak to her. Deal?"

Gobbrox sighed. "Fine! Fifty–fifty it is. Do you want their top halves, or their bottom halves?"

He held Amy in both hands and made to break her in two. Grunta stopped him at the last second as she squawked in terror.

"No, you idiot! I mean, you hand in the girl, and I hand in the boy!"

"Oh, right," said Gobbrox. "Yeah, that's an even better idea."

Yanni bellowed in pain – the changeling was going absolutely berserk inside the bag now, biting and scratching his back to escape. It felt like being attacked by a swarm of wasps. Grunta held him up, frowning.

"Hang on – there's something in his bag!" he muttered. "I'd better check it for weapons…"

He unzipped the backpack, peering close at the tiny opening…

"No!" Yanni cried.

Everything happened very fast. The changeling

flew out of the backpack and dug its claws straight into Grunta's face. Grunta shrieked in agony, dropping Yanni and his club to the ground. Yanni tried to scramble away, but the chain held fast to the changeling, who was still clamped tight to Grunta's face. Yanni had to roll across the floor and leap out of the way as Grunta charged around in circles, stamping his feet in pain and getting his ankles tangled in the chain.

"GOBBROX!" he screamed. *"GET IT OFF ME!"*

Gobbrox looked at Yanni, looked at the changeling, looked at Grunta's club on the ground – and beamed with delight. "I've got it! I've got it! I've got it!"

He dropped Amy, grabbed the club, leaned back with all his might, and swung it straight at the changeling. The changeling sprang free at the last second … and the club smashed into Grunta's face. Grunta made a sound like a dinosaur choking on porridge, spat out all of his teeth, tripped over his tangled ankles and passed out on top of Gobbrox. Gobbrox collapsed to the ground, Grunta's metal helmet smashed into the top of his head … and knocked him out cold, too. Within two seconds, both goblins were sprawled unconscious on the floor.

Yanni stared in shock. The changeling was still stuck fast to the golden chain snagged around Grunta's ankles, thrashing and hissing. Quick as a flash, Amy was on her feet, untangling the chain, and stuffed the changeling back into the bag. It fought for a moment longer, before the dark quickly calmed it and it fell quiet again.

"Wh-what just happened?" asked Yanni. "Something made it go completely nuts!"

"Good thing it did," said Amy. "A few more seconds, and we'd have been prisoners."

Amy was right – it had been a lucky escape. But the guards could wake up again any second. "Quick – what do we do now?"

Amy's eyes widened. "Why do you keep asking me that? I don't know how to break into a goblin lair any more than you do!"

Yanni racked his mind. "What if this was ORC'S QUEST? What would Saphiana do?"

Amy paused in her panic – and all of a sudden, her eyes lit up. "She wouldn't go through the main doors. She's smart. She'd find a side door and sneak inside that way. There's *always* a side door." She pointed. "Like that one!"

Yanni turned around. Sure enough, hidden behind one of the statues was another doorway. Amy was good at this. She raced over to Grunta and pulled a heavy ring of keys from his belt.

"Bingo!" she said. "By the time these two wake up and sound the alarm, we'll already be inside and looking for the keep!"

Yanni blinked. "But you heard what the signpost said – there are thousands of goblins inside. How are we going to walk around the fortress without them noticing us?"

Amy grinned. She heaved off Grunta's massive spiked helmet and wiggled it about excitedly.

"Did someone say … *disguises*?"

THE GOBLIN FORTRESS

Yanni carefully unlocked the door and peeked inside.

The wall of heat hit him immediately. If the cavern had been hot, the inside of the fortress was absolutely rash-inducing. He couldn't see a thing – just steam and smoke. The sound of hammers filled the air, along with hissing water and orders being bellowed. Whatever the goblins were making, they were evidently busy.

"Is it clear?" came a muffled voice behind him.

Yanni glanced over his shoulder. Amy was standing unsteadily in place behind him, wearing Grunta's helmet and breastplate. Both were far too big for her – the bottom of the breastplate reached her ankles. Even with her face concealed by the visor, the disguise was pretty ropy.

"Are you *sure* we're both going to fit under that?" said Yanni nervously. "It looks really heavy…"

"We need to look goblin-sized, remember?" said Amy, her voice reverberating inside the metal visor. "Besides, there's only one helmet. Come on! I'll sit on your shoulders – you can be the legs."

Yanni frowned. "Why can't *you* be the legs?"

"Because I'm not strong enough to carry you *and* the armour!" she snapped. "Come on – we have to go before they wake up!"

She nodded at the two still-unconscious goblins. Yanni groaned. Once again, she was right. He crouched down and let Amy clamber onto his shoulders, then he tried to stand. His knees buckled. As predicted, the armour weighed an absolute ton, and he already had the changeling in the backpack strapped over his shoulders. Yanni had to grit his teeth with the effort of holding them all up.

"Right – onward!" Amy commanded, wobbling on his shoulders unsteadily.

Yanni stumbled forward on shaking legs, letting Amy swing the door open before he staggered into the fortress. The heat and the smoke and steam hit him again; he could barely breathe, let alone see through the tiny chink in the breastplate. It was so hot inside the armour that it felt like being trapped inside a faulty boiler. Within seconds, sweat was pouring down his face. How on earth were they supposed to find the keep like this?

That wasn't the only problem. For some reason, the changeling was kicking off again, hissing and scratching and shrieking with anger in the backpack. Yanni fumed. He never thought he'd miss Ari's screaming, but at least she didn't maul him.

"What's – OW! – wrong with it?" he hissed. "If it keeps making that kind of noise, we'll – OW! – get caught immediately!"

"Stop distracting me," muttered Amy, wobbling in place. "I need to focus on looking where we're going or— *Watch out!*"

Yanni stopped at the last second. He peered down at his feet, and his stomach flipped. The floor directly ahead fell straight away, down into a great roaring furnace. No wonder the fortress was so hot: far below them, a lava flow ran from one end of the cavern to the other, surrounded by hundreds of goblins tapping off streams of molten metal from a vat into troughs and moulds. The air was filled with sparks and steam as they hammered away at anvils, forging weapons and shields and throwing them into clattering piles.

Amy gasped. "Of course – don't you see? It's *iron*!" She pointed to the furnace. "Everything the goblins use is made from it: their armour, their weapons… That's why the changeling's so upset! Faeries hate iron, remember?"

Yanni grimaced. *That* was why the changeling was

slashing and biting to get free – it was surrounded by the material it hated more than anything. It wasn't angry – it was in pain.

"*OW!* Well, for God's sake, let's – *OW!* – find this keep and get out of here before it—"

He stopped. He had just seen something far below them.

At first he thought it was just another burning torch; then he realized this torch was floating in mid-air, swimming in a pale green glow. It was the blackthorn log that Lorde Renwin had thrown into the fire ... and one end had already started turning to ash, leaving a ghost of itself behind. The goblins didn't seem to be able to see it: as Yanni watched, one of the goblins even walked straight through it without noticing.

Yanni understood what it meant – the log wasn't really there. It was a message from Lorde Renwin. He was gloating at him; he was showing Yanni that he was running out of time. Yanni gritted his teeth. He wasn't going to give the faerie the satisfaction.

"Well, come on," he said. "Let's – OW! – find this Toadstone before—"

"STOP RIGHT THERE!"

Yanni spun round so fast that Amy almost toppled off his shoulders. Two goblin guards were standing right behind them, both holding clubs the size of snooker tables. Sure enough, they each had the shopkeeper's scowling face.

"What are you doing in here?" grunted the first one. "That's class three armour you're wearing – you're supposed to be on Door Duty!"

"Identify yourself!" growled the second, his grip tightening on his club.

Yanni's blood turned cold. This was it – they were done for. There was no way that the goblins would be convinced by their terrible disguise. They couldn't even make a run for it now; their only choice was to give themselves up before—

"How DARE you talk that way to your superior, you WORTHLESS MAGGOT!" Amy roared.

Yanni almost fell over – even the changeling stopped squirming. Amy had shouted at the top of her lungs – no, shouting wasn't the right word for it. She had *bellowed*, transforming her voice instantly into the grizzled bark of a furious goblin.

"Answer me, SCUM!" she boomed at the guards. "And stand up straight when talking to your commanding officer!"

The goblins were completely befuddled. "What's a commanding officer?"

"HOW DARE YOU ANSWER ME BACK!" Amy roared in reply. "The temerity – the GALL! I should have you both shaved and salted! I should come over there and give you a taste of the back of my hand!"

There was a pause. She gave Yanni a kick under the armour.

"I said, I SHOULD COME OVER THERE AND GIVE YOU A TASTE OF THE BACK OF MY HAND."

Yanni snapped awake and stumbled forward, dazed. He couldn't believe it – awkward Amy had completely transformed. She was pushing around the two goblins like her life depended on it. Which, to be fair, it did.

"I've met a few worthless morons in my time," she bellowed, "but never, NEVER two snots as insubordinate as you! To confuse *me* with a mere Door Duty goblin…"

One of the guards pointed in confusion. "But … you're wearing class three armour…"

"OF COURSE I AM!" Amy boomed, not missing a beat. "For the top-secret mission I'm on, commanded by the Goblin Queen herself! And you two IDIOTS just nearly gave the whole thing away!" She glared at the two guards. "Well? Do you want to answer to her *yourselves*?"

The guards both fell to their knees in horror. "No – no, sir, have mercy!"

"Don't tell her, please!"

Yanni was speechless. Amy had the two goblins eating out of the palm of her hand. She dismissed them with a flick of her wrist.

"*Pah!* You two grubs aren't worth the effort. Now, if you could just tell me where the keep is before you leave…"

One of the guards frowned. "You don't know?"

"*I ASKED FOR DIRECTIONS, NOT OPINIONS, YOU STINKING PILE OF DOG OFFAL!*" Amy screamed.

The guard wailed with terror and pointed a trembling finger to a set of double doors behind them. "Y-you're standing right next to it, sir!"

"I know I am!" said Amy. "Now for the last time, GO!"

The goblins needed no further encouragement. They scrambled to their feet and raced off, practically tripping over their own clubs to get away. Yanni watched them go in wordless amazement.

"Amy – that was … that was…"

"I know," she said glumly. "Terrible. I got the voice all wrong. I totally messed up their ranking system, too."

Yanni was thrown. Amy hadn't been terrible at all – she'd been incredible. What was she talking about?

Before he could say any more, the changeling sank its teeth into his back again. Yanni howled. "Quick – the keep!"

He pinballed off the walls and charged through the doors with the last of his strength. He didn't even have time to check if the room was empty – the changeling was attacking his back like it was on fire. He crashed to the floor in agony.

"Quick – close the doors!" he wailed.

Amy scrambled out of the armour and slammed the double doors just in time. Yanni crawled out of the breastplate and tore off the backpack; finally freed from the iron armour, the changeling stopped fighting. Yanni lay on the floor, groaning with blessed relief. After the heat of the furnace, the skin of his back almost sizzled on the cool stones.

"Oh my God," he gasped. "After this, I'm *never* complaining about Ari ever again…"

Amy didn't reply – she was too busy staring at what was inside the keep. Yanni sat up, looked around … and his mouth dropped.

The Goblin Keep was filled with gold: piles and piles and piles of it. It was heaped right to the ceiling, which was held up by hundred-foot stone archways that were almost completely hidden by gleaming golden dunes. And not just gold, either – there was every kind of jewel under the sun, sapphires and emeralds and rubies as big as footballs, all flung in thoughtless piles. There was no telling how much it was all worth. Millions – *hundreds* of millions maybe. If the precious Toadstone was going to be hidden anywhere, then it was in here.

But which one was the Toadstone?

Yanni glanced around in growing dread. He had no idea how big the Toadstone was, what colour it was, what shape it was. It could be right in front of him, or hidden beneath a thousand tonnes of gold.

"Yanni," whispered Amy nervously. "Which one is it?"

Yanni finally understood how fiendish Lorde Renwin's task was. They had sneaked inside Goblin Mountain, made their way through the Goblin Maze, overcome the guards, and found the Goblin Keep against all odds ... and it was still impossible.

He swallowed. "We'll just have to check every single one, and hope we find it before—"

"INTRUDEEEEERRRRSS!"

Yanni spun round – and his stomach dropped. The doors behind them had been flung open; in the entrance stood a dozen heavily armed goblin soldiers. Standing at the front was Gobbrox.

"That's them, Your Majesty!" he cried. "I told you we had intruders!"

Yanni's eyes widened. Gobbrox wasn't standing on his feet – he was dangling in mid-air, his meaty toes barely scraping the floor. A muscular hand was holding him up by his head. The hand was enormous – the arm it was attached to was even bigger, the neck even more so. And the head that it led to...

Yanni gazed up, shaking with terror. Once again, he was staring at the gruesome, scowling face of the shopkeeper — but this one only just managed to fit through the huge double doorway. She was twice the size of the other goblins, twice as muscular, her tusk-like teeth twice as sharp. And sitting on her head was a gigantic iron crown.

It was the Goblin Queen. She had found them ... and she was very, very angry.

THE GOBLIN QUEEN

THE ROOM HELD ITS BREATH. GOBBROX BROKE THE silence, jabbing a finger at Yanni and Amy.

"That's them, Your Majesty! The ones who overpowered me ... and, er, hit Grunta in the face. I told you I wasn't making it up!"

The Goblin Queen flung him to one side and stormed into the keep, the stone floor cracking beneath her with every step, making the columns of the room tremble and the golden mountains sing.

"GUARDS!" she roared. "SEIZE THEM!"

The guards surrounded Yanni and Amy in a tight circle of spears and clubs. Two leaped forward to grab Yanni; another two grabbed Amy. The second their iron armour came close, the changeling started shrieking inside the backpack.

Gobbrox leaped up from the stack of rubies he'd landed on.

"Look in the bag!" he cried. "Look at what they've brought with them!"

A fifth goblin ran over and tore open the backpack. The changeling shot out at once, springing off the goblin's armour like it was red hot and screeching with pain. It tried to escape, but it was no use – the chain on its wrist held it tight. The Goblin Queen's eyes widened.

"THEY'VE BROUGHT IN A FAERIE!" she boomed. *"THE SWORN ENEMY OF THE GOBLINS!"*

It all happened too fast. A soldier raced forward with a huge set of iron tongs and clamped it around the changeling's chest, snatching it in mid-air. The scream of pain that came from the changeling's throat was hideous; it suddenly transformed into the shape of an adder, flinging itself in every direction and slithering wildly to escape, but it was no use – the tongs held fast.

Yanni cried out in horror. "Stop! You're hurting it!"

But the Goblin Queen wasn't listening. With one swing of her colossal arms, she snatched Yanni up like a paper puppet and held him trembling before her face.

"HOW DARE YOU!" she bellowed, her breath blasting him like a hurricane. *"TO DARE SET FOOT INSIDE MY KEEP…"*

Yanni was utterly terrified. But he had to keep his head. "Please, you don't understand! We were sent here by Lorde Renwin…"

Every goblin in the room gasped at the same time. The Goblin Queen stopped dead. You could have heard a pin drop.

"L-Lorde Renwin?" stammered the Goblin Queen. "You work for *him*? The Pale Stranger?"

Yanni had no idea what the Goblin Queen meant by *Pale Stranger*, but at least she was listening to him. "Yes, that's him! He stole my sister and set me a challenge to—"

"The Riddle King?" she continued. "The Prince of Two Faces? The one who took over Hallow Fall, tried to murder me, and forced the goblins to hide inside Goblin Mountain for over three hundred years? You work for *HIM*?"

Yanni could feel her hand gradually closing around his ribcage. The edges of her eyes had started to develop blood vessels. He thought very, very carefully about what the best thing would be to say next.

"No?" he tried.

It didn't work. The Goblin Queen raised him above her head.

"They're not intruders – THEY'RE ASSASSINS! Assassins sent by the Pale Stranger himself!" She spun round to the goblins. "Guards, prepare the three deepest, darkest dungeons you can find! Make them as cold and lifeless and desolate as you can!" She roared with laughter, her eyes bulging out of her head. "That's right!

You three will never see sunlight again! You're going to rot down here for the rest of your lives!"

Yanni was overcome with despair. Their challenge was already over – and now he and Amy would never see their families again. Yanni looked at the changeling, still trapped in the form of an adder, writhing in agony in the iron tongs and knew he had to do something. He fought against the Goblin Queen with everything he had.

"No – don't, please! You have to listen to me…"

He stopped – the keep had suddenly fallen silent. The guards were frozen to the spot. The Goblin Queen had stopped waving him around, too. The only sound was the gentle chime of something bouncing on the stone floor.

Yanni looked down. It took him a moment to recognize what it was. There, rolling to a stop at the Goblin Queen's feet, was the fifty-pence piece. It must have fallen from his pocket when he was struggling. The Goblin Queen picked it up in her enormous fingers, holding it so that its edges twinkled in the lamplight.

"It is … *beautiful*!" she gasped.

The other goblins crowded around her, oohing and aahing.

"Such metalwork!"

"Such craftsmanship!"

"Such artistry!"

"Which bit do you stab people with?"

The Goblin Queen put Yanni down. The guards were so captivated that they even let go of Amy, and dropped the tongs holding the changeling. It snapped back to its faerie child form, gave a quick hiss and hid in a corner. Yanni stared at the enthralled goblins in confusion.

"It's nothing special; it's just—"

Amy elbowed him savagely in the ribs. "A gift, Your Highness! A priceless coin forged from our most precious human metals. We're not assassins – we're gift-bearers!"

The Goblin Queen gasped. "This is for *me*?" Her eyes shone with wonder. "What our goblin metalworkers could achieve with such a priceless artefact to study…"

Yanni finally saw the answer. *This* was how they could finish the challenge. "That's right! So how about we make a deal? You give us the Toadstone, and we'll give you—"

Things escalated rapidly. In five seconds, every goblin in the room had their weapons pointed at Amy's and Yanni's throats.

"HOW DARE YOU!" bellowed the Goblin Queen. "To DARE to suggest that we give you *anything* from the Goblin Keep…"

"It's not the only gift we brought!" Amy said hastily. "Behold! We also have, er … these!"

She reached into her pocket and held out the two

plastic dice. Yanni winced – this was desperate. But to his surprise, the goblins lowered their weapons and gasped even louder than before.

"So small!"

"So light!"

"So … not made of iron!"

"Which bit do you stab people with?"

Yanni couldn't believe it – it was working. "You see? You don't *have* to make things from iron. With these to study, you could make whatever you want. Surely that's worth trading the Toadstone for?"

The Goblin Queen thought it over. "This does seem reasonable. But tell me – why don't we just *take* your gifts, and lock you in the dungeons anyway?"

Yanni looked blank. It was an excellent point. "Um…"

This time, it only took two seconds for every weapon in the room to be pointed at their throats. The Goblin Queen smiled patiently.

"So? Give me *one* good reason why I shouldn't lock the three of you in the heart of Goblin Mountain for the rest of your lives!"

Yanni panicked. There had to be something – *anything* – he could offer the goblins to convince them to let him leave with the Toadstone. But what?

"Er … how about this?" he suggested.

*   *   *

Ten minutes later, Yanni, Amy and the changeling were back outside Goblin Mountain. The Goblin Queen stood at the entrance, the rest of her army peeking excitedly through her legs.

"So it is agreed," said the Goblin Queen. "In exchange for the Toadstone, you will leave us the coin and the dice … *and* you give us your *sworn word* that you will return when you are done, and bring us this legendary *one-pound coin*."

Yanni nodded. "I promise I'll get it to you, one way or another."

The goblins muttered with excitement. The Goblin Queen rubbed her hands together. "And it is true, what you say? That it is made of gold, and even *smaller* than this fifty-pence piece?"

Amy waved her hands dramatically. "A thing of beauty, Your Majesty! A nugget of finest gold, its edges carved with the most intricate of letters…"

The Goblin Queen licked her lips greedily. She raised herself up to her full height.

"Very well! Never has such a deal been arranged in goblin history! But times have changed; now we goblins will forge all manner of tasteful nick-nacks. Behold – the sacred Toadstone!"

She reached into her crown, tugged out a stone, and dropped it into Yanni's hand.

"Quick!" cried the Goblin Queen. "Run, before they change their minds!"

The goblins charged back into the mountain and slammed the doors behind them. Yanni was certain he could hear them giggling. He looked at the jewel in his hand – compared with the other treasures he'd seen in the keep, the Toadstone was downright ugly. An amber lump the size of a ping-pong ball with a black hole in the middle. He couldn't help but feel like he recognized it somehow.

"*This* is it?" he spluttered. "*This* is what we nearly died for?"

"So?" Amy shrugged. "We finished the first task! And it only cost one pound fifty and a couple of dice. I'd say that's a bargain."

Amy was right – it didn't matter if the Toadstone was ugly. They were one step closer to saving Ari. Soon he'd be back home, with Mum and Dad and...

"What is that, by the way?" Amy suddenly asked, pointing. "You keep holding it."

Yanni looked down and gave a jolt. Once again, he'd absent-mindedly clutched the *mati* for comfort under his T-shirt. He felt a flush of embarrassment, but then he stopped. Why *should* he be embarrassed? He had no reason to be. He pulled the necklace out from under his T-shirt.

"It's something my yiayia gave me," he said.

"Yiayia?"

"My grandma."

Amy nodded. "It's nice! Lucky you."

And that was it. Yanni was surprised. He'd been worried that Amy might tease him for wearing a necklace – especially after how horrible he'd been to her. But Yanni was beginning to see that Amy wasn't like that. There was something grumbling at the bottom of his stomach – something demanding to be said.

"Amy?"

"Yes?"

"I'm really sorry for throwing away your manual."

Amy blinked. "You've already apologized; you don't have to—"

"No, I really mean it," he said. "I'm properly sorry. I'll make sure I get you a new one, when we get out of here. I'm really grateful for all your help. What you did in there was really cool."

Amy brushed it off. "It was nothing."

"It *wasn't* nothing!" he protested. "The disguises, the acting … you were amazing!"

Amy blushed. "Well, you did good, too. Especially attached to that thing the whole time."

She pointed to the changeling, who was now sat on the path beside them in its moss nappy, chewing stones. It had finally calmed down after its ordeal.

"Poor little thing," said Amy. "That iron must have really hurt it."

"It hurt *me*, too," muttered Yanni.

Amy sighed. "You know, I don't think we should keep putting it in the backpack. It's not *right*. It might not be human, but it's not a *thing*, either." She paused. "Come to think of it, we should stop calling him *it*, too. He's part of our quest now. Quests are always better in a gang of three!"

Yanni gawped at the tiny baby eating rocks. "How do you know it's a boy?"

"Gustiver said, remember?" Amy pointed out. "We should give him a name, too. Like Theoren! Or Dyranor. A good faerie name."

Yanni glowered at the changeling. "I vote for Dumbnut."

"No," snapped Amy.

"Fishlips?"

"Stop it! Give him a proper name, not an insult."

Yanni sighed. "Like … Biscuits, or something?"

"He's a faerie, not a dog," she huffed. "Imagine if he was your brother – what would you call him?"

Yanni's mind drew a blank. All the men on Dad's side of the family had the same name: Yanni, or Yannis, or Ioannis, or Giannis. If he called the changeling *that*, it was just going to make things confusing. And all the

171

men on Mum's side of the family had super-English names, like…

"Kenneth?" he suggested.

Amy rolled her eyes. "Does he *look* like a Kenneth to you?"

Yanni stared at the changeling. He did not look like a Kenneth.

"Stop being difficult, and choose one that feels right," Amy ordered.

Yanni had no idea what felt right – after all, he was such a strange-looking creature, with his tiny eyes of midnight black, his alabaster skin, his grey hair…

"He looks like an evil Ari," he said.

Amy spluttered, mishearing him.

"*Larry?* Whoever heard of a faerie called *Larry*! If you're not even going to try…" She stopped – and smiled. "Hey, look!"

She pointed at the changeling – and Yanni saw, to his surprise, that the changeling's raven eyes were fixed on him, as if listening intently.

"I think he likes it!" said Amy. "Larry? You like that name?"

Yanni couldn't believe his eyes. The changeling was *smiling*. Yanni realized, for the very first time, that the little faerie was actually quite cute.

"Fine – Larry it is," he said. "Now, come on – we

have to give the Toadstone to Lorde Renwin and find out the next task!" He started to run. "It could take for ever now we're not carrying Larry around in the…"

He made to yank at the chain, and found he didn't need to. Larry wasn't pulling against him any more – he was running alongside him.

"Oh!" said Yanni, surprised. "Um … never mind."

They set off together back to the dark tower, the sound of their feet making a rough harmony along the path.

THE PALE STRANGER

YANNI AND AMY STOOD BY THE RUINED ARCHWAY, gazing up at the dark tower. They were both too surprised to speak.

"Does it seem ... *different* to you?" Amy asked eventually.

It did. When they had left, the tower had been a sleek black needle darting to the moon. Now the black stones were old and worn, as if eroded by an unseen force. The walkway was chipped and crumbling. It was as if ten years had passed since they were last here. Yanni could have sworn the tower had *shrunk*, too. He frowned. How could a building change so much in so short a time?

He clutched the reassuring weight of the Toadstone in his pocket. He couldn't waste time thinking about it – everything had different rules in the Land of Fae. He had to get inside and complete the first task.

"Right – I'll find out what the next object is," he announced. "You wait out here again."

Amy's face fell. "Why do I always have to wait outside?"

"Because I don't know what's going to happen when I give Lorde Renwin the Toadstone, that's why!" he said. "Just be ready to catch us if we suddenly appear in mid-air again, OK? Come on, Larry."

But Larry wasn't going anywhere. The second he realized Yanni was going back to the tower, he started squawking and trying to run away. Yanni had to practically drag him across the walkway. The inside of the tower had aged, too: the once-gleaming candles had begun to gutter out, making the hallway look close and murky. The paintings were all coated with a thick film of dust.

And as for the man inside them… He had changed, too.

The faerie's appearance had aged, just like the building. His skin was less smooth, and his eyes were less bright. At first, Yanni wondered if it was a trick of the light – but then he looked down, and saw that the plaque at the bottom had changed as well.

The Pale Stranger.

Yanni blinked – it was the name the Goblin Queen had used for Lorde Renwin. He glanced at the next painting along, and the next one, and the next. Sure enough, in each one the faerie had a different name. One plaque said he was *The Man Upstairs*; another called him *The King of the Cats*; another proclaimed him *The Night Marcher*; another, *Sperrit Grey*; and one, *Old Tom Tuttle*.

Yanni sent a dry swallow down his throat. It was as if the faerie was wrapped in layer after layer of beautiful veils, and now a single one had been removed. He was getting closer to the truth that lurked at the bottom: the real Lorde Renwin. Something that was dark and poisonous and not beautiful at all.

"C-come on," said Yanni. "Let's get upstairs before—"

Larry suddenly raced over and clamped himself to Yanni's leg. Yanni was shocked. The changeling was holding on to him for protection, burying his face into his leg and shaking. Larry really, really didn't want to go back upstairs. At least Yanni wouldn't have to drag him now.

He clambered awkwardly up the staircase, step by step, heaving Larry on his leg like a meat boot. Thankfully the staircase seemed no longer quite as tall as before. The ballroom that met him had changed as well – it was shabbier, darker, smaller somehow. The mirrors on the walls had begun to cloud. The food on the tables was beginning to turn: the platters of sauce had developed a skin.

"Ah! Back so soon?"

Yanni felt his guts clench. Lorde Renwin, too, was on the turn: just like the paintings downstairs, he had dark shadows beneath his eyes. He no longer sat proudly on his throne, sagging wearily to one side instead.

He grinned. "Look who it is, my little dumpling!"

Yanni glanced at the floor – and his heart clenched. There was Ari, swaddled in her ridiculous nightgowns at the base of the throne. Normally she would have grabbed for Yanni the moment she saw him; now she didn't even bother to look up. She was playing with what appeared to be a small furry ball with arms and legs that ran around her in circles. Her face had changed, too – the edges of her eyes were turning black. She was slowly becoming a faerie.

Yanni swallowed down his fear; he couldn't let himself be distracted. He marched towards Lorde Renwin and held out the Toadstone. "Here – I finished your first task."

Lorde Renwin's lip curled.

"*Pah!* Yes, yes, I know you did. That *stupid* Goblin Queen – I should have known she'd hand over the Toadstone for a few worthless trinkets!"

Yanni was taken aback. How did Lorde Renwin know about all that? It was like he'd been beside them the whole time.

The faerie waved him away. "*Ugh!* I've no use for that worthless piece of tat. You might as well keep it."

Yanni felt a sudden surge of rage. "Worthless? I nearly *died* trying to get this for—"

"Now!" said Lorde Renwin, his face brightening. "Let's see how much time you've lost, shall we?"

He turned to the fireplace – the only part of the room that was still bright. In the heart of the flames sat the log of blackthorn, floating in a pale green miasma. It looked exactly like it had when Yanni saw it in the Goblin Fortress – but this time, even more of the wood had burned away to ash. A good third of it was now gone, leaving a faint outline of itself behind.

"My, my! You took your time, didn't you?" Lorde Renwin tittered. "And that task was the easiest of the lot! You'll have to speed up if you want to save your sister before midnight…"

Yanni felt a wave of dread. If that task was meant to be *easy*, what was the next one going to be like?

Lorde Renwin turned to the raven, still sat on the back of his throne.

"Gustiver! Take the boy downstairs and explain his next task – he's got plenty of catching up to do!"

Yanni frowned. "Can't you just tell me?"

"The rules say that *Gustiver* has to explain what each object is, remember?" Lorde Renwin snapped. "You *have* been following the rules, haven't you?"

The faerie started laughing and didn't stop. Yanni watched, uncertainty and dread creeping up inside him as the faerie howled and cackled. Gustiver flew out of the door and Yanni scrambled after him, Lorde Renwin's laughter following him down the staircase. He'd thought that he was gaining ground; now it felt like a part of the floor had been pulled from beneath him. He was still far, far, far from saving Ari. How could he *ever* hope to complete this challenge?

By the time he and Larry reached the bottom of the staircase, Gustiver was waiting for them on the banister.

"Right!" the raven huffed. "Let's go outside so I can explain—"

Yanni grabbed the banister in despair. "Gustiver, I can't do this. You know I can't do this! You're my only hope. Tell me something – *anything* – that will help me!"

Gustiver was taken aback. "I *can't*, lad. I cannot disobey my master's wishes. He has my name – my *true* name. That means he may do with me as he pleases."

Gustiver's voice had changed in that final sentence. Yanni realized, with surprise, that the raven was frightened. "What do you mean, he has your name?"

Gustiver glanced back up the stairs. He looked like he was wondering whether or not to continue talking.

"That's how faeries take their powers," he explained

quietly. "A person's name holds great magic. The more names a faerie takes, the more magic they possess – and my master has taken more names than any faerie in history."

Yanni glanced at the paintings in the hallway around him, with their different plaques. "Is that why Lorde Renwin has so many different names? The Goblin Queen called him the Pale Stranger, and the Riddle King…"

Gustiver nodded. "Precisely. When my master arrived at Hallow Fall, he fought every faerie who lived here and stole their names, one by one. That is how he took the magic from Hallow Fall. Lorde Renwin is not even his real name. His real name – his *true*, secret name – is hidden away where no one will ever find it, so that no one will ever steal it from him and take his powers. Even *I* do not know where it is." He gave Yanni a grave look. "That's why he is so keen for you to fail. No name holds more power than the name of a human child. If you lose the wager tonight, and he takes your sister's name, you'll make him twice as powerful as he already is."

Yanni felt his guts clam up. What on earth would that mean for Hallow Fall? What would someone like Lorde Renwin do with even more power?

"But … I don't understand," said Yanni. "How can someone *take* a name? How did he take yours?"

Gustiver was silent for a moment.

"This is not relevant to the task," he said softly. "Let us make our way outside, so I can explain the next task."

"But—"

"I said *no!*" Gustiver snapped. He shot a glance back up the stairs. "For the last time, let us go. *Immediately.* Away from the tower. So I can explain the next task. Do you *understand*?"

He fixed Yanni with eyes of midnight ink. And all at once, Yanni did understand. It was what the signpost had warned him about – that he should spend as little time in the tower as possible. Gustiver couldn't give Yanni any clues, and he couldn't disobey his master's orders – but he was secretly trying to help him. He was on his side.

"Y-yes, I understand," said Yanni. "Thank you, Gustiver."

"You have no reason to thank me," said the raven sternly. "Now come. You're running out of time."

And with that, he flew outside without so much as a glance behind him.

THE ENCHANTED RUIN

B Y THE TIME YANNI AND LARRY MADE THEIR WAY back to the path, Gustiver was wearily perched on a branch, and Amy was several minutes deep into a monologue.

"As for the fundamentals of this magic system," she was asking, "how does magic manifest itself in the Land of Fae? Does Lorde Renwin's power wear down like a fuel? Or rather, is the application of magic here more like a *studied discipline* that…"

"You're here," said Gustiver gratefully, catching sight of Yanni. "Thank God. Let's just get on with the explanation." He spread his feathers wide. "The second object is the elixir of life. You'll find it in the Fount of Eternal Youth, hidden in Hallow Fall. You are to gather a vial of the elixir and bring it back to my master." He glanced up at the window at the top of the tower. "And from now on, you should *tread carefully* – understand?"

Yanni didn't understand, but he knew that it would be important – Gustiver was trying to give him a clue. "Thank you, Gustiver."

"I told you not to thank me," the raven snapped. With that, he leaped from the branch and flew away before Amy could ask him any more questions. She watched him leave, crestfallen, and then turned to Yanni.

"Hey – you've still got the Toadstone!"

Yanni glanced down – he'd forgotten he was still holding the worthless jewel.

"Lorde Renwin didn't even want it," he muttered. "I think it was just a way to get us locked in a dungeon until midnight. He knew everything we did on that last task, too. The Goblin Queen, handing over the dice – *everything*. It was like he was with us the whole time."

Amy's eyes widened, and she glanced over her shoulder. "Do you think he can see us now?"

Yanni shuddered. "I hope not. Let's just pray the next object isn't so worthless."

He made to chuck the Toadstone into the gorge, but Amy stopped him at the last second.

"Don't! It could be useful later."

"How?"

Amy rolled her eyes. "It's obvious you've never played ORC'S QUEST. You never know when something might come in handy. Keep it in the inventory, just in case."

She unzipped the backpack and dropped it inside. Yanni shrugged – he didn't see what use the Toadstone could possibly have, but he wasn't prepared to argue. "Come on – let's find this Fount of Eternal Youth, then."

The three of them raced back down the path as fast as they could until the crossroads appeared. The signpost gave them another cheerful wave.

"Well, look who it is!" It beamed. "Any help I can offer on this fine evening?"

Yanni didn't waste any time. "We're trying to find the Fount of Eternal Youth – do you know where it is?"

"Of course!" said the signpost. "I'm a signpost."

"Great!" said Yanni. "Can you tell us where it is?"

"No!" said the signpost.

"Thanks, that's really…" Yanni's face fell. "Wait – *no*?"

"The Fount of Youth lies inside an enchanted ruin," the signpost explained. "I can't tell you the location of anything that's enchanted – the magic prevents me. Sorry!"

Yanni felt a renewed wave of despair. Lorde Renwin was right – this task *was* going to be harder than the last one. They didn't even know where to begin looking. "What do we do?"

Amy's eyes flickered between the different paths that led off the crossroads.

"We can work it out. Everything in Hallow Fall

is linked to Fallow Hall, isn't it? The dolmen is Lorde Renwin's tower. The village shop's Goblin Mountain. So if we want to find the Fount of Eternal Youth, we just need to think of something like it in Fallow Hall."

Yanni blinked. "Does Fallow Hall *have* a fountain?"

Amy shook her head. "Er … no, it doesn't. To be fair it doesn't have an enchanted ruin, either."

Yanni racked his brains. He'd only seen Fallow Hall once, but he *must* have come across something that was like a fountain. He pressed his hands against the sides of his head, as if trying to squeeze out any thoughts left at the bottom of it. *A fountain, a fountain, something with water inside it…*

He opened his eyes. "I've got it!"

The church had changed.

When Yanni had visited that morning, the little stone building had been surrounded by a neatly trimmed graveyard. A raked gravel path led right to the church doors. *This* was very different.

"It's, um … a bit bigger," he said.

In front of them stood a vast, sprawling cemetery, stretching like an ocean of death as far as the eye could see. The ground was scorched; the path that wound through it was crooked and treacherous. The headstones were scattered in every direction like teeth; between them were stone crypts, crosses, statues with shattered stumps for wings, so old and worn that the stone had turned rotten.

And there, rising from the centre of the graveyard like an island, stood the enchanted ruin.

It was an abbey – or at least, it had once been an abbey. Now all that was left was a gutted skeleton of its four walls, like the remains of a bonfire. The glass was gone from the windows; the doors were charred to ash; the roof had long since caved in. It didn't look enchanted – it looked cursed. Perhaps, Yanni thought, they meant the same thing.

"Are you *sure* that's it?" Amy asked.

"It has to be. When I went inside the church today, there was a stone font from 1703. That's over three hundred years ago – about as long as Lorde Renwin's been here. This all must have something to do with him."

Amy nodded. "And the sign?"

She pointed to the high spiked fence that stood before them. The thorns of the forest had twisted through the rails like barbed wire. Above the entrance, the briars themselves had formed into words, spelling out the message:

THE SLEEPING GUARD AWAITS

"The Sleeping Guard?" said Amy. "What does *that* mean?"

Yanni swallowed, piecing it all together.

"I think it's a warning. The elixir must be protected by something. I think that's what Gustiver meant when he said I had to *tread carefully*. That's the task: I have to take the elixir without waking this ... Sleeping Guard."

Yanni gazed at the abbey, and a wave of fear swept over him. What kind of monster would be waiting for him inside that desecrated ruin? What would it *do* if Yanni woke it up?

He pushed away the fear; he had to be brave now. "R-right. Well, wish me luck…"

He made to step through the entrance – but couldn't. Larry was bolted to the ground, whining.

"Come on," Yanni groaned. "We *have* to go in!"

But Larry had absolutely no intention of going inside the graveyard. Whenever Yanni pulled the chain, Larry dug his fists into the ground and pulled back, scooping up great handfuls of earth. Yanni stormed towards the changeling, fuming.

"Fine! If you won't come, then I'll *carry*— OW!"

The moment Yanni made to grab him, Larry sank his teeth deep into Yanni's hand. Yanni howled with pain and leaped back as Larry flew up the nearest tree.

Amy gasped. "Yanni! What did you do?"

"What did *I* do? He just bit me!"

He held up the bite marks on his palm – and stopped. There was a gap in the middle of the row of punctures – as if Larry was missing a tooth. Yanni frowned. When had *that* happened?

"Of course he bit you," snapped Amy. "He's terrified!"

"*He's* terrified?" Yanni pointed at the graveyard. "In ten seconds, I have to go in *there* and steal an elixir from a sleeping monster! How can I *tread carefully* if it's making a racket like that?"

Amy gave him a cold look. "*His* name is Larry, remember? And you're five times bigger than he is. Stop being a bully!"

Yanni spluttered with indignation, but before he could reply, Amy pushed past him and held out her hand to Larry, who was clinging to a branch and hissing.

"Don't!" warned Yanni. "He'll…"

Sure enough, Larry swiped at her hand viciously when she came near, but Amy kept her cool. Her movements were level; her voice was calm and soft.

"*Shh, shh.* It's OK. I'm a friend. See?"

She reached out her hand again; Larry eyed it warily, but this time he let her touch him. Amy started gently stroking his head.

"There, that's better, isn't it? Poor little thing."

Yanni couldn't believe his eyes. Larry's grip on the

branch was loosening. Soon he had relaxed so much that he even let Amy pick him off the branch and cradle him in her arms. She held him out to Yanni. "Right, your turn."

Yanni baulked. "He'll bite me again!"

"He will if you keep shouting like that," she muttered. "Come on – help him feel safe. He's frightened."

Yanni wanted to shout, *Well, I'm frightened, too …* but he knew, once again, that Amy was right. They were only going to win this task if Larry was quiet. Amy placed the changeling into his arms, and he and Yanni looked at each other warily.

"Er … nice changeling?" said Yanni.

"Try harder," ordered Amy. "You've looked after your sister before, haven't you?"

Of course he had. But this was different – his sister had just wanted to be held by him. It was all she ever wanted. Larry, on the other hand, looked like he was considering whether or not to bite him again. Yanni tried to remember what Mum and Dad did to calm Ari down on those long sleepless nights.

"Um … *Frère Jacques, Frère Jacques…*"

He rocked Larry from side to side, singing softly under his breath. He must have looked completely ridiculous, singing a French lullaby to a faerie outside a haunted graveyard.

But, as if by magic, it worked. Larry's grip softened.

His eyelids began to flicker and fall, and his head slumped into Yanni's chest, and in a matter of moments, he was fast asleep and curled up in Yanni's arms like a kitten.

"I … I did it!" said Yanni in amazement. "I put him to sleep!"

Amy nodded. "See? He was exhausted. He might be a faerie, but he's still just a baby."

Yanni looked down at the sleeping changeling. Larry fitted into Yanni's arms like it was the only place he was ever meant to be. Yanni suddenly saw how small and frightened and vulnerable he was. Despite everything, the faerie completely, utterly trusted him.

Just like Ari had.

The guilt was like a knife in his chest. Ari had only ever wanted to be with him – and he had always resented it. But that wasn't his fault, was it? If she hadn't been so difficult, so demanding, then maybe Yanni would have *wanted* to be with her more…

Or maybe, said the voice in his head, *you just weren't a very nice brother.*

Yanni swallowed, and gazed at the enchanted ruin ahead. There was only one way to make up for it now – he had to finish the challenge. He had to face whatever monster lay inside.

"Right," he said quietly. "You wait here and—"

"No." Amy shook her head. "You can't keep leaving me outside. I'm coming in with you."

Yanni gawped at her. "But ... but it's *dangerous.*"

"I know it is," she said softly. "That's why I'm coming."

Yanni was speechless. He could see how terrified Amy was, yet she was still helping him. That was Amy all over. She was nice. Not like him.

"Thank you," he said.

"*Shh,*" said Amy, giving him a weak smile. "No talking now – *tread carefully*, remember?"

Yanni nodded. From now on, they had to be completely silent; their lives were depending on it. Holding the sleeping child in his arms, he paused to take a breath, and then together he and Amy stepped through the gates and into the graveyard, their feet silently tracing the path that led to the looming ruin ahead.

THE FOUNTAIN

Yanni and Amy crept through the cemetery in silence. There was no wind here: the air was dead. The stillness only amplified the sounds of their breathing, the quiet pucker of their footsteps on the broken path, the steady hammer in their ribs like a counting clock.

They made their way past the rows of headstones. It was wrong to call them rows – they looked like they'd sprouted from the ground by accident. Most were simple stone grave markers, but here and there a plot was taken up by a crypt or a statue. Yanni gazed around. Come to think of it, he had never seen so many statues. There were hundreds of them, all turned away from the abbey. It was as if something so awful had happened inside the ruin – something so unspeakable – that they couldn't bear to look at it. Some had even bent double to hide their faces.

Yanni looked closer as he passed by one – and felt

a lurch in his chest. He was wrong. The statues weren't hiding their faces.

They didn't have any faces.

He swallowed, gazing around the cemetery. It was true: every single statue had a flat blank plane where a face should be, as if someone – or *something* – had shorn away the stone from chin to crown.

He looked at Amy – and saw the same horror in her eyes. What if these weren't statues? What if they were victims? Was *this* the punishment for people who tried to steal the elixir of life? Was this what the Sleeping Guard did to those who didn't *tread carefully*? Was Yanni going to find himself confronted by a monster that slunk from the shadows, and feel the cold creeping up his body as his own flesh was petrified and the Sleeping Guard reached out its claws to remove his face?

He froze – Larry had just shifted in his arms. Yanni had tightened his grip in fear without realizing it and almost woken Larry up. The changeling grumbled and then fell back asleep, pressing his face into the crook of Yanni's elbow for warmth.

Yanni swallowed – he couldn't let that happen again. If Larry woke up and saw any of this, he'd be terrified. One single scream would surely summon the Sleeping Guard from wherever it was hiding.

Somehow, Yanni made his legs start working again,

and he and Amy walked the final few steps towards the ruined abbey. There was no entrance to speak of: the only way inside was through a great gaping hole above a pile of rubble. Inside was dark: very dark. Yanni and Amy looked at each other, and nodded. They were going to have to clamber over it – and the rubble didn't exactly look stable. One wrong step would send it scattering to the ground.

With excruciating slowness, they began to pick their way over the rubble. Every step filled Yanni with dread – whenever he or Amy set down a foot, the broken stones shifted and crackled beneath them. It was all he could do to keep himself steady and hold Larry still. By the time they reached the top of the pile, Yanni's palms were slick with sweat and he was shaking with the physical and mental effort.

He gazed inside the abbey; it was now little more than an empty ruin filled with an undersea darkness, lit by the moonlight cast here and there through holes in the roof. It was silent – but not *true* silence. It felt like a trap: an act, feigning stillness. But no matter where Yanni looked, he could see no sign of any Sleeping Guard, no monster in the shadows. Only those terrible stone statues, lining the abbey walls on every side like trophies, standing out in silhouette in the moonlight coming through the empty windows and twisting away in horror…

And there, high above the floor in the centre of the abbey, was the burning blackthorn log. Its pale green light flickered across the walls, counting down the seconds in ash. They were running out of time.

Directly beneath it, as if under a spotlight, was the Fount of Youth.

At first sight, it made Yanni think of the great gleaming fonts he saw in the churches that he visited with Yiayia and Pappou. But like everything else in Hallow Fall, the fountain was a dark and twisted version of ones he knew. It was twice the size of the font in Fallow Hall, and made of carved ornate stone. There was no doubt about it: the elixir would be inside.

A row of empty glass vials stood at the base of the fountain, twinkling in the pale moonlight. All Yanni had to do was walk across the abbey floor, fill one up with the elixir, and get out again.

Amy made to step off the pile of rubble, but Yanni suddenly shook his head violently.

What? she mouthed, confused.

Yanni had to get his point across without using his hands. He mimed moving his head around the abbey, looking this way and that, mouthing as best he could.

You stay here. Lookout.

Amy's eyes flashed with understanding behind her broken glasses – she had to watch for the Sleeping Guard and warn Yanni if it was coming. Yanni turned to face the fountain. This was it – it was all up to him now. He gazed up at the statues lining every wall and every empty window around him – had *they* got this far? Or was it only when they tried to take some of the elixir that the Sleeping Guard had found them?

There was only one way to find out. He held Larry tight, swallowed down what little courage he had left … and stepped onto the abbey floor.

It felt like he was making a journey of a thousand miles. Every one of his footsteps sounded as loud as a gunshot on the stone floor, echoing inside the dead space and beating off the walls. Yanni knew he was imagining it. It was this silence – it made even the quietest of noises feel warped, out of joint. He glanced around the shadowed corners, but he could see no movement in the dark, hear no sound of approaching steps. Perhaps Yanni simply couldn't hear them over the urgency of his breath, the dull, steady thud of his heartbeat, the dry rasp of his own tongue against his teeth. He glanced down at Larry, still sleeping peacefully in his arms.

Please stay asleep. Please don't wake up.

Finally he stood before the fountain. He could now see that it wasn't all made of stone: the lid was glass, six inches thick. Yanni stood on tiptoes and peered inside. Sure enough, at the bottom lay a rippling pool of white clouded water, dull as a blind eye, swaying silently in the darkness.

The elixir.

He glanced back to where Amy stood on the rubble at the far wall. She gave him a shaky double thumbs up – all clear. He was suddenly so grateful, grateful beyond words, that he wasn't doing this on his own. He simply had to take one of the vials and fill it up.

And then what? Would the Sleeping Guard leap from the shadows the moment his fingertips touched the elixir? Or would it not even be as sudden as that? Would Yanni fill up a bottle, only to turn around and find that a smiling monster had been waiting beside him the whole time, its mouth slowly opening…?

Yanni shook his head. He couldn't keep frightening himself like this. Every second he hesitated was another second that the Sleeping Guard might wake and find him. He adjusted Larry in his arms and, with a shaking hand, stooped down to pick up one of the vials. Its glass base scraped on the floor as he lifted it: the sound sang through the abbey, echoing off the stones. Yanni stayed bolted to the spot, his breath held, waiting for the roar of a waking … but there was nothing. He glanced back at Amy – still two thumbs up. He let out a tremble of tension. Now he just had to find a way to get to the elixir inside.

He crept around the fountain, looking for any kind of clue … and stopped. There was something hidden on the other side: a metal hand, cast in bronze. It hung from the edge of the font, draped elegantly as if waiting to be kissed. Beneath it lay a thin metal spout. So that was it – the elixir had to come out of the spout somehow.

He carefully shifted the weight of the changeling, and slowly, painstakingly, lifted the bottle to the spout. It took all his strength to keep himself steady, to stop himself shaking, to make sure he didn't rattle the lip of the bottle against the metal tube… At last the vial was safely in place. He looked at Amy – two thumbs up still. Yanni swallowed with relief – they were almost there. He glanced around for the tap that would let the elixir pour out.

Nothing. There was no lever to turn, no button to press. Yanni looked over the surface of the fountain, but there was nothing. Only the outstretched bronze hand, stuck above the spout…

And suddenly the memory hit him: Yiayia and Pappou, bending down to kiss the hand of the priest as he walked past. Yanni stared at the bronze hand in alarm. Was *that* what he had to do?

He looked over his shoulder. Amy was staring at him, frozen in place, waiting to see what would happen. Yanni swallowed, and turned back to the bronze hand.

It had to be there for a reason. He reached out, brushing its surface with a trembling finger…

The hand came to life instantly, clamping around his wrist. Yanni almost cried out in fear but held back just in time; the elixir was streaming out of the spout and into the vial now, a thin coil of white water drilling against the glass. The sound rang through the abbey like an alarm bell. Yanni's heart raced. There was no way – absolutely no *way* – that it would not be heard by the Sleeping Guard. But there was nothing he could do – the bronze hand held on tight as the bottle filled up, millilitre by millilitre, right up to the brim. Then, just as quickly as it started, the hand let go of his wrist and hung lifelessly from the font once more, and the flow stopped.

Yanni swung around, his heart thundering, his gaze flying from corner to corner. Surely that was it? Surely any moment now he would hear a scream, and turn around to find the Sleeping Guard charging from the shadows…?

But there was nothing. Just the same chill silence as before; nothing but him, Larry and Amy and the statues at the windows. He looked up at Amy – and sure enough, she gave him two thumbs up. It was clear.

He stifled a gasp. His mind was playing tricks on him again – perhaps the sound of the elixir hadn't been as loud as he'd thought. He gazed at the vial in his hand.

There it was – the elixir of life. It felt heavier than water somehow; it was freezing cold, too, the chill spreading fast through the glass. Yanni had a feeling it was only going to get colder – the faster he handed it over to Lorde Renwin, the better. He stepped quickly across the abbey floor, giving Amy a final glance…

She was silently screaming at him, waving her hands frantically.

Yanni was filled with a fine, white-hot terror. He understood immediately. The Sleeping Guard was coming – it was here. His head snapped from side to side in panic. Where was the monster? What had Amy seen? He looked up at the walls and ceiling, searching for any sign of it, any clue, any…

The statues were gone.

Yanni stood, frozen to the floor with horror. His eyes weren't deceiving him – a moment ago, there'd been dozens of statues, lining every single window and every single wall. Now they weren't there any more – the plinths were abandoned. The windows were empty. Where had they gone? How could they possibly have—

Scrape.

Every hair on Yanni's body stood on end. The sound was almost too quiet to notice – but Yanni had heard it. It was the sound of stone dragging across stone … and it was coming from behind him.

Scrape.

Slowly, his body rigid with fright, he turned around. Something was heaving itself out of the darkness. Yanni knew exactly what it was – he just didn't want to believe it. He didn't want to believe that the thing crawling across the floor towards him was real: the shattered stumps, the crumbling skin, the blank void where a face should be…

It was one of the statues. It was alive, hauling itself inch by inch across the abbey floor by its fingernails. There was another one beside it, and another, and another, and another. He turned, terrified. There were dozens of them, crawling down the walls like beetles, dragging themselves over the flagstones towards him. Amy's face was a frozen mask of horror as she waved her hands over and over and over and over…

And the truth of it finally hit him. The statues weren't victims – they were the Sleeping Guard. *They* were the cursed monsters who stalked the enchanted ruin, and guarded the elixir from anyone who tried to take it.

And Yanni had just woken them up.

The Sleeping Guard

YANNI STOOD, BOLTED TO THE FLOOR WITH TERROR. The statues crawled down the walls towards him on every side, lit by the flickering green of the blackthorn log. Yanni was completely surrounded: no matter where he turned, the statues blocked his escape, tightening in a decreasing circle around him. He could only stand and watch, paralysed, as the statues dragged themselves closer and closer across the flagstones towards him, pushing their chests off the floor to crane their necks as if looking for something…

No, not looking – *listening*. Yanni suddenly realized, the statues had no eyes: they had to use their ears to find their way. They were heading for the noise that had woken them – the elixir from the fountain. They were searching for even the slightest sound that would reveal where Yanni was.

The floor was now completely covered in slithering

statues, and there were more coming down the walls every second. Yanni and Amy looked at each other – they both knew what Yanni had to do. The only way out of the abbey was *through* the ring of statues. He had to walk right past them. And he had to be completely silent when he did it. If he made a sound now – even one – then the statues would know where he was.

He glanced down at the vial of elixir in his hand – and at Larry, still fast asleep, totally unaware of the seething nightmare around them. Yanni had to keep it that way. He could only pray that his breathing, his heartbeat and the sound of his own teeth rattling inside his head wouldn't wake him up.

With agonizing care, he stepped on the heel of one shoe and pulled his foot free – then he did the same with the other, until he stood in his socks on the stone. The first wave of statues was getting closer and closer. Yanni wanted to turn and run screaming in the other direction – but he couldn't. There was only one way out now.

He left his shoes where they were and slowly, steadily, silently, stepped towards the statues. They grew closer, centimetre by centimetre, until finally the first statue dragged itself past him, so close that Yanni could sense the grinding of its body over the stone floor. Yanni held his breath and kept walking forward. He almost couldn't bear to look; he couldn't afford to lose concentration now for even a second. Each time he lifted a foot from the floor, Yanni was certain – *certain* – that a statue would hear the hush of material peeling from stone, and clamp a hand around his ankle… But it seemed like the sound of their scraping bodies covered his footsteps. So long as he stayed steady and silent, he—

The nearest statue suddenly reared up like a cobra, twisting its blank void of a face towards him. Yanni's strength failed him: the statue was so close that he could see the grain of the stone where its eyes should have been. For a dread moment, Yanni thought that this was it – his moment had come; this was where his task would end, and he would finally find out once and for all what the Sleeping Guard did to those who dared to steal the elixir…

But he was wrong. The statue turned its head from left to right, completely unaware that Yanni was standing in front of it. It was drinking in the sounds around it, searching for any signs of the intruder. Yanni stood like a statue himself, not even daring to swallow, praying that the thunder in his ribs wouldn't betray him now that he was standing so close…

The statue found nothing. It lowered back to the floor and continued its slithering path to the fountain. Yanni's heartbeat fell from its fever pitch. He had to keep going. He looked up at the rubble-strewn hole where

Amy still stood waiting, her eyes wide and desperate, and made his way towards her on shaking legs. More and more statues were pouring down the walls; Yanni weaved between them as they crawled past him, his body trembling as if he were carrying a weight far greater than the changeling. Slowly, step by step, the hole in the wall grew closer, until finally he was almost there, and Amy could almost reach out her arms and touch him…

WHAM.

Yanni froze. The statues had stopped – all of them. Amy pointed a trembling hand to the abbey behind him. Yanni turned around, dread building in his stomach.

One of the statues beside the fountain was slamming its palms onto the floor, drawing all attention towards it. It had found his shoes: now the statues *knew* that Yanni was here. Every one had frozen in place, totally silent, their backs arched and their heads raised, searching for the slightest sound that would reveal where the intruder was standing.

Yanni was trapped. He was mere footsteps from the hole in the wall, but there was no way he could go through it. The second his feet touched the rubble, the statues would know where he was. His only hope was that if he waited long enough, they might start moving again and make enough noise to cover his footsteps…

Yanni froze. Something had just stirred in his arms.

Larry was waking up.

Yanni stared down in panic. Larry was gazing back up at him, blinking his raven eyes awake. The sound of the statue striking the ground must have woken him. Yanni shook his head hopelessly, trying somehow to will the changeling back to sleep and stop him seeing the horrors around him...

No, no, no, no, no!

But it was no use – Larry knew that something was wrong. He must have seen the look of terror on Yanni's face, felt the fear radiating from his body like fever. He sat up and twisted his head to see what was going on.

Larry saw it all – everything. The darkness, the rotting abbey, the faceless stone statues scattering the floor like corpses...

And screamed.

The sound rang through the abbey like thunder. The statues swung round as one, their terrible faceless heads fixed on the exact spot where Yanni was standing. The silence that followed the scream was even more horrific – just long enough for Yanni to understand, truly understand, what was about to happen to them.

And then all at once, the statues were on their feet and flying towards him, moving far faster than Yanni could ever have possibly imagined. He turned to Amy and let out a blinding shriek of terror.

"RUN!"

Silence didn't matter any more. Amy flew out of the hole in the wall and Yanni tore after her, scrambling over the rubble. His shoeless feet slipped and skidded painfully on the loose stones, sinking to his ankles just as the statues reached the bottom of the pile behind him. He only just managed to pull himself free as the closest statue flung itself through the air, its hands slamming on the rocks as it tried to grab him. Yanni tore over the last of the rubble and dived onto the broken path that led back to the gates.

His blood froze. The cemetery was filled with statues – hundreds of them, scrambling over the crypts on every side, scuttling on all fours between the headstones towards him.

Amy was streaking down the path as more statues closed in on her from either side. The moment that she raced through the gates, the statues ceased following her. It was as if their powers only extended to the edge of the cemetery. Now all their attention was fixed on Yanni.

"BEHIND YOU!" Amy cried.

Yanni snapped around: the statues were crawling out of the abbey, clambering over one another in a blind heap to reach him. He tore himself from the path and flew between the headstones, slipping and dodging and doubling back on himself as statue after statue flung itself out of the darkness towards him. Fear pulsed through his body; his brain was a buzzing hornets' nest. Larry was screaming constantly now, a low, wild moan of terror, pushing and fighting to get away from him, but Yanni held him tight. They had to find some other way out of the cemetery, another entrance, a hole in the fence, *anything…*

But there was nothing. The spiked metal fence stood unbroken on every side. A wave of statues was already heading towards him from the other side of the abbey, blocking his escape. There was nothing left to do but hide. Yanni flung himself behind a high white crypt and pressed his back to the rough stone, clutching Larry close as he screamed.

"No – stop!" Yanni cried. "They'll hear us!"

But Larry was beyond listening. His eyes were bulging out of his head, his shriek high and fast, his tiny heartbeat hammering. Yanni was struck, once more, by how small he was – how much he looked like Ari, crying herself into a frenzy. Amy was right – Larry was just a baby. He held him close and rocked him.

"*Shh* – it's OK, it's OK! You're OK…"

It wasn't working. Larry kept struggling and crying in his arms as the statues grew closer and closer, drawn by the sound of his screams. Yanni gripped him tight, trying to pour safety into him, keeping his own voice steady and calm.

"Nothing's wrong; it's all OK. I'm here. See?"

Larry stopped crying and gazed up at him, chest heaving, eyes filled with fear.

"Yes – that's right," soothed Yanni. "You're safe with me. Everything's fine."

Yanni glanced up – and saw that it wasn't fine at all. The statues were closing in, tightening in a ring of death, clawing their way around the gravestones towards them. Yanni realized that there was no way out. He gazed down at the vial of elixir, still clutched in his hand – but there was no help that it could give him now. It was as worthless as the Toadstone. He held Larry tight as the statues drew nearer and nearer.

"Th-that's right," he whispered. "We're OK. It's all going to be OK. *Frère Jacques, Frère Jacques…*"

Yanni glanced to one side and saw a stone hand creeping around the nearest edge of the crypt. The statues were clambering over the crypt itself, crawling around it on every side, tracking the sound of his voice. They were so close that Yanni could see every tiny blemish in the stone.

"Dormez-vous, dormez-vous…"

And Yanni understood, with a strange clarity, that there was no saving them now. He was going to die. He would never see Mum and Dad or Ari ever again. Amy was safe, at least – there was a chance she would get home again. But the thing that cut through all of it, the thing that pained him most, was that he had doomed Larry. He was just a baby – none of this was his fault. He'd been made a pawn in Lorde Renwin's sick game, and now he was going to die in this horrible place. Yanni would have given anything – *anything* – to have it otherwise.

The nearest statue was mere inches away, slapping its hands over the ground to find them. It didn't matter if it heard him now. It was over. All that Yanni could do was hide Larry from the truth. He held the child close, and shielded his face so he wouldn't see.

"We're safe," said Yanni. "I promise we're safe."

The statue's head snapped towards him – it had heard. It reached out its hand, clawing the last of the air between them. Yanni closed his eyes and took his final breath, and cradled the child tight in his arms.

"I'm sorry," he whispered as the statue's hand came down.

A CRY IN THE DARK

A SOUND CUT THROUGH THE GRAVEYARD. A SCREAM. Yanni's eyes snapped open. For a moment, he was certain what he was hearing: *Amy*! She must have come back into the cemetery to try to save him, and now the statues had found her...

But then the scream came again, and this time Yanni could hear that it wasn't Amy's voice.

It was his own.

"Here! Over here!"

Yanni wasn't imagining it. It was his own voice, coming from the other side of the cemetery. The nearest statue was frozen in place in front of him, its fingertips mere centimetres away – but now it had turned to face the scream. All the statues were doing the same.

"That's right! Over here! Come and get me!"

The statues threw themselves to their feet and tore towards the scream. Yanni stayed with his back pressed against the crypt, clutching Larry tight as wave after wave of statues thundered past them. Within seconds, the cemetery ahead was empty: they were alone. Yanni waited until the sound of the statues had faded into the distance, and then peered around the edge of the crypt, shuddering like a blade of grass in the wind.

The statues were charging in a giant crowd towards the other side of the abbey. Yanni could see now there was no way – absolutely no way – he could possibly have got past them all. There were hundreds of them, chasing something that always remained just beyond the statues' grasp. Yanni could still hear the sound of his own voice, taunting them.

"This way! Over here!"

Yanni had no idea what was happening – and no intention of staying to work it out. He threw himself to his feet, the vial of elixir in one hand and Larry in the other arm, and tore towards the gates in his shoeless feet like a man possessed. He bashed his knees against headstones and snagged his socks on the broken path. Twice he almost lost his balance and went sprawling, but he didn't break speed for even a second. He ran and ran until finally he was flinging himself back through the gates, where Amy stood waiting, ashen-faced and shaken, almost in tears.

"Y-Yanni! Omigod, omigod – that *scream*! I thought the statues…"

Yanni shook his head, his chest heaving. "It ... it wasn't me. Look! Over there!"

He pointed to the other side of the abbey, where the statues were still tearing after the voice.

Amy stared in confusion. "But ... it sounds exactly like you."

Yanni nodded. "I know – and it came just at the right moment, too. One more second and the statues would have got us!"

Amy frowned. "But if it's not you, then who is it?"

Yanni didn't have a clue; there was no explanation for it. Who was trying to help them – and why? As if it wasn't already strange enough, the voice now suddenly disappeared as quickly as it had arrived. The statues began shrieking with rage, clambering over one another and sightlessly swiping the air to try to find who had tricked them.

Yanni was as confused as they were. "Whoever it was, they just saved us," he said. "They saved *both* of us."

He gazed down at Larry, still clutched tightly in his arms, and his heart sang for joy. They were alive; they were safe. And what's more, they'd just completed the second task. He held up the vial with trembling hands. Inside it lay the elixir of life – the liquid now so cold that it almost burned him.

Amy gasped. "You did it!"

Yanni smiled. "*We* did it! Now come on, let's get it to the tower before…"

But Amy wasn't listening – she was looking at Larry. "Er … is he OK?"

Yanni looked down. Larry had changed again. He had now taken the form of a kitten and was clinging to Yanni, purring.

"He must be able to change form sometimes," said Amy. "Like when he turned into an adder in the Goblin Keep. Maybe it's whenever he feels a really strong emotion."

Yanni was puzzled. "Why's he doing it now?"

Amy gave him a look that was almost pitying. "Why do you think? Look at him! He *loves* you!"

It was true. Larry's eyes were absolutely bursting with love. After all, Yanni had protected him. Yanni felt a strange warm feeling in the pit of his stomach, and blushed.

"Whatever. At least he'll be easier to manage now."

"Sure," said Amy with a smirk.

"I mean it," said Yanni, still blushing. "It's not a big deal."

"Right, right, whatever you say."

"Stop giving me that look."

"I'm not giving you any look!"

Yanni's face was now as red as a prize tomato. "Let's go, then."

Embarrassed as he was, Yanni couldn't help but

smile as they raced back down the road together. He was closer to saving Ari than he could ever have hoped. But it wasn't just that: something else had started to change, too. He could sense it. Maybe it was the feeling of being alive after being so close to death. Maybe it was Larry trusting him more. But whatever it was, he felt as if he were running on air.

Once again, the signpost was waiting for them at the crossroads.

"Three weary travellers! Did you manage to find the Fount of Eternal Youth?"

"We did!" exclaimed Yanni, waving the vial. "Two tasks down and closer than ever!"

"He was brilliant," said Amy. "So brave."

Yanni blushed even more. "It was nothing."

"It *wasn't* nothing!" she retorted. "I could *never* have done that!"

"You were with me, too, you know."

"But not like *that*!"

The signpost watched in bemused silence as Yanni and Amy said nice things to each other.

"I mean, you came in after me, even when you didn't need to…"

"Well, *you* let me get away from the statues…"

"We'd have never even gone inside if you hadn't calmed Larry down!"

215

"All right, all right, it was a joint eff—"

"*Oi!*"

Yanni and Amy spun round. A familiar figure stood in the shadows behind them – the stone frog from earlier, scowling at them.

"That's right. I still haven't forgotten about you!" It gave them a furious glare. "Now go on – admit it! Which one of you took my eye?"

Yanni and Amy looked at each other. The frog picked up a handful of gravel and held it threateningly.

"I *said*, admit it! Before I break every single bone in your—"

"Get lost," said Yanni.

The frog stared at him in shock. "What?"

"I *said*, get lost," Yanni repeated. "We're not frightened of you any more. *Shoo.*"

It was true. After everything that he and Amy and Larry had just gone through – Lorde Renwin, the goblins, the abbey – an angry frog was nothing.

The frog began to tremble from head to toe with rage. "*HOW – HOW DARE—*"

"You heard him!" snapped Amy. "Go and pester someone else; we haven't got time for this."

The frog was totally stunned. "Hang on a minute. You can't just—"

Larry cut it off with a hiss, and the little gang of

three turned back to the path that led to the tower and disappeared down it together. There was nothing the frog could do except watch.

There was a muffled snicker beside it – the signpost was covering its mouth with its arms, trying not to laugh.

"Shut up," muttered the frog.

THE BLACK PIANO

"IT'S CHANGED AGAIN," SAID AMY.

She was right – Lorde Renwin's tower had become even more derelict than before. The structure was bent to one side like a crooked finger. The black stones were warped and broken, the raven statues dropping crumb by crumb from the walkway into the sightless gorge beneath.

Amy shook her head. "Why does it keep changing like this? It doesn't make any sense."

Yanni gazed up at the top of the tower. There was the sound of chimes, ringing from the window like before, but now they had changed, too. They were quieter. And slowly, piece by piece, it all began to make sense.

"It's because of these tasks," he said. "It's because we're winning. We're wearing down Lorde Renwin's magic!"

He couldn't explain it, but he knew – just *knew* – that he was right. The closer they got to winning the wager, the less strength Lorde Renwin had. He glanced down at Larry clinging tightly to his neck and felt another surge of courage. The changeling didn't seem as frightened any more. It filled him even more with hope. After so many setbacks, the end was in sight.

"Right – time to find out the last task!"

Yanni raced over the weak and wobbling bridge with Larry in his arms and burst into the hallway. It was the worst it had ever been: the floor was warped and greasy with cobwebs, the air as damp and mouldy as something left to wither underground for a hundred years. Yanni wondered if it had *always* been like this, and only now was he seeing the truth of it for the first time. He was another step closer to what lurked beneath the veils. He turned to the nearest painting to see what the master of Hallow Fall looked like now … and stopped.

The paintings didn't show Lorde Renwin any more. Each one showed a completely different person. Yanni knew at once that they were all faeries: they all had the same bone-white skin, the same long fingers, the same sleek grey hair. The names on the plaques all seemed to suggest faerie names, too: *Lorde Fairchild, Lady Alinora, Earle Mosswind*…

But all the paintings had their faces ripped out.

Yanni gazed around the hallway in shock. It was true: each and every face had been torn from the canvas, as if by claws. Larry tightened his grip and whined. Yanni swallowed. Had Lorde Renwin done this?

He stopped. There was a sound echoing down the staircase from the ballroom, but it wasn't the sound of bells this time.

It was the sound of people crying.

It took all of Yanni's courage to make the short climb. When he arrived, he saw the ballroom was in an even worse state than before. The food on the table was a heap of decay, oozing with flies. The smell was indescribable. The once-grand and beautiful room was grim and murky, surrounded by filthy mirrors. The only light came from the sickly green glow of the fireplace.

Yanni looked around. The throne was empty; there was no sign of Lorde Renwin. Where had all those screams and sobs been coming from?

"*Aha!* He returns!"

Yanni jumped. Lorde Renwin was hidden in a corner, sat at a beautiful grand piano. The piano was polished to a sparkle: its ebony surface gleamed like obsidian, the white keys shining like teeth in the darkness. The faerie, on the other hand, looked even worse than before. He was haggard and old and exhausted; his once-fine clothes – now dirty and stained – hung from him. Yanni was shocked by the state of him. He felt fear trickle down his spine, remembering those shredded paintings downstairs. But he wasn't going to let himself be frightened now. He stepped forward and held out the vial.

"Here – I finished your task."

Lorde Renwin pounded his fist on the piano. "*Gah!* How did you manage it? Those statues were supposed to tear you limb from limb, not run away!"

Yanni frowned – once again, Lorde Renwin seemed to know what had happened during the task. Except *this* time – for some reason – he didn't know about the voice that had drawn away the statues. Was it a sign that his powers were waning?

"Well?" he said, holding out the vial. "Aren't you going to take it?"

Lorde Renwin gasped, his eyes wide and desperate. "The elixir of life? Oh, please, boy, quick – hand it over, before it's too late!"

He reached for the vial; Yanni could see that his hands were shaking. He paused – would drinking the elixir somehow bring Lorde Renwin back to his full powers? Perhaps Yanni shouldn't give it to him. But if he didn't hand it over, he wouldn't complete the task. He couldn't afford to risk losing more time; he gave Lorde Renwin the vial and the faerie lifted it to his lips with shuddering hands.

Then he hurled it at Yanni's feet, shattering the vial into a thousand pieces. Yanni yelped with pain – the elixir was soaking into his socks and stabbing into his bones, the cold so intense that it burned like hot coals. He dropped Larry and fell to the floor, frantically tearing off his socks as Lorde Renwin howled with laughter.

"*Ha ha ha ha ha!* The look on your face – priceless!" He wiped away a tear. "You stupid boy, do you *really* think I'd have any need for that filthy bog water?"

Yanni stuffed the wet socks into his pocket, glaring with rage. "You do, actually. You look terrible. And I know the reason why!"

He pointed to the fireplace. There was the log of deepest blackthorn, burning away in a cloud of green. Almost half the log was still left.

"I'm beating you!" said Yanni. "You were so certain that you'd win my sister's name, you used up all your magic to make this wager. That's why your tower looks so awful. And now I've only got one more object left to find!"

Larry leaped back into Yanni's arms, and together they stood against the faerie. Lorde Renwin's face sagged with misery.

"Oh, how right you are!" he cried, weeping bitter tears. "Woe is me! I should have thought twice before meddling with a brave, clever lad like you! To think that now you might actually *beat* me!"

Yanni shifted uneasily. There was something that felt

false about the faerie's words — something that didn't feel right. "S-stop stalling and give me the final task."

Lorde Renwin sat up brightly, all misery gone. "Of course! But before you go — shall we have some music?"

He turned back to the gleaming grand piano. Yanni frowned. What was going on? "I don't care about your stupid piano. Tell me what the last task is."

"*Stupid?* Oh no, this piano is my greatest creation!" said Lorde Renwin, stroking the keyboard with genuine affection. "Where else do you think I keep my prisoners?"

Yanni paused, despite himself. "P-prisoners?"

Lorde Renwin gave him a wide grin. "Of course! The faeries that used to live in Hallow Fall! Where do you think I put them after I stole their powers?"

Yanni suddenly remembered the hallway. "Those shredded paintings downstairs..."

Lorde Renwin sneered with distaste. His face suddenly darkened, like a spoiled Victorian child.

"*Ugh!* Yes, that's them. The whole stinking village used to be full of them! How I *hated* them, with their stupid rules and laws! Do you know, when I first arrived here, I politely asked them to hand over their powers and make me their king — and they *refused*!" He looked scandalized. "The audacity! Well, I wasn't going to stand for that. No, sir! So I took Hallow Fall by force, and I made sure those faeries suffered. I beat them with holly until they bled, and stole their names from them one by one, until I had every single one of their powers. No other faerie in history has managed it! And where do you think I put them afterwards? *Between the keys, of course!*"

He turned back to the piano and began to play with a flourish ... but the sounds that came out of it were not music. They were screams. Each press of a key produced a wail of pain and despair that split the air in two. Yanni's hairs stood on end – *that* was the sound he had heard downstairs. It was the sound of Lorde Renwin torturing his prisoners in that grotesque piano, filling the ballroom with sobs and shrieks. No wonder Hallow Fall was such a broken, horrible place. But it couldn't be true. Lorde Renwin *couldn't* have trapped all those innocent faeries inside there...

"Y-you're lying," he said faintly. "You can't hide something between the keys of a piano."

"Oh, on the contrary!" said Lorde Renwin. "That's what faeries do best – hide in the gaps! Whenever you see a crack, you can always bet there's a faerie watching!" He smirked at Larry and hammered down his fists on the keys, drawing out a chorus of agony. "Even *that* one's stupid parents are trapped in here somewhere!"

Larry shrieked in terror and pressed his face to Yanni's chest. Yanni's blood ran cold. He'd assumed that Larry was Lorde Renwin's own child, used like some kind of pawn. But the truth of the matter was even worse. His parents were stuck inside that piano, tortured and imprisoned. Was *that* where Larry would end up, too? And what about Ari? If Yanni lost the wager, would she—

He froze.

"Where is she?"

The faerie stopped playing and looked up. "Where's who?"

Yanni panicked. "My sister. The baby you stole. What have you done with her?"

He spun around, but Ari was nowhere to be seen. He'd been so distracted by everything else that he hadn't even *thought* about her – what was *wrong* with him?

"Baby?" said Lorde Renwin. "There's no baby! I'm the most powerful faerie in existence; I think I'd know if there was a *baby* in my..." He suddenly clicked his fingers. "Ah, yes! *The baby!* I remember now. She's over there, I think."

He waved a hand at the heaps of rotting food on the table. Yanni gasped – there was Ari, balanced on the edge of a chair. She was filthy – her lace nightgowns were torn and covered in stains, and her hair was caked with old food. She was steadily, blankly, cramming more faerie food into her mouth. The sight of it filled Yanni with horror.

"For heaven's sake, you're not even looking after her properly!" he cried, running over to her. "She could have fallen or choked or—"

Yanni reached out to grab his sister – and the moment his hands came near, she hissed at him. He leaped back, blinking in disbelief.

"Wh-what are you doing? It's me – your brother!"

But Ari stared at him with pure hatred. There was no love left in her eyes, no shred of recognition. The black rings around the edges of her irises had grown even thicker. She was turning more faerie with every passing second.

Lorde Renwin hobbled over and picked her up. Yanni watched as his baby sister clung to the faerie's filthy chest – to the monster who had trapped and tortured thousands. She looked perfectly at peace.

"Yes, my sweet!" said Lorde Renwin. "You don't want to be with that nasty *human*, do you?"

And suddenly Yanni was filled with vile fury, stronger than anything he had ever felt in his life.

"Give me the task," he spat. "Right now. I'll be back with your worthless item – and this time, I'll rub your face in it. I'll make you beg. By the time I'm done with you, you'll be even more disgusting and pitiful than you already are!"

His words filled the darkness of the ballroom, echoing back at him over and over. With shock, Yanni realized what he sounded like. He sounded exactly like Lorde Renwin.

The faerie's mouth opened in a wide, triumphant smile, and Yanni saw, for the first time, that he was missing a tooth.

"Gustiver? If you would be so kind?"

On Lorde Renwin's command, the raven leaped from the throne and flew straight out of the window, disappearing fast into the night.

"Wait – where's he going?" said Yanni. "Doesn't he need to tell me what the task is?"

"Of course he does!" said Lorde Renwin, the grin still plastered across his face. "So you'll have to catch up with him, won't you?"

Yanni's stomach dropped. The raven was flying away as fast as he could – and until Yanni caught up with him, he wouldn't be able to find out what the final task was. The faerie's eyes sparkled in the shadows, and Yanni saw that Ari's eyes were doing exactly the same.

"Off you go, boy," whispered Lorde Renwin. "I hope you like running."

THE GALLEON

YANNI CHARGED OVER THE CRUMBLING FOOTBRIDGE in his bare feet, Larry clutched tight to his chest. Amy appeared on the path up ahead, blinking in confusion.

"Where's Gustiver?" Yanni cried. "Where did he go?"

Amy pointed. "He just flew that way! But…"

There was no time to stop and explain. He grabbed her hand and tore down the path, dragging her behind him.

"Lorde Renwin's tricked us again! We have to catch up with Gustiver to find out what the final task is – we can't let him get away!"

There was no time to lose. Who knew how far Gustiver would get before they caught up with him – they could spend the rest of the challenge just trying to find him. The signpost was appearing ahead. This time, Yanni didn't even stop for greetings.

"Gustiver – Lorde Renwin's raven. Where did he go?"

The signpost understood immediately. It pointed down the fourth and final path. "That way!"

Yanni looked down the road. He knew exactly where it led – there was only one place left to go. "It's the playing field! Come on!"

"OK," Amy groaned, panting for breath. "But can you not drag—"

Yanni raced off, yanking Amy behind him with a squawk. Larry leaped from his arms and the three of them flew down the final path together. Yanni gritted his teeth in determination. He was going to catch up with Gustiver. He wasn't going to let Lorde Renwin beat him when he was so close.

And whatever this final challenge was, Yanni would be ready for it.

"Ah," said Yanni.

The three of them stood at the end of the path. There was Gustiver, flying into the distance … but they couldn't take another step further.

An ocean was in the way.

Yanni gazed around in disbelief. On this side of the gateway, the waterlogged playing field was a boundless desert of water, stretching in every direction. The swollen moon hung before them, perfectly reflected over the horizon like a vast set of gloating eyes. Gustiver was flying straight towards it. If they wanted to follow him, there was only one way to do it now.

"I ... I think we have to use *that*," said Yanni.

Anchored in the water before them was an enormous wooden galleon, creaking in the swell of the waves. It looked as if it hadn't been touched for a hundred years. Its rotten hull was rimed with salt; a tattered flag hung from its mast, showing a stag's skull emblazoned on black.

"That ... doesn't look very safe?" Amy hazarded.

"That's the whole point," said Yanni. "It's the final task – it's going to be the hardest one yet. Come on, before he gets away!"

He stepped to the edge of the path and gazed down. The water below looked very, very cold. Larry gave a squeak of protest and leaped back, pulling on the chain. Amy didn't look much happier.

"We can't sail that!" she cried, pointing at the galleon. "It's a million years old!"

"We don't have a choice," said Yanni, determined. "It's our only hope of saving my sister."

Amy blinked frantically behind her broken glasses. "But ... I don't know a thing about boats! And how are we even going to get to it? I'm hopeless at swimming, and..."

Yanni groaned. "Why do you keep doing that?"

Amy was confused. "Doing what?"

He turned around. "Saying you're bad at everything. You say you can't do voices, yet you're amazing at them. You say you never have a clue what to do, and then you come up with a brilliant idea! If it wasn't for you, I wouldn't have lasted ten seconds in Hallow Fall. Why can I see that, and *you* can't?"

Amy stared at him, shocked. Yanni grabbed her by the shoulders.

"You don't have to be like Saphiana to do things, you know. You can be yourself. You're brave, and smart – and kind! That matters!"

Amy rolled her eyes. "Anyone can be *kind*, Yanni…"

"But not everyone is, though," he said. "*I* wasn't. But you are all the time – easy as breathing. You helped me when anyone else would have left me behind. And when we get home, I'm going to make it up to you." He looked her straight in the eye. "When school starts, we're going to make that lunchtime ORC'S QUEST club, just like you wanted. And if Chloe wants to hang out with that other girl Cecile instead? Fine! It's her loss."

Amy's eyes lit up like fireworks again. "Really?"

"Of course," he said. "I mean, you'll have to teach me to play it first. I still haven't a clue how it works."

Amy was too excited to care about technicalities. "Omigod! We could make a club plaque, with our own insignia! We should get rings made, too!"

"Absolutely," agreed Yanni. "Maybe let's think about all that when we get home, though?"

"Oh! Yes, the challenge, sorry."

Larry chirruped and leaped back into his arms; Yanni squeezed Amy's hand.

"One last task," he said. "All of us together – a gang of three!"

Amy beamed. "A gang of three!"

They took a deep breath, and plunged together into the freezing waves. The water was even colder than Yanni expected – all three of them came up spluttering for breath – but he felt brilliant. The same couldn't be said for Larry – he'd clambered on top of Yanni's head, squeaking with anger, jamming one foot over his eye and the other in his ear. Amy was already swimming out to the galleon.

"See?" Yanni shouted across to her. "I knew you'd end up being good at swimming!"

They swam frantically to the slimy rigging that hung from the galleon and hauled themselves onto the empty deck. Yanni grimaced: the ship was in an even worse state than he'd feared. The salt water had worn through each and every metal fitting; the wood was warped and twisted. Yanni was amazed it was still afloat. He glanced around the creaking vessel. In films, galleons like this were controlled by teams of sailors working like an orchestrated ballet. How were the three of them supposed to do *that*?

He didn't have time to worry about it – by now Gustiver was barely a speck on the horizon. "Come on – let's get going! Haul anchor!"

"I think you mean *weigh anchor*," Amy corrected.

Yanni shot her a look. "So much for you knowing nothing about boats…"

He ran to the edge of the deck with Larry still clamped to his head and peered down into the water. Sure enough, a thick and rusted chain hung from the boat's prow, strung with tendrils of slime.

"There's the anchor!" he called. "Amy, can you see a lever or anything that brings it up?"

There was no reply. Yanni turned around.

"Amy? I said, is there a…"

He trailed off. Amy was behind him, standing in the exact same spot where he'd left her on the deck.

So were a hundred other people.

It took a few seconds for Yanni to process what was happening. The boat – which, moments before, had been completely empty – was now packed with people, gazing at him in silence.

But they weren't people – they were ghosts.

Larry squawked in terror, scrambling off Yanni's head and burrowing inside his T-shirt. Yanni looked around in disbelief. They were ghosts, all right. They covered every part of the deck, the rigging passing straight through them. They looked like they'd been shaped from sea mist, barely a tracing-paper version of themselves...

And they were walking towards him.

Yanni acted fast. *"Amy, run!"*

He grabbed her as the ghosts drew forward, their mouths open in soundless howls of fury. Yanni spun round – but now the ghosts were behind them, too. They were trapped. He backed against the mast in terror, dragging Amy with him.

"G-get away! All of you!" Yanni cried.

But Amy wasn't panicking. She was looking at the ghosts, frowning. "I – I don't think they want to hurt us. Look – they're not angry; they're sad."

She pointed at the ghosts; and Yanni saw what she meant. Their hands weren't clawing; they were reaching out. Their mouths weren't howling; they were pleading, desperate to be understood.

"I think I know what's going on here..." said Amy.

She pulled free of him before Yanni could stop her.

"Amy, no!"

She marched right up to the ghosts ... and sure enough, they stopped before her, silently mouthing messages imploringly. Some of them even fell to their knees. Yanni could see how grateful they were, how long they'd been waiting for someone to listen to them. Amy's eyes darted around, trying to take it all in.

"I – I can't understand you," she said. "One at a time: is this your boat?"

The ghosts understood her; they shook their heads. A few pointed up the mast. There, at the very top, the tattered black flag with the stag insignia fluttered in the wind.

"A stag…" said Amy thoughtfully. "Antlers – like Gustiver. Hang on, is this Lorde Renwin's ship? Are you faeries?"

At the mention of Lorde Renwin's name, the ghosts shook their fists in the air with rage and mimed spitting on the floor. Amy was right – now that Yanni looked closer, he could see that the ghosts all had bone-white faces and raven eyes. He'd never have noticed it without her. Amy nodded, piecing it together.

"You really hate him, don't you?" she said. "He's making you do this against your will – did he summon you back from the afterlife to be the crew of this ship? And he won't let you return?"

The ghosts nodded miserably, placing their heads in their hands, rending their clothes and moaning in silent grief. Yanni's heart went out to them; they looked so lost, so sad, so broken. They were clearly desperate to pass back into the afterlife – who knew how many years they'd been forced to stay here on this miserable boat.

"Don't worry – we can help you," Amy promised. "Is there anything we can do that would help you pass on?"

Yanni gasped. "We don't have time for—"

But the moment she said it, something very strange happened. The ghosts all nodded frantically; they were pointing at Yanni, mouthing words he couldn't read. In fact, they weren't just pointing at him – they were pointing at his eyes. Yanni gazed around in confusion. The ghosts were trying to tell him something, only he couldn't understand what it was. "What are they saying?"

Amy looked between Yanni and the faeries. "Hang on – I think that *you* can free them. I think you can help them pass back over. Maybe if you give them a task... Is that right?"

The ghosts nodded again, almost weeping with gratitude. Yanni was filled with hope – now they had a chance to finish their quest. He pointed to the fading speck in the distance, only just visible against the moon.

"There's a way you can help us," he said. "Can you sail the galleon and follow that raven?"

The ghosts gave one final nod – and in an instant, the deck became a whirlwind of movement. Yanni's breath was taken away by their speed. They raced from one end of the ship to the other, drawing up the anchor, loosing the sails, turning the wheel... Within seconds, the galleon was swaying and twisting to face the horizon.

Yanni beamed. "Amy, what did I tell you? You were amazing!"

He meant every word. Once again, only Amy had seen the truth. She stood on the deck, her face flushed, breathless with excitement. Her eyes were gleaming with happiness behind the broken glasses.

"Omigod, I did it! I *was* amazing! And you know what the best bit was? I didn't do it as Saphiana – I did it as *me*! Amy!"

It was wonderful to see her so happy. Yanni could swear that she even looked taller: and then he realized that she was. She was standing up properly, for the very first time.

"That's right! Me, Queen of the Ghosts! How d'you like *them* apples, Chloe? Want to sit next to Cecile, do you? Be my guest! All her stories are boring anyway!"

The sails swelled and the boat leaped towards the horizon. For a moment, it was as if Amy was master and commander, and the wind that sent them racing across the waves was powered entirely by her pride.

THE FINAL TASK

THE GALLEON CUT THROUGH THE WAVES LIKE A knife, and the world of Hallow Fall disappeared behind them. This far out, Yanni could see the lands that lay beyond Hallow Fall, stretching further into the Land of Fae. On one side, he saw a misty headland covered entirely in white roses and carousels, its riderless horses blinking silently in the brume. On the other, Yanni could make out a towering elm tree, its canopy so vast and wide that it covered the land like a thundercloud. In the heart of its branches sat a sparkling stone castle, a waterfall pouring from its doors and tumbling to the world below.

The gang of three watched in silent awe. It was incredible to think that this all lay hidden beneath the real world. Yanni wondered how many more marvels lay beneath the dull and everyday.

"I've never done anything like this," Amy whispered.

Yanni knew exactly what she meant. He didn't feel like a child any more – he felt invincible. Now more than ever, it felt like victory was in sight. Soon he'd be out of his shackles and back home with Ari, away from all this and…

And the realization hit him. *What about Larry?*

He looked at the faerie child poking his head out of his T-shirt, squinting against the wind. Yanni had been so busy completing the tasks that he hadn't thought once about what was going to happen to Larry when all this was over. He couldn't take the changeling home with him; he couldn't leave him behind, either. Would he end up inside that piano, too, with his parents? Or would Lorde Renwin do something worse to him, something even more cruel?

If you leave him behind, said the voice inside his head, *then you're no better than Lorde Renwin.*

Before he could find an answer, the ship lurched; Yanni had to grab the rail to stop himself falling over. The ghosts had stowed the sails and spun the wheel, and the galleon was drifting to a stop. Yanni gazed at the water below, and his heart leaped. There, perched on a white branch that stuck straight up from the waves, was Gustiver. Yanni could swear he was smiling.

"Even faster than I expected," said the raven, impressed.

Yanni smiled back – but there was still no time to lose. "Quick! Tell us the final task!"

Gustiver held out his wings. "The final task is right here."

Yanni frowned – there was nothing around them but miles of water. "What do you mean, here? How can it be...?"

He trailed off. He'd finally realized what it was that Gustiver was perched on.

It wasn't a branch; it was a bone. A skeletal arm rising from the water and gripping a huge longsword. The blade was covered in seashells; seaweed draped from its rusted handle. Gustiver folded back his wings and explained their final task.

"Long ago, the lands beneath this water were ruled by the Erlking. He was a great and powerful sorcerer, who knew how to capture magic and use its powers. But the Erlking had no desire to share his magic with anyone: he wanted it all for himself. He wandered the Land of Fae stealing every ounce of magic that he could find, forging it into a crown for his own head until he had claimed powers beyond reckoning. He became as strong as a god; there was no one who could defeat him."

Yanni glanced down at the dark and twisting waters below. What did all this have to do with the task?

"The Erlking and the faeries fought for centuries,"

Gustiver continued. "But so long as the Erlking had his crown, the faeries were powerless against him. His magic was simply too great." He ruffled his feathers. "Then came the day of their final, terrible battle. It raged for weeks and months – it seemed there would be no end to the bloodshed. In a final act of desperation, the Erlking drew deep from his crown's magic and summoned a spell to make him grow as tall as a giant and crush his enemies – but his spell was too powerful, too quick, too careless. His head and body grew, but the crown did not – it split in two and unleashed all his stolen magic at once. It brought a vast flood, filling the valley from end to end and creating this ocean."

Gustiver looked down. "The Erlking's body and his broken crown lie far beneath us on the ocean floor, untouched for centuries. That is your final task. Journey to the uttermost parts of the sea, find the drowned Erlking, and take the broken crown from him."

Yanni almost choked. "Are you serious?"

He stared at the twisting waves beneath him, panic rising in his chest. The water was fathomless. How was he supposed to get down there? "No – this isn't fair! It's impossible!"

Gustiver shook his head sharply. "The terms of the wager were very clear: *no task is impossible*. No matter how difficult it may appear, it can always be completed.

My master relies on you thinking otherwise. Do you understand?"

Yanni shook his head. "But—"

"No!" the raven suddenly shouted. "I won't let you come this far to give up. *I will not let him do to you what he did to me!*"

His voice echoed across the water. Yanni stared at him, shocked.

"*That's* how he took your name? You lost a wager with him?"

Gustiver gazed at the horizon. It was as if he was looking at something that wasn't really there – something Yanni couldn't see. For a moment, it didn't even look like he was going to reply – and then he did. But not with his own voice.

"*Tell me your name, child, and I will give you all the treasures of the world! You can tell me your name, can't you?*"

It was a pitch-perfect impression of Lorde Renwin. Gustiver looked back at Yanni.

"I believed him," he said quietly. "My parents had just lost all their money. I thought I could help them. I was young, you see. Young and human. Humans make mistakes most easily, I have found."

Yanni couldn't believe it. "You used to be ... human?"

Gustiver nodded sadly. "I was, once."

The raven gazed back at the Land of Fae and gave a deep sigh.

"I have said too much. I must leave you now, and return to my master. Good luck, lad. Finish the task. Save your sister. Take her away and never look back."

With that, he launched himself from the bone and flew gracefully back towards Hallow Fall. Yanni watched him go, his mind reeling. He finally understood the truth about Gustiver and why he wanted to help. It was too late for the raven to save himself, but he could still help save Ari. He could stop her from becoming trapped in Hallow Fall like him. Yanni realized that Gustiver was probably the bravest person he had ever met.

Amy suddenly grabbed him and spun him round.

"Right! You heard what he said – you can't give up. We have to get you to the bottom of the ocean, now!"

Yanni stared at her hopelessly. "*How?* How am I supposed to get to the bottom of the ocean, find a magical crown and get back up again, all in one breath?"

Amy gritted her teeth. "There has to be a way. We'll get the ghosts to drop anchor and then…" She gasped. "Omigod – that's it!"

She peered over the edge of the boat and pointed at the rusted metal dripping from the bows.

"*That's* how you get down to the ocean floor! You hold on to the anchor while it sinks to the bottom, then get the ghosts to haul you back up again afterwards!"

Yanni gazed down at the water; his heart filled with dread. The heavy anchor would definitely get him and Larry to the bottom faster than swimming. But that was only one part of it. "How am I supposed to find this crown when I get down there?"

He turned around ... and trailed off. The ghosts stood in silence, waiting on the deck. They had formed two rows, making an aisle that led to the back of the boat.

"I ... I think they want us to follow them," said Amy.

Yanni, Amy and Larry stepped silently between the ghosts to the back of the boat. There, just beyond the quarterdeck, stood a broken figurehead: a wooden stag's head, practically perished to driftwood by centuries of salt and sea wind. Something hung from its antlers, sparkling in the moonlight.

Yanni gasped. It was a necklace: the most delicate necklace he had ever seen. A clear pendant hung from a golden gossamer chain, the glass no thicker than the skin of a bubble. Inside it, a single pearl lay suspended in brine. It sparkled as if it was brand new, but Yanni knew, deep down, that it was incredibly old. He could feel the magic radiating from it, hear the faintest clamour of tiny bells ringing through the air as he stepped closer. It was his first taste of unbroken magic: radiant, true, clean and pure as morning dew on a spiderweb.

The ghosts were pointing at the necklace and then at Yanni.

"They want you to put on the necklace," said Amy. "I think they're saying it'll help you with the task. Is that right?"

The ghosts nodded enthusiastically. Yanni gulped. He had no idea how the necklace was supposed to help him – but frankly, a magical necklace was better than nothing, no matter what it did.

He passed Larry to Amy, and gently lifted the necklace from the figurehead. It was so light he could barely feel it in his hand. He hung it around his neck beside his *mati*, and felt the change at once. The thrum of magic, beating its way into his blood. It almost made his head spin. It was intoxicating – no wonder Lorde Renwin and the Erlking had wanted to hoard so much magic for themselves. He took Larry back and swallowed nervously.

"R-right," he said faintly. "Let's do it, then. One more task."

He made his way back to the anchor and climbed carefully over the side, resting his bare feet on the dripping metal hooks. He gazed down at the water churning beneath him, and felt his insides flip. Somewhere down there was the body of an ancient king – and Yanni had to steal his crown. What would happen when he did?

Would it be like the abbey all over again – would there be something down there that wanted to stop him? How would Yanni ever get away from them if he was trapped at the bottom of the ocean?

"Ready?"

He looked up. Amy stood beside the lever that controlled the anchor.

"I'll be here the whole time," she promised. "When you reach the ocean floor, strike the anchor once to let me know you're OK. Then when you need to come back up, strike the anchor three times, and the ghosts will reel you in. Got it?"

Yanni swallowed. It wasn't much of a plan. The anchor's chain was thick with rust. What if it broke when he was halfway down, and he never came back up? What if he died down there, at the bottom of an ocean in another world, never to return home or see his parents again?

"Wait – Amy," he said. "I – I need you to look after something for me."

He reached into his T-shirt and brought out his *mati*. He held it tight, and then pulled it over his head. It was the first time he had taken it off since he had stepped into Hallow Fall – the first time he would be without Yiayia close to him. He gave it one final kiss and handed it over.

"Please – take care of this. If I don't make it back, give it to my mum and dad, OK?"

Amy was shocked. Her hand shook slightly when she took it from him. "Are ... are you sure?"

Yanni nodded. He was sure. But there was one final thing he had to say.

"I'm really frightened."

He would never have admitted it a day before – but then, Yanni felt like he'd grown up more in the last few hours than in the rest of his life put together.

"I don't know if I can do this. I know I act brave, but I've been terrified since the very first moment we got to Hallow Fall."

"Yeah, I know," said Amy.

"And I don't know if I can—" He stopped dead. "Wait – you *knew*?"

"Of course! It was pretty obvious. You're not a very good actor." She smiled. "There's nothing wrong with being scared. You should have just said."

Yanni gazed at the sightless depths beneath him. "But ... I *have* to be brave. I have to look after Larry. I have to save my sister. If I'm scared, I'll never be able to defeat Lorde Renwin..."

"I don't think it works like that," said Amy. "I think you *have* to be frightened to be brave." She put her hands on the lever. "Are you ready?"

Yanni looked down at the changeling, still clinging to his chest – so small, so vulnerable – and saw that his raven eyes were steady and determined. He was ready to follow Yanni right to the uttermost parts of the sea. If that tiny faerie could be brave, then he could be brave, too. They looked at each other, took a deep breath together – and nodded.

Amy heaved against the lever – and Yanni's stomach leaped into his chest. The anchor plummeted, and the last thing he saw before he hit the freezing water was Amy's face above him, her eyes shining with tears behind her broken glasses.

THE BROKEN CROWN

THE COLD OF THE WATER KNOCKED OUT YANNI'S breath, a whole lungful in one go. He opened his mouth in shock, and seawater poured right in. He flew instantly into a blind panic, thrashing his arms and opening his eyes to meet the white sting of salt water…

Only, his eyes weren't stinging; he could see through the water as clearly as glass. He could breathe perfectly well. He wasn't drowning at all.

He looked down, and saw that Larry wasn't drowning, either. The changeling was gawping at him in mild surprise and blinking his raven eyes. They were gripping the anchor tight and sinking through the ocean at a rate of knots, calm and comfortable and respiring just fine. How?

Yanni caught sight of the glass necklace – and gasped. It was floating before him, pulsating with a faint white light. The shackle on his wrist was doing the same; so was the chain that linked him and Larry. Now Yanni understood why the ghosts had wanted him to wear it – it gave him the power to breathe underwater. And as long as he was magically shackled to Larry, that meant the changeling could breathe, too.

Yanni would have laughed for joy … if he hadn't seen what loomed below them in the ocean depths.

The skeletal arm that Gustiver had perched on was the top of a towering totem of bones. It snaked right down to the ocean floor, a stack of ribs and skulls and femurs leading to the uttermost depths of the sea. Yanni followed it all the way down … and felt a lurch in his chest.

The seabed was a carpet of bones. Yanni couldn't believe how many there were. They spread in every direction like a coral reef, as far as the eye could see. They were the remains of the final battle – thousands of faerie skeletons still strapped inside their rusted armour, their hands still clinging to their bronze weapons that gleamed like oil in the salt water. Some stretched over the ground, their long pale hair swaying like meadow grass in the currents; others had delicate white sea flowers sprouting from their eye sockets, crabs crawling from their open jaws. Yanni could even make out the skeletons of the stags they rode into battle, their antlers teething with barnacles.

Yanni felt a small hand tightly clutch his own – Larry. He squeezed back. Once again, he was very, very glad he wasn't doing this by himself.

The anchor finally came to rest on the ocean floor, sending up a cloud of powdered bone. Yanni gazed around in stunned disbelief: it was a whole underwater world, perfectly preserved in brine, exactly as it would have been on the day of the final battle. The seabed swelled and dipped like the valley floor it had drowned; in the distance he could even make out underwater trees, fish swimming between their branches, their leaves bleached white with brine. He and Larry were the only other living things in sight.

Yanni looked around the battlefield, and felt a wave of dread. Was the broken crown hidden somewhere beneath these bones? Was that his task – to search and search a thousand skeletons to find it, like the Toadstone in the keep? How on earth was he supposed to succeed...?

Yanni stopped: he had just seen the answer, right in front of him.

In the distance, suspended in the water high above them, was the log of deepest blackthorn, its magical green flames flickering even down here in the deepest ocean. Barely a quarter of the wood was left now: Yanni was running out of time.

But once again, the final object lay beneath it.

A single rock stood on the ocean floor, rising from the bones like a dolmen. Sticking out of the top of it was a worn metal ring, a handspan in width. Yanni knew at once what it was. He could feel the broken magic beating off it, a half-step out of tune, a tremor of ancient electricity that rippled through the water and sang through his teeth.

The broken crown.

It didn't look anything like he'd expected. He'd thought the crown would be beautiful and ornate; instead it was a simple ring of metal, jammed into the top of the rock, so that only a semicircle was visible. Yanni simply had to pull it free.

But Yanni knew how these tasks worked now – he knew that the moment he tried to take the crown from the rock, something would appear to stop him. Would it be the Erlking, risen from the dead and ready to defend his crown? Or would it be a sea monster – or even the skeletons themselves?

Yanni gulped. He had to make sure he was ready. He steeled his nerves and released the anchor, stepping onto the ocean floor in his bare feet. The brined meadow grass crunched beneath him. He let go of Larry, reached down and carefully picked up a bronze sword and shield from the seabed, trying not to disturb the bones. Then he took a helmet from the seabed and placed it on his head.

He was shocked to find that the helmet fitted him, and the sword and shield felt light and easy in his hands. It felt like he was in a dream, and everything had been waiting for this moment. He turned to Larry, who floated in the water beside him, the white glow of the chain casting a sheen across the battlefield.

Are you ready? he thought.

He didn't know why he did it. There was no way that Larry would be able to hear his thoughts – let alone understand them – but to his surprise, the changeling nodded. It was as if he'd sent a message through the chain that connected them. Yanni suddenly remembered the message for Amy and, turning back a final time, he struck the anchor as hard as he could with his sword. The sound rang through the water, strangely muffled … and then, after a pause, another came back in reply, faint but resonant. He glanced up at the wooden hull floating on the ocean's surface like a cloud. It seemed a long way away. But Amy was up there, waiting for them, ready to haul them in at a moment's notice. They weren't alone.

He turned to the rock, the broken magic singing in the distance. Slowly, his heartbeat a dull steady thump in his ears, Yanni made his way across the carpet of bones as Larry floated through the water beside him. Yanni kept his sword held high, scanning the horizon for any signs of movement … but there was nothing. Just the rock, getting closer, the faint chimes of its broken magic growing louder and louder around him.

Finally he stood at the rock's base. Up close, the broken crown looked even more dulled and twisted – the half of it that he could see, anyway. The bottom half lay buried in the stone. The protruding semicircle of metal hummed with its sickly magic, close enough to reach. All Yanni had to do was lean forward and...

There was a sudden sound beside him – a scuttle of bones. Yanni snapped round, heart racing, expecting to see that they were no longer alone and there behind them was the drowned Erlking in all his terrible glory, ready and waiting to fight ... but there was nothing. Larry gave a whimper of fear and swam towards him, clinging to his shoulder. Yanni gazed directly at him.

Don't worry, he thought. *I won't let anything hurt you. Just be ready to swim back to the anchor, OK?*

Larry nodded, as if he understood every word. Yanni turned back to the crown. This was it. He placed his shield and sword on the seabed. Then, slowly, he pressed his whole body against the rock, the magic throbbing into his chest. He leaned forward, centimetre by centimetre, until his fingertips could finally brush the metal rim of the broken crown...

He clasped his hand around it. Then he shut his eyes, gritted his teeth, and pulled.

Nothing. The crown didn't budge; it was stuck far too deep in the stone. Larry whimpered, desperate to get away. Yanni gulped – he understood what he had to do. He was going to have to stand on top of the rock and pull the crown out with both hands.

Slowly, heart pounding, he climbed onto the rock and stood up. He could feel the magic throbbing up through the soles of his bare feet. Yanni took another glance around him. The ocean was silent; nothing moved.

It was now or never. He leaned down and clasped the rim of the crown with both hands. Then he squeezed his eyes shut, braced himself, and heaved on the crown with all his might…

The scream filled his head like an explosion, wild and terrified. Yanni spun around. Larry had leaped from his shoulder and was scrambling back through the water, pulling on the chain for all he was worth. Yanni felt a burst of blinding adrenaline: he knew what it meant. Something was coming for them. He had to get the crown out and escape now, while he still could.

He turned back to the crown between his feet … and felt his insides wither in terror.

A pair of vast white eyes were open on the rock face beneath him, as deep and desolate as abandoned wells. Yanni bellowed in fear and fell back, clattering onto the carpet of bones and scrambling away from the rock. But it wasn't a rock – it was a giant stone head, rising from the ocean floor, scattering bones like sand as it revealed a mouth, a neck, a chest…

It was the drowned Erlking himself. He was still down here, after all these years – still a giant, still defending his crown. Yanni could now see that the broken metal ring was embedded in the space between his eyes – the place where it had split when the Erlking had cast his final spell, his body growing faster than he could control. The crown had snapped and dug into his flesh, flooding his body with broken magic and turning him into a monster. He was the single biggest creature Yanni had ever seen … and his wild, furious eyes were fixed on him and Larry.

The Erlking opened his mouth and roared.

THE DROWNED ERLKING

THE POWER OF THE ERLKING'S ROAR HIT YANNI LIKE an explosion, driving him back across the ocean floor. He was sent tumbling over the bones as if by a rip tide, tangling in the chain that linked him to Larry. Yanni knew nothing except fear. There was no way to fight the Erlking, no way to hide from him. Their only hope was to flee.

Yanni scrambled to his feet and half ran, half swam towards the anchor, dragging Larry with him. The Erlking slammed his fists onto the seabed and bore after them like a tidal wave, bellowing with rage and trembling the ocean around them. Yanni leaped onto the rusted anchor and hammered it again and again, hoping that Amy would get the message in time…

But with a single swipe of his arms, the Erlking struck the chain and shattered the rusted links to smithereens. Yanni was sent tumbling to the ocean floor again as the chain sank through the water beside him. Yanni sent a thought to the changeling, shrill and fast…

Run!

Yanni started to tear through the water to escape – but found he couldn't move. Larry was tugging in the other direction, stopping them both in their tracks. The changeling's screams were continuous now, a ringing shriek inside his head. Yanni could barely see a thing through the storm of erupted sand and bone around them. But the Erlking could see *him* – there was no way to hide the glowing chain that linked him and Larry, beaming through the water like a lighthouse.

No, no, no! Yanni cried. *We have to move together or—!*

Too late – the Erlking slammed down his fist on the golden chain between them and pinned them to the ocean floor. Yanni reeled with terror – surely there was no escape now? But through the chaos of sand and bone, he could see that the Erlking's fingers were scrabbling to find purchase on the thin chain. Larry was thrashing to pull free, his eyes wild with fear. Yanni sent the thought straight to him, praying that he would understand.

Listen – we have to work together! Do you trust me?

Larry's eyes met his own – and even though he was terrified, the faerie nodded. Yanni held out his hands.

To me – quick!

Larry shot towards him; at the last second Yanni yanked the chain from beneath the Erlking's grip, and they both swam free. The Erlking roared with rage and pounded the ocean floor, sending up another blizzard of sand and bone. Yanni swung around, looking for any way out – *anything* – but he couldn't even make out the ship any more. The only thing in sight was the tower of bones, twisting up from the seabed beside them.

Follow the tower – it'll lead us back to the boat!

Their only hope was to swim to the surface before the Erlking could catch them. They heaved through the water and scrambled up the tower, handful by handful...

But it was no use. The Erlking struck the tower and shattered it with a single blow, filling the water with a tumbling mist of bones. Their only hope toppled to the seabed. Yanni had no idea which way was up any more, which was down. He was filled with despair – there was no way they could outrun the Erlking now. So long as he and Larry were held together by the glowing chain, the Erlking would always be able to find them...

And that was when Yanni noticed it.

The golden chain was completely undamaged. One blow from the Erlking had broken the anchor's chain like it was made of gossamer, and another had destroyed an entire tower of bones; but the golden chain looked as new as the moment it had first been made. Gustiver's words suddenly echoed in his head:

The shackles binding you together are made of eldritch magic and cannot be broken.

That was it – the only thing they had that was stronger than the Erlking. Yanni held Larry tight.

Listen – we have to use the chain!

The Erlking was sweeping his head through the water beside them, twisting his vast eyes to find them. They didn't have much time. Yanni pointed.

If we swim either side of his neck, we might be able to stop him!

It was their only hope. If they could tighten the chain around the Erlking's neck, then they might just be able to bring him down. It was their only way to defend themselves – and they had to do it now. The Erlking had found them. With another bone-shuddering roar, he flew towards them, his mouth wide open and his eyes filled with fury…

Now!

Yanni and Larry leaped towards his neck – but they landed too high, slamming into his face. They clung on for all they were worth as the Erlking reared up with rage, trying to shake them off. Yanni grabbed hold of anything that could keep him there, anything that could buy him more seconds, anything that might keep them away from the Erlking's bellowing mouth…

Yanni felt something throb up his arm – without realizing it, he had grabbed the broken crown. It was still embedded in the space between the Erlking's eyes, pulsating with the last of its cursed magic. Yanni could *feel* the Erlking's pain bursting through it, singing through the metal and into the muscles of his arm…

That was it. *That* was how the Erlking was still alive, after all these years. The broken crown was his only source of power. The plan came in the space of a heartbeat.

Larry – the crown! You have to swim through it!

The space between the crown and the Erlking's face was tiny – barely a handspan in width. Yanni could only pray that the changeling was small enough to fit through. It was their only chance to survive. Larry scrambled over the Erlking's face and squeezed himself through the loop of the crown as the Erlking's hands swept through the water towards him … but it was just as Yanni feared. Larry's hips got jammed halfway through the crown: he was stuck. He screamed with fear and thrashed to escape, twisting and squirming as the Erlking's fingers closed around him…

Larry!

In a snap, Larry changed – suddenly he was in the form of a stoat, twisting through the crown just as the Erlking's fingers grabbed for him. The plan had worked.

The golden chain was wound through the ring of the crown like a thread through a needle. Yanni sent the message to Larry, hard and urgent:

Swim, as hard as you can! We have to pull it out!

Yanni launched from the Erlking's face and he and Larry swam with all of their might, the chain snapping taut between them. The Erlking bellowed in agony, churning up the water around them like an earthquake, but it was hopeless. The crown was buried too deep in the Erlking's skull – they would never be able to pull it free. Yanni felt a flood of panic – he could see the Erlking's hands swinging up through the water to grab them...

No!

Too late. He felt the Erlking grasp the chain. Yanni twisted round in horror and saw that all was lost. The Erlking had finally caught them – there was no escape. The monster opened his mouth to utter a roar of triumph, and Yanni saw that what lay inside was a cavern of horrors: a black bottomless throat, shards of broken teeth scuttling with crabs. The Erlking was going to eat them. He wrenched Yanni and Larry towards his gaping mouth, pulling hard on the chain...

...and tearing the crown straight from his own head.

The sound that burst from his mouth was horrific. The Erlking had torn a crater in the space between his eyes; Yanni watched as the skull around it crumbled to dust, collapsing in a ripple effect across his face. The power that had held the Erlking together for centuries was gone; he was falling apart, piece by piece, his eyes widening in horror before they, too, collapsed and disintegrated. Then his neck, then his shoulders, then all along the length of his body until there was nothing left but two pillars on the sand where his legs had been…

And from the cloud of dust, something emerged on the golden chain: the broken crown, strung along its length like a necklace. Yanni looked at Larry and saw the same expression of stunned amazement. They had done it: they had the crown. They'd defeated the drowned Erlking and completed the final task. Yanni let out a scream of delight.

Larry – we did it! We've got the—

And then it happened. With the final shreds of his evil magic, the Erlking's hand burst from the cloud of dust and tore towards them, its nails as sharp as jagged clamshells. Yanni jerked his head back, but it was too late. The fingers latched on to the whisper-thin chain of the glass necklace around his neck, pulled tight … and snapped it.

Yanni felt his chest crush like an empty can as an explosion of bubbles erupted from his mouth. The magic of the ghosts' necklace was gone – he couldn't breathe. He couldn't even see. The ocean squeezed in at him from every side, crushing his skull, blinding his eyes, pressing every last ounce of breath out of him. All he could feel was the chain yanking and thrashing on his wrist – and knew that meant Larry couldn't breathe, either. They were both drowning.

LARRY!

Yanni thrashed in the water, spinning his head this way and that, but it was no use – he couldn't see a thing. The sound of his own heartbeat hammered to a crescendo in his ears as he fought, and fought, and fought…

No, no, no – not here, not now!

And then all of a sudden, the panic ebbed. His arms suddenly felt heavy. A blackness was settling down on top of him, one which he knew there was no use fighting. It lowered him down like a gentle wave, shutting his eyelids and calmly laying him to rest on the ocean floor as the sea was swallowed in darkness around him…

THE DREAM

WHEN YANNI OPENED HIS EYES, HE WAS STANDING IN his old house.

It was all exactly as he remembered it. The cosy living room, the cars driving past the windows, the old sofa they'd left behind. His heart swelled to see it again. He'd forgotten how much he'd missed it all.

"Ah! A text. They are here!"

Pappou strode out of the kitchen, staring at his phone like someone reading a compass. Yiayia followed close behind him, wiping her hands on a tea towel. Yanni blinked – what were they doing here? Before he could think too much about it, Pappou clamped a hand on his shoulder.

"Yiannaki, an important day for you, yes? Today is the day you are a brother!"

Yanni looked at Pappou and Yiayia sadly. He understood what this was: he was inside a memory.

And he knew exactly what memory this was.

The door opened. Mum and Dad stood framed inside it, next to the old front door, blue with gold numbers. They were dressed in the same clothes they'd been wearing when they left two days before. They looked utterly delighted, and utterly exhausted.

Mum walked inside first and sat down weakly. Dad followed close behind, carrying a car seat like it held the single most precious object in the whole entire world. Pappou and Yiayia clapped their hands and cooed.

"Here she is," said Dad. "Her first day home."

He settled the car seat down on the floor, looking inside it so lovingly that it made Yanni's insides hurt. He'd never seen Dad look at anything else like that before. Mum beckoned Yanni over.

"Yanni, come and say hello to your new sister."

Yanni walked over and gazed inside the car seat. All he could see was a squashed pink face in a smother of white fabric. He remembered exactly how he had felt at the time: he hadn't felt love or excitement upon seeing his new sister. The truth was, he'd felt a knot in his stomach, being pulled tighter and tighter. From now on, he knew everything would be different.

"We've decided on a name," said Mum. "Do you want to know what it is?"

Yanni opened his mouth to answer – but before he could

266

say anything, his baby sister suddenly opened her eyes and looked straight at him.

"Right," she said, "you're going to wake up any moment, so listen to everything I'm about to say."

Yanni stared at her, blinking in confusion. "Wait — sorry, did you just talk to me?"

"It's important. OK?" said Ari. "We don't have much time."

Yanni looked around. Mum and Dad and Yiayia and Pappou were all smiling and nodding, as if none of this was happening.

"But … it didn't happen like this," he argued. "You didn't talk. You're only a day old!"

"Will you stop being so difficult?" Ari snapped. "This is the only way I can get you to listen to me!"

Yanni was stumped. What was going on? "Who are you?"

"It doesn't matter," said Ari. "You'll forget about all this when you wake up anyway. But I'm going to plant some things in your head for now: they'll help you understand what to do later."

Yanni was utterly bewildered. "What do you mean, I'll forget about all this?"

Ari ignored him. "First of all — your mati. The one you gave to Amy. You have to get it back. You have to make sure you're wearing it, all the time, and never take it off again.

Secondly – and this is really important – you kill a monster by saying its name. Understand, Yanni?"

Yanni shook his head. "No, not at—"

"Just remember those two things," ordered Ari. "Nothing else matters. Get the mati back, and you kill a monster by saying its name."

"But…"

Ari opened her fist – and Yanni saw that there was a blue glass eye embedded in the surface of her palm. It was a mati – and it was broken. A single crack split it in two across the middle. It looked more like an eye than ever before.

Then it blinked.

"Yanni? Yanni, wake up!"

"Yanni, wake up!"

Yanni was lying on something rough and hard. He could hear voices, creaking wood, wind. He could taste the faint tang of salt in the air. There was a face gazing down at him: a single eye behind a cracked lens…

"Please, wake up!" Amy begged. "Oh, please, please, please…"

Yanni rolled onto his side and vomited up a lungful of water. His vision bobbed and swayed. He was back on the galleon. Amy was crouched on the deck beside him.

"You're alive!" she cried. "Omigod, I can't believe it, you're al— Wow, that's a lot of puke."

Yanni's head was swollen to bursting. The memories came back at once: the ocean floor, the broken crown, the fight with the Erlking, the necklace breaking, Larry…

"Where's Larry?" he cried. "Where…?"

All the air was slammed out of him at once as Larry threw himself on top of him, squealing with happiness. There he was – soaking wet and shaken and shivering, but back in his faerie form, alive and well. Yanni couldn't believe it.

"He's OK!"

Amy nodded. "Oh, it was awful… When the anchor chain broke, I thought you were gone for good. I tried talking to the ghosts to work out some way we could save you, but then I heard something crying out on the other side of the boat – it was Larry! He'd turned into a fish and swum you both back up to the surface. But you were floating on your front – I thought … I thought…"

Yanni gazed at Larry in amazement. The changeling had saved his life. And he'd done it because he loved him – Yanni could feel it in his hug, in the message passing over and over and over between the chain that linked them.

And strung along the chain between them, lying on the deck…

The broken crown.

Yanni picked it up with shaking hands. He could

feel, instantly, that its magic was finally gone. It was nothing more than a ring of dead metal now. In fact, it wasn't even a full ring: it had fractured in the middle so it didn't quite meet, both ends frayed to molten splits. But it was theirs: the final task was complete. He staggered to his feet.

"Quick! We have to go back to the tower, right now!"

Amy frowned. "You almost drowned. Maybe give it five minutes to—"

Yanni shook his head. "No – I saw the blackthorn log. We're running out of time! We have to get this back to Lorde Renwin to win the wager." He turned to the ghosts, who stood waiting in silence on the deck. "Quick! Take us back to Hallow Fall!"

The ghosts obeyed at once, transforming the deck into a whirlwind of movement. The ship reeled around to face the headland, the sails swelled, and they darted through the water, leaving the final remains of the ancient battlefield far below them.

Yanni faced the headland, his heart racing. He couldn't believe it. The end of their task was right in front of him. Never in a million years had he thought that they would be able to take on such impossible tasks, fight against so many odds and win. But he was going to save his sister. He had done it.

No – *they* had done it. He and Amy and Larry

together, a gang of three. They had shared the hardship and the fear and the pain – now they were going to share the victory. Amy clambered up the rigging, pointing to the shore, and Larry clung on to Yanni tight. The three of them faced the horizon: back to Hallow Fall, to the tower, to the end of their quest. Yanni had never been so grateful to have other people in his life.

Then suddenly, out of nowhere, there was a nagging thought – something important, right at the back of his head.

"Amy – do you still have my *mati*?"

She glanced at him. "Of course, right here. You didn't think I'd lose it, did you?"

Yanni laughed. "It's not that. It's—"

He tried to explain … but nothing came out. He knew it was important that he have it, but he couldn't explain why.

"It's nothing," he said. "Can I have it back?"

Amy handed it over, and he quickly hung it around his neck, back where it belonged. And all at once, the nagging thought disappeared. Yanni couldn't remember why it had been so important. Within seconds, he had forgotten he'd even had the thought in the first place.

VICTORY

THE GALLEON SWEPT TO A GRACEFUL STOP AT THE shore's edge. Yanni and Amy and Larry vaulted over the ship's side and landed on the path. Yanni turned and gave the ghosts a final wave.

"Thank you for everything!" he cried. "You've fulfilled your duty – does that mean you can pass over or…"

He trailed off – the ghosts were already fading from view, as quickly as they'd appeared. It had worked – they were finally free. But Yanni didn't have time to celebrate. He grabbed Amy's hand.

"Come on! We have to get to Lorde Renwin's tower, now!"

They tore back to the crossroads, back down the path, back through the forest. Sure enough, the black tower was in a worse state than ever before. It was little more than a squat ruin, a shadow of its former self; the bridge that crossed the gulf was barely standing. The hum of broken magic that radiated off it seemed fainter, beating off the trees in sickly waves; the sound of chimes had never been so quiet.

"He's even weaker!" said Amy. "You're going to do it, Yanni!"

Yanni looked down at the changeling in his arms. He'd made up his mind on the way here – he knew what he had to do now. "That's right. And we're not just going to save Ari, either. We're going to save Larry, too."

Amy blinked. "We are?"

"Who knows what that monster will do to him after we leave! Larry saved my life; now we have to save his. If Lorde Renwin's powers are weaker, then there must be a way we can beat him!" He grabbed her arm. "And this time, you're coming with me. We're going to finish this together – just like we should have started it. A gang of three!"

Amy beamed. "A gang of three!"

They flew across the crumbling footbridge hand in hand and ran inside the tower. The hallway was worse than ever, rotten and stagnant and thick with decay. This was no longer a place of decadent beauty; this was a place where no gold sparkled, where no candles shone. The portraits had disappeared completely; the walls were now covered with something dark and wet, like…

Amy reached out in shock. "Is that … *soil*?"

She was right. It was cold, wet soil, packed against the walls and floor. They were finally seeing the place for what it really was, what it had always been beneath the glamour of Lorde Renwin's magic. Whatever was waiting for them upstairs would be in its final form, too.

"He's just trying to distract us," said Yanni. "We have to get upstairs and finish the challenge, now!"

They raced up the staircase, the rotten wood threatening to cave in with every step, and came to the ballroom. The room was now just a cramped and dingy cell, filled with broken furniture. Lorde Renwin was slumped in his throne, Gustiver perched high above him.

"Well, well! You've brought your friend!"

Yanni was expecting the worst, but the sight that met him was still a shock. The faerie's beauty had withered away: the whites of his eyes were sallow and bloodshot, and his once-sleek hair was matted with filth. His clothing hung in mouldering threads: the body beneath it was bony and stained. The gap of his missing tooth stuck out like a hole in a windowpane.

And there, sat in his lap, was Ari. Her eyes were now almost completely black; she was gazing at Yanni like he was a stranger. He felt Amy's hand grab his. It was the first time she had been inside the ballroom – the first time she had seen the faerie with her own eyes. But if she was frightened, she didn't show it.

"Finish the task!" she cried. "Now!"

Yanni glanced at the blackthorn log floating in the fireplace. Sure enough, there was barely any left. The time had come. Yanni threw the broken crown at Lorde Renwin's feet, the clatter of metal ringing off the corners of the dismal room.

"There! That's it – the final object. Stop the clock!"

Lorde Renwin glanced at the crown disdainfully. "*Pfft*. And what would I do with that worthless piece of rubbish? Take it away before—"

"Enough!" snapped Yanni. "I've done what you asked. I've completed your stupid tasks. I fulfilled my end of the bargain, fair and square! Now finish the challenge!"

Yanni's heart was soaring. After all they had been through, after everything they had suffered, it was finally over. He faced the feeble, withered faerie on his desolate throne and held Larry tight to his chest, swelling with confidence.

"You thought I'd fail, but I didn't. You thought I'd give up, but I didn't. Now I'm taking back what's mine – and I'm taking Larry from you, too. I won't let you do to him what you did to his parents!" He raised an arm and pointed to the child on his lap. "Now, for the last time, *give me back my sister*!"

His words rang off the walls and echoed into silence.

Lorde Renwin didn't move; he just stayed exactly where he was, still smiling.

Then, slowly, his smile began to widen, and kept on widening. Something inside Yanni faltered. The faerie didn't look like someone who had just lost. He looked like a predator taking its final steps forward.

"Oh no," he said calmly, his voice soft and playful in the darkness. "No, I won't be doing *that*. The wager's not finished."

Yanni glanced at Amy. "Of course it is. Three objects. That's what we agreed."

Lorde Renwin shook his head. "No game is over until the last hand has been played. Let's add up all the penalties first, shall we?"

Yanni felt something shift inside him. The temperature of the room dropped.

"Wh-what penalties?"

Lorde Renwin giggled. "For all the rules you broke, of course! You remember the rules that Gustiver explained at the beginning of the wager? You broke *ever* so many!"

Yanni glanced at Gustiver, but the raven stared straight ahead, betraying nothing. The room was changing around them: he could feel it. "N-no – I didn't break any rules. I finished all your tasks fair and square…"

Lorde Renwin wasn't listening. He turned to the

burning blackthorn in the fireplace, and made a steeple of his fingers.

"Let's start from the beginning," he said. "You asked the signpost where to find the Toadstone. Correct?"

Yanni frowned. "Well – yes, but it said it could—"

"All tasks must be completed by yourself and the changeling," said Lorde Renwin. "Does it say anything about the signpost helping you? No! That means you broke the rules."

Whoomph.

Yanni gasped: a centimetre of the blackthorn log had suddenly turned to ash, leaving a ghost of itself behind. "Wait – that's not fair! You never said—"

"What about those ghosts?" said Lorde Renwin. "You asked them for help, too. You weren't supposed to do *that*, either…"

Whoomph.

Another centimetre of the log burned through. Yanni felt like the floor was slipping away from beneath him. Once again, Lorde Renwin knew everything they had done. "I had to ask the ghosts for help! You trapped them here…"

But Lorde Renwin still wasn't listening. He fixed Amy with a mocking glare.

"And as for this friend of yours – you accepted *all sorts* of help from her! Where do I even begin?" He counted off on his grimy fingers. "Opening the door to Goblin Mountain, tricking the goblins, calming down the changeling, talking to the ghosts…"

Whoomph. Whoomph. Whoomph. Whoomph. Whoomph.

Yanni watched in horror as the final fragments of the log were eradicated in front of him, piece by piece. The faerie was changing, too: his clothes were patching themselves up, his skin growing taut and youthful and dazzling in the firelight. The truth was beginning to dawn on Yanni: Lorde Renwin had never been getting weaker, not really. It had all been another trick. The faerie had known that Yanni was breaking the rules all along, and he'd kept it a secret until this moment.

Yanni gazed up through eyes that were wet with tears. The blackthorn log was almost completely gone now – barely a millimetre of wood was left burning at the end.

"Please," he whispered. "Please let that be it…"

But Lorde Renwin smiled, his eyes even more sickening and hateful.

"And last, but by no means least – the *graveyard*. Something saved you from the statues at the very last moment. It took me ever such a long time to work it out!" He sat back. "A voice called out and drew them away – and there's only one person it could have been. Someone who's been trying to help you all along, it seems."

Lorde Renwin looked up.

"Isn't that right, Gustiver?"

Yanni's head snapped up. The raven was trembling on the throne like a leaf. Yanni had never seen anything look so frightened before.

"M-Master, I would never dream of—"

"You flew into the graveyard," said Lorde Renwin. "You copied the boy's voice to confuse the statues. You made sure to do it in a place where I wouldn't see. You tried to trick me, Gustiver. I really am most terribly, *terribly* angry with you."

Yanni panicked. "No! I never asked him to—"

Gustiver shot towards the window, trying to escape, but it was hopeless. The faerie clicked his fingers, and the room filled with a sickening *snap*. Gustiver's body twisted in mid-air and fell to the floor like a stone. Larry screamed; Amy clamped her hands to her mouth in horror.

"There!" said Lorde Renwin. "He broke a rule; I broke his neck. That seems like a reasonable trade, don't you think?"

"Gustiver!" Yanni cried.

He dropped Larry and ran over to the raven, crouching down beside him ... but Gustiver wasn't a raven any more.

He was human; he was a boy, just like Yanni. His

hair was neatly combed; he wore a woollen pullover and shorts. Yanni understood, at once, that he was looking at the real Gustiver: the human one, the boy Lorde Renwin had stolen away all those years ago. When the boy spoke, he spoke with his true voice.

"I'm sorry," he whispered. "I tried. I couldn't let him do it. I couldn't let him take another one."

Yanni shook his head in horror. "Gustiver, no, no, no, please, don't..."

Gustiver's eyes suddenly shone with remembrance. "No – Gustiver's not my name. It's ... *John*. That was my name, back in Fallow Hall."

Yanni gasped, remembering the name of the missing boy that the old lady in the church had told him about. Gustiver was the boy who'd been stolen from Fallow Hall, all those years ago. He'd been stuck here all that time, never able to see his parents again. "Wait – hold on, I can find a way to save you."

But the boy suddenly grabbed Yanni close and pulled his face right down to his, so his voice was barely a whisper. Yanni could see, straight away, that he was missing a tooth.

"I lied," he hissed. "When I said I didn't know, I lied. It's there, with all the others. The very, very, very last one."

Yanni didn't understand. "But..."

He stopped. Gustiver – John – couldn't hear him any

280

more. His lips stopped moving, the shine fell from his eyes and Yanni knew at once that he was dead.

Larry gave a great wail of misery. Amy stayed frozen to the spot. Yanni kneeled on the floor beside the boy's body, shaking from head to toe. John was dead. He had given his life trying to help Yanni, and now it was all for nothing. Yanni had witnessed many strange and terrible things that night ... but this – oh yes, this – was the worst by far.

"What a shame!" sighed Lorde Renwin. "Still, that's what happens if you break the rules. And *speaking* of breaking rules..."

Whoomph.

Yanni felt his insides lurch. The last of the pale green light disappeared.

He turned around ... and saw that the final fragment of the blackthorn log had burned through, the ash drifting down like fine snow. The look on Amy's face said it all: their challenge was over. They'd run out of time.

Yanni had failed.

THE NAME-TAKING

YANNI STARED AT THE EMPTY FIREPLACE IN HORROR.
The reality of it was almost too enormous for him to
contemplate. The log was gone. The challenge was over.
And that meant…

"Well!" said Lorde Renwin briskly. "Let's get down
to business, shall we?"

He snapped his fingers, and the shackle on Yanni's
wrist flew apart. Larry shrieked and sprang from
Yanni's side, trying to make a dash for the door –
but Lorde Renwin simply twirled his fingers, and the
changeling was hauled back across the floor with a
terrible cry.

Yanni leaped up. "NO! Don't you dare hurt him!"

It was no use. A gilded cage materialized like smoke
in one corner of the room. Larry was flung inside it and
the bars became solid gold, slamming shut around him.
He cried out in fear, changing into every form that he

could to try to escape – a snake, a sparrow, a stag beetle, a wildcat – but it was no use. He was trapped.

"Let him go!" Amy cried. "He's just a baby. He hasn't done anything…"

"I have his name – I can do with him as I please!" snapped Lorde Renwin. "Perhaps he can replace Gustiver as my manservant. I'll have to wait until he's a bit older, though." He tapped his chin. "If only I had someone else to replace him until then…"

He gazed at Amy … and smiled.

Yanni gasped. *"No, don't!"*

But it was too late. Lorde Renwin's hand shot towards Amy; her knees buckled instantly and her head slumped. She turned to Lorde Renwin with a dreamy expression, her eyes swimming in her skull.

"That's right." The faerie nodded. "Don't fight it, child – just tell me your name…"

Yanni ran to Amy and shook her, trying to wake her up before it was too late. "No! Don't tell him!"

But it was hopeless – it was like Yanni wasn't even there. Her eyes saw only Lorde Renwin.

"Amy, Master," she said faintly. "My name's Amy."

Lorde Renwin howled with glee – in an instant, she was wrenched from Yanni's arms and dragged across the floor as if being pulled by an invisible rope. She woke up just long enough to scream.

"Wh-what's going on? *Help!*"

Quick as a flash, Lorde Renwin passed a hand across her mouth and yanked something out. Amy shuddered as if an electric shock had passed through her; a dissonant clang of broken chimes immediately rang out across the room. Yanni had no idea what Lorde Renwin was doing to her, but it was wrong, deeply wrong, unspeakably wrong.

"No! Get off her!"

He ran forward to grab her ... but Amy wasn't there any more. All that was left was a pile of clothes slumped on the floor, and a pair of cracked glasses. Yanni looked up, and there on the back of Lorde Renwin's throne, where Gustiver had sat only moments before, was a raven with antlers. It was Amy: she had been turned into Lorde Renwin's new servant, trapped for all eternity. She stared at Yanni with petrified eyes.

"No – no, not Amy, please!" he cried. "Change her back!"

Lorde Renwin simply shook his head. "Enough, boy. I believe *you* owe me a name. Pay up."

Yanni gasped and looked at Ari, gazing at him blankly on the faerie's lap. This was it – the moment that he lost her. "No! I won't let you have her!"

The words froze in his throat. Lorde Renwin leaned forward.

"A deal in blackthorn cannot be unmade, boy. Give me her name, and do it fast. I want it while she still has *some* human left in her..."

His pale fingers were dancing in the air; Yanni could *feel* something rising up from inside him, like it was being reeled from the end of a fishing line. His stomach churned; his tongue twisted in his mouth. It was the name, trying to make its way out of him.

Lorde Renwin giggled.

"Ah! There it is! I can feel it! Ooh, it's wriggling!"

Yanni clamped his mouth shut. He had to fight it; he had to keep it inside him. But it was hopeless: he could feel his teeth being drawn apart, the word rising up out of his throat, as the faerie leaned closer with gleaming eyes.

"That's it! Give it to me! Give me what's mine!"

Yanni fought back with everything he had, but Lorde Renwin was too powerful. His mouth was wrenched open as if by invisible hands, and with a final cry of despair the name came flying out of his throat...

"Ari!"

It felt like a piece of his heart had been pulled out; like a family photograph had been burned with a poker, a face lost for ever. The faerie shrieked and bent forward, passing his hand over Ari's mouth – just like Amy, her whole body convulsed. It was awful, truly awful, to see.

"No!" Yanni cried. "Don't you *dare* hurt my sister!"

But it was too late. The sound of broken chimes rang out; Lorde Renwin looked up, his face calm and sinister.

"*Your* sister? I don't believe she's *yours* any more, boy…"

He held up Ari – and Yanni's heart broke. Right in front of his eyes, her face was changing: the skin draining to the colour of bleached bone, grey hair pouring from her head, cheekbones filing to points. The eyes that looked back at him were now purest midnight black. She wasn't human any more. Her transformation was complete: she was all faerie.

"I did it! I tricked you!" cried Lorde Renwin, raising a clenched fist in triumph above his head. "Two human names! *Two human child names, in a single night!*"

Yanni gasped. The room was transforming around them. The remaining darkness was disappearing, the filth cleaning itself from the floor, the low ceiling stretching to the lofty heights of a glorious ballroom. Every surface was exploding with gold and diamonds. The broken chimes clamoured off the walls, louder and brighter than ever. Lorde Renwin was growing taller, too, even more beautiful, every inch of his skin swelling with power and shimmering with grace until it was almost terrible to behold. The faerie turned to him in triumph, raw magic surging in his eyeballs like flickers in a lightning cloud.

"You understand what you've done now – don't you, boy? You've given me more power than any faerie in history! You thought you could beat me, and you were wrong! You never had a hope of winning! *I TRICKED YOU!*" He leaned back in his throne, and waved a dismissive hand. "Now go – All Hallows' Eve will be over soon. I have no further use for you."

Yanni stood frozen with disbelief, tears streaming down his face. It was too awful to comprehend. A child lay dead on the floor. Larry was locked inside a gilded cage. Ari and Amy were lost for ever. And what about the creatures of Hallow Fall? The signpost, the goblins, Lorde Renwin's prisoners, still trapped. He had failed everyone. The guilt and desperation were indescribable.

"Please," he whispered. "Give them back. I'll do anything…"

Lorde Renwin gazed at him in amusement – and started cackling with laughter. "What on *earth* do you have left to give me, boy? I've already taken everything you have!"

It was true – Yanni had nothing left. Everything that he had grown to love had been taken from him. There was only one thing he had left now, and that was…

He looked up, blinking away the tears. It was unthinkable – it was madness. But it was his only chance to save them.

"I do have something left, actually," he said. "My name. You never did manage to take it from me, did you? No matter how hard you tried."

Every hair on Lorde Renwin's head stood on end. Yanni stepped closer, dreading the words even as he said them.

"One more challenge. Double or quits. If I win, you let them all go free. Ari, Amy, Larry ... all of them." He swallowed. "But if I lose ... then you can have *my* name, too."

Yanni couldn't believe the words coming out of his mouth. He knew the consequences of making a wager with Lorde Renwin. But it was the only option he had left.

Amy flapped her wings madly, trying to stop him. "*No*, don't do it! Leave while you still—"

The faerie flicked his fingers, and her beak was bound shut. Lorde Renwin gazed at Yanni with fascination. He almost looked sorry for him.

"You *stupid* boy," he whispered. "After everything that's just happened – after all you have just seen – you would risk losing your own name, too? You would become a slave for the rest of eternity – just for a *chance* to save them?"

Yanni nodded. He didn't care about himself any more. He couldn't let his friends – his family – suffer for what he'd done. The faerie bent closer, his eyes gleaming.

"As you wish. Name your terms, boy."

Larry cried out with misery in his cage, as if trying to

stop Yanni, too. Yanni ignored him; he had to make sure he got this next part right.

"First of all – I can ask for help this time, without any penalties. As many times as I want."

Lorde Renwin snorted. "Ask for all the help you want! Not that it will do you much good."

Yanni saw Ari on the faerie's lap, gazing at him like he was a piece of stone. He swallowed down the fear. "Secondly – there's no time limit. You have to stop time, so I can finish the challenge and get home before All Hallows' Eve is over. You're the most powerful faerie in existence now, aren't you? Surely you can stop time!"

It was the only way to save himself from being trapped.

Lorde Renwin raised an eyebrow. "Hmm, perhaps you're right. Let's see…"

He clicked his fingers – at once, the room shifted and lurched around them. The light seemed different all of a sudden, the air thicker and heavier. It felt like a dial had been turned in Yanni's blood.

"There!" said Lorde Renwin. "I've stretched out the gaps between time – every second now lasts an hour. Is that good enough for you, boy?"

Yanni nodded. It would have to be. He steeled himself. Was he *really* about to do this?

"Final demand – this time, you have to tell me the

challenge first, before I agree to it. I have to know exactly what I'm looking for, and where to find it."

Lorde Renwin gave him a withering look. "Why on *earth* would I agree to that?"

"Because otherwise I won't do it," Yanni snapped. "Think about it – this is the best wager you'll ever be offered. Two human child names in one night is one thing, but *three*… Imagine the power you'll have if I lose. You might not see that opportunity for another thousand years – and you don't like waiting, do you?"

Lorde Renwin's eyes flashed with greed; the whole room seemed to swell and shift around him again. His smile widened.

"As you wish. Here's your challenge." He gestured at the three prisoners. "You want their names back? Go and find them."

Yanni blinked. "What do you mean? Their names are here – I just saw you take them."

Lorde Renwin gave a shrill titter. "Oh, I'd never keep them *here*! The source of all my power?" He opened his fists to show his empty hands. "No, no, no, they're far too precious. I've magicked them both to my stronghold in the Lower Kingdoms. That's where I keep all the names I take. The changeling's name will be in there, too. Your challenge is this: travel to the Lower Kingdoms, break into my stronghold, and bring back three names of your choosing. Whoever they are whose names you bring back, I'll let you keep them."

Yanni shook his head. "No – not three names. Four. I have to save John, too."

Lorde Renwin stared at him for a moment – and then howled with laughter.

"You mean … *Gustiver*?" He pointed to the body that still lay on the floor. "There's no saving him, boy – he's dead! I might be the most powerful faerie in history, but even *I* can't bring back the dead!"

Yanni felt another stab of guilt. So that was it – there was no way he could ever save John.

Lorde Renwin wiped away a tear of laughter and leaned forward. "But otherwise, boy – a wager it is. Agreed?"

Yanni gazed at the faerie, holding out his hand once more. He looked at what was once his baby sister, sitting on Lorde Renwin's lap; at the raven that had once been Amy, perched on the back of the throne; at Larry, trapped in a golden cage. This was it – his one and only chance to save them. He gathered up the broken crown from the floor and put it into Amy's backpack. Then he stepped forward, took Lorde Renwin's hand, and shook it.

"Yes," he said firmly. "I accept."

He closed his eyes, waiting for the sudden shriek

of triumph, the revelation that once again he'd been tricked … but it didn't come. The room was silent. When he opened his eyes, Lorde Renwin was simply smiling at him.

"What are you waiting for, boy?" he said. "Off you go. You've got some names to find."

THE
LOWER
KINGDOMS.

ALONE

IT FELT LIKE AN ETERNITY BEFORE YANNI HAD MADE his way back down the staircase and over the new walkway. He took one final look at the tower behind him: it was vaster than ever before, dwarfing even the moon behind it. The sound of broken chimes was deafening now, tolling across the treetops and drowning out all other sounds. The crumbling stone archway was fixed, resplendent with fresh ivy.

Yanni rubbed the mark on his wrist, where the shackle had worn at the skin. He never thought he'd miss having it there, but its absence was an aching reminder of how alone he was now. How was he going to do this by himself, without Larry or Amy beside him?

He gritted his teeth. He wouldn't let Lorde Renwin win. He had to find the Lower Kingdoms. What would Amy do?

"Step one," he said out loud, "check your inventory."

He opened up the backpack and looked inside. There wasn't much: the Toadstone, his soaking wet socks, the broken crown … nothing that would help him now. He gazed at the forest around him – and saw something jutting from the undergrowth.

"Amy's book!"

There it was – the ORC'S QUEST manual, still lying where he had thrown it away. Surely there would be something in it about the Lower Kingdoms? He opened it up and searched through it, page after page … but there was nothing. No mention of the Lower Kingdoms anywhere. He ignored the piercing worry in his gut and placed it on the path. It was too heavy to carry around with him.

"I'll ask the signpost," he said to himself. "It must know where the Lower Kingdoms are!"

He marched to the crossroads, but was shocked by what he found when he got there. The signpost was bent double beside the road, trembling and moaning. It turned to Yanni in misery. "Oh, child … what have you done?"

Yanni was horrified. "Wh-what do you mean?"

The signpost raised an arm to the treetops, to where the sound of stricken chimes tolled over and over.

"You've given him more power than ever before!" the signpost cried. "Don't you understand what that means for us? For the Land of Fae?"

Yanni shook his head. "D-don't worry – I'm going to fix it! I've made another wager to win back the names! Once I have them, Lorde Renwin'll lose his new magic and—"

The signpost recoiled in shock. "*No!* No more wagers! Leave now, before you make it any worse!"

Yanni was dismayed. "But if you don't help me—"

The signpost didn't reply; it simply turned away and fell silent.

Yanni swallowed. He was going to have to find someone else to help him search for the Lower Kingdoms.

"The goblins!"

But when Yanni arrived at Goblin Mountain, everything had changed. The mountain was churning out smoke faster than ever, turning the sky black. The stone doors had been sealed shut; Yanni pounded his fists against them. After frantic scuffling from inside, a small hatch opened above him, and a set of piggy eyes leered out.

"Yes? What do you want?"

Yanni recognized the voice. "Gobbrox – I need your help! You have to help me find the Lower Kingdoms and—"

"Where's the one-pound coin?"

It took Yanni a moment to remember what the goblin was talking about. "I don't have it yet. This is more important! I need to find the Lower Kingdoms before—"

"Don't come back until you have it!" snapped Gobbrox. "Haven't you heard those chimes? The Pale Stranger's stronger than ever! The Goblin Queen has given me *strict instructions* to *stay out of the way* and make sure no one gets through these doors. She even let me have a weapon!"

Gobbrox waved a small cake fork out of the hatch. His hand was covered in plasters, presumably from where he'd accidentally stabbed himself with it.

"Now get lost," he ordered. "And don't come back until you've got the one-pound coin!"

The hatch slammed shut. Yanni stared at the doors in mounting horror. Lorde Renwin was right: he could ask for all the help he wanted now, but no one would heed him. After all, he had doomed Hallow Fall.

"It's fine – I don't need any help!" he cried out loud to no one. "I can find the Lower Kingdoms by myself!"

But wherever he went, all he found was emptiness and silence. Plants shrivelled up when he stepped near; birds flew and hid; the forest filled with the sound of scattering creatures. No one would speak to him; no one would help.

At long last, Yanni found himself back at the crossroads – and realized that there was only one path left for him to take. The one that led back to his house.

"There has to be a way to the Lower Kingdoms down here," said Yanni. "There has to be!"

But there was nothing. He searched every inch of the dead and silent path and found only shadows. Even the stone frog, it seemed, had fled. Finally he came to the bridge of twisting trees that stood before his house: the place where all this had begun, mere hours before. It felt like a lifetime ago.

Yanni was struck by a sudden thought. The fireplace was still inside; the gateway would still be open. If he wanted to, he could step back through and leave all this behind. He could see his mum and dad again.

Yanni's heart wrenched. Of course he couldn't. He could never go home again, not now. He had made a deal in blackthorn; he was bound by faerie magic. Even if by some miracle he *could* leave Hallow Fall, what good would it do him to go back without Ari? Without Amy?

He gazed into the gorge that the bridge crossed over. The darkness below was absolute, the depths unfathomable. It was the only place left in Hallow Fall he hadn't already been.

Yanni stopped. Was *that* the way to the Lower Kingdoms?

He stepped slowly towards the edge of the gorge, his heart pounding as he looked down into the depths. It was a sheer drop; there was no way of climbing down, no rope that would let him scale the sides. Perhaps the only way down was to jump?

Yanni closed his eyes. If it would save Ari, save Amy, save Larry, then so be it. He clenched his fists, summoned all his bravery, thought of Mum and Dad—

"Oi."

Yanni opened his eyes. He hadn't seen the figure sat in the shadows beside him, knocking away pebbles with its fishing rod.

"I wouldn't do that if I were you," said the stone frog glumly.

Yanni groaned. This was the last thing he needed now. The frog glared at him.

"That was rotten, what you said earlier," it muttered. "You didn't have to be so rude."

Yanni wanted to tell the frog that maybe it shouldn't have chased him and kicked him, but he couldn't be bothered with an argument now. He turned back to the gorge and tried to summon his courage again. If he could just convince his legs to move…

"There's nothing down there, you know," said the frog.

Yanni sighed. He was about to lose his temper and tell the frog to get lost … when he realized that it was the only thing in Hallow Fall not running away from him.

"Why aren't you hiding from Lorde Renwin?" asked Yanni.

The frog snorted. "That show-off? No point. He

never tells me where my eye is, either. You faeries are all the same."

Yanni blinked. "I'm not a faerie."

"Sure you're not, mate."

There was a long pause. The frog waddled over and sat grumpily beside him.

"Look – I just want my eye back. That's not much to ask, is it? *It's my eye.* You don't know what it's like, having something precious taken away from you."

Yanni's heart ached. "I do, actually."

There was another pause. An unseen wind blew deep inside the chasm. The frog waited for the right moment, scuffed its foot, and looked up at him hopefully.

"You … you don't know where my eye is, do you?"

The frog blinked miserably at him with its empty socket. Yanni couldn't help but feel sorry for it. It was so pathetic, so pitiful – so obsessed with getting something back that was clearly lost for ever. Yanni wondered if this was going to be his own fate – to spend eternity wandering Hallow Fall, begging for help, descending into madness as everything that saw him ran away…

Yanni stopped. He had just noticed the frog's remaining eye: a polished amber globe with a black centre. He suddenly realized why it looked so familiar.

"Hang on – is this it?"

He unzipped the backpack and pulled out the

Toadstone. The frog's face lit up like a sunbeam.

"My eye! I *knew* you had it!"

"It was with the goblins," said Yanni.

The frog didn't care – it grabbed the Toadstone greedily and stuffed it back into its empty socket, blinking experimentally. "*Oof!* That's better! I tell you what, I've missed that depth perception."

Yanni smiled sadly. The frog looked so happy. At least he'd finally managed to help someone, even if he had failed everyone else. The frog didn't seem very grateful, though – it gave Yanni another bitter glare.

"*Hmph.* Suppose you want a reward now, don't you?"

Yanni shook his head. "There's nothing you can give me." He gazed miserably down at the darkness. "Unless you know a way to the Lower Kingdoms."

The frog snorted. "The Lower Kingdoms? Sure I do."

Yanni swung round. It was like a bolt of lightning had passed through him. "You do?"

"Course!" The frog shuddered. "Everyone does. No idea why you'd want to go down *there*, though. It's horrible."

Yanni's heart was pounding. "Can – can you show me where it is?"

The frog sighed, then stood up and faced Yanni with its hands on its hips.

There was a long pause.

"Well? Are you going to get out of the way, or what?"

Yanni was confused but did as he was told. The frog gave a sorry shake of its head, reached down to the grass where Yanni had just been standing…

…and opened up the ground.

Yanni gasped. A door had been lifted in the spot where he'd been standing. Beyond it lay a stone spiral staircase, twisting down into the bowels of the earth, the walls lined with flaming torches. The frog jumped inside and started waddling down the stairs, its stone feet chinking on the steps. It stopped just before it turned a corner and glanced up at Yanni.

"Well?" it asked. "You coming, or what?"

THE RAFTSMAN

YANNI FOLLOWED THE SOUND OF THE FROG'S footsteps down the stairs. The air grew colder as they descended further and further into the Lower Kingdoms, the torches more spaced out, the darkness heavier. Just as Yanni felt that the staircase might never end, it did. The frog stood waiting for him at the bottom, tapping its foot impatiently.

"Well, here you are. The Lower Kingdoms."

Yanni gazed ahead in awe. Before him stood a vast, empty cavern. The floor was made of flat and featureless stone, stretching into resounding darkness. If there were walls here, they lay too far away to make out. The only things in sight were the rows of towering pillars, stretching up to a hidden ceiling high above them.

"I need to find Lorde Renwin's stronghold," said Yanni. "Where do I go?"

The frog shrugged. "Ask him."

It pointed into the distance – and Yanni saw that the cavern wasn't completely empty. There was a single figure, out there in the darkness. It was so far away that it was almost impossible to make it out.

"What … what is that?" Yanni asked nervously.

But the frog was already bounding up the stairs two at a time, sprinting back to Hallow Fall as fast as it could. Once again, Yanni was on his own. He gulped. He wanted more than anything to turn around and follow the frog back up the steps, to get away from this horrible dark place. But he couldn't flee now.

You have to do this. For Ari. For Amy. For Larry.

He walked across the cavern, his bare feet making no sound on the dusty stone. The figure grew closer and clearer in the darkness, until Yanni could see that it wore a long grey hooded robe that covered it from head to foot. The figure made no movements, just stood and waited in silence. When Yanni was within earshot, he called out.

"H-hello?"

Nothing. The figure didn't seem to hear him. Yanni carried on walking towards it, trying to calm the pounding in his ribcage. It was only as he drew closer that Yanni realized the figure was standing on a raft, which floated on a river carved deep into the stone floor. The river ran from one end of the cavern to the other; the water inside it was dark and rippling.

Yanni stood before the raftsman. The hooded figure did not turn to face him, nor did it greet him; he simply waited on the raft with his head lowered, a long pole gripped in his hands.

"I – I'm looking for Lorde Renwin's stronghold," said Yanni, his voice shaking.

Nothing. The man didn't even move. Yanni caught sight of his hands, and saw that the skin was as dry and worn as old paper left in the sun. He swallowed, and lifted the raftsman's hood. The face that lay beneath it was the same as his hands: dry eyelids sealed over dry sockets; lips shrivelled over teeth. He was dead – and had been dead for hundreds of years.

Yanni pushed down a feeling of sickness and tried to prise the pole out of the dead man's hands: nothing. The desiccated fingers clung on tight, and no amount of strength could pull the pole from their grip. Desperately Yanni searched his backpack, looking for something – *anything* – that could possibly help him. But it was hopeless: all he had left was a broken crown, and two old socks that were still damp with...

Yanni froze.

...the elixir of life.

Yanni touched the socks – and immediately felt a chill shoot through his fingertips, dulling his arm. There was still some elixir left in the fabric, maybe only a drop … but it might be all he needed. He carefully lifted the socks out of the backpack and held them against the raftsman's dry lips. Then, in one quick movement, he wrung them as tightly as he could.

A single drop ran out of the fabric, trickling between his knuckles and down his fingers. He cried out as the burning cold shot up his arm, but kept his grip steady: if he lost this drop, his one and only hope was gone. He watched as it hung from his trembling fingertip, hovered for a moment, then fell into the raftsman's mouth…

The dead man wrenched backwards, barking out a great plume of dust. Yanni fell back in fright. The raftsman's body was swelling and inflating before him; a pair of shining eyes emerged from the darkness of his sockets, and the skin of his face patched itself together right in front of Yanni's eyes, and the dry rasp seething from his throat became a human cry…

And then the raftsman was alive and awake, heaving for breath against his pole. Yanni felt a wave of grief. Could he have used the elixir to save John? But it was too late now.

"I need to find Lorde Renwin's stronghold," he said again.

The raftsman stepped to one side, and gestured to the raft.

"There is only one way," he said.

Yanni looked down at the raft: it was made of black-thorn logs. The very last thing he wanted to do was climb onto it and get any closer to the raftsman, but he had no choice. He summoned all his courage and stepped on with shaking legs. The logs dipped and swayed beneath him; a trickle of thick black water ran over his bare feet, strangely warm to the touch. He glanced down – and saw that the water wasn't black at all. It was a deep, rich red.

"Th-that's blood," murmured Yanni weakly.

The raftsman drove down his pole and pushed them along the river. "It is all the blood spilled in the world above. Everything finds its way down to the Lower Kingdoms. We must follow it to reach the stronghold."

The raft was moving faster and faster now. Within seconds they were flying at a frantic pace, the rows of pillars swinging past them in a grey blur. Yanni had to crouch down and grip the logs to stop himself falling overboard. The craft trembled and shook as the raftsman kept pushing them along, shooting through the endless darkness at an impossible speed…

But no – it wasn't endless darkness. Up ahead, a tunnel was emerging. Even from this far away, Yanni could feel the air roaring out towards him, hot as a furnace. The moment he felt its breath on his skin, a burst of sickening rage shot through him, twisting down to his core.

"Cover your ears," ordered the raftsman. "That is the wind of all the words spoken in anger in the world above. Everything finds its way down to the Lower Kingdoms. We must pass through it to reach the stronghold."

Yanni clamped his hands over his ears just as the raft shot inside the tunnel's mouth and total darkness snapped around them again like a set of jaws. It was like entering a lightning storm. Wind hit them from all sides at once, buffeting them in the pitch-blackness.

Yanni felt it at once: the ceaseless, hammering rage flooding his body, straining at his muscles and poisoning his blood. He gritted his teeth – he was angrier than he had ever been in his life, so mad it felt like a sickness. He wanted to rip apart the raft he sat on, shatter it to firewood, pull out his hair and scream until his lungs gave in. He wanted to tear Lorde Renwin limb from limb, stamp his tower to dust and leave all Hallow Fall in ashes… But he knew he had to withstand it. He kept his hands clamped over his ears, his teeth clenched shut and his whole body shaking with fury as the wind built to a relentless roar around him…

They shot out of the tunnel, and Yanni collapsed, gasping for breath. The sickness that had taken hold of him disappeared as fast as it had come. They were inside another vast cavern now, flying past yet more towering pillars; but this cavern was no longer silent. It was filled with noise, a roar that echoed back at itself over and over again. Yanni could feel something pounding through the wood of the raft beneath him. He looked up, and saw that the wall they were heading towards was moving. It was a waterfall, stretching from one end of the cavern to the other.

"Hold on," came the voice of the raftsman. "We are coming to a waterfall of all the tears shed in the world above. We must sail up it to reach Lorde Renwin's stronghold."

Yanni gasped – the waterfall stretched higher than his eyes could make out. How on earth were they supposed to sail *up* it? Surely that was impossible? But then he felt the white spray of its water as they drew closer – and it was like a knife of grief twisting inside him. All this fighting, all this effort, was worthless. He saw John's face as he lay back on the floor, John who he could have saved; and Larry in his cage; Amy's desperate eyes; Ari's cold, uncaring gaze. And then he saw his parents back home, weeping to have lost both their children, and he knew that he would never see them again. He had already lost; he had already failed them, all of them, and there was no way of ever getting them back...

The waterfall loomed closer and closer, the raft shuddering with the force of the falls until Yanni was certain they were going to capsize. He closed his eyes.

The despair pulsed up through him, wave after wave … and still it grew worse. Each bite of spray stung like a needle on his face, and he realized that the ceaseless roar he could hear was not the sound of water but the sound of a million cries of sorrow, growing louder and louder until the raft struck the waterfall and the weight of a thousand million tonnes of human tears hit him all at once…

And then there was nothing. Silence. Calm.

The raft was still.

Yanni opened his eyes, heaving for breath. The waterfall was gone; the river of blood was gone. The raft was floating inside a tiny stone cavern, little more than a pocket of air.

"We have arrived," announced the raftsman, his voice bouncing off the cavern walls. "Lorde Renwin's stronghold lies right ahead."

Yanni gazed in shock. Before him lay a shingle cove, the waves gently lapping against the stones. A door stood directly in the cavern wall. It looked like it didn't belong here at all; it looked as if it had been transplanted from another world.

And in a way, it had been.

Yanni recognized it at once. He would know that door anywhere: the blue paint, the gold numbers.

It was the door to his old house.

THE STRONGHOLD

YANNI GAZED AT THE STRONGHOLD DOOR, HIS heart pounding. He wasn't imagining things. There, in the cavern wall ahead, was the door to his old house, his *real* house. The home he'd left behind. What was it doing down here in this terrible place?

The raftsman landed the boat with a hiss on the shingle. Yanni stepped onto the shore with shaking legs, but the man did not follow.

"This is as far as I can take you," said the raftsman. "The elixir will soon wear out. I must return to where you found me."

Yanni took heart from that – he couldn't have saved John, not really, not for more than a few minutes.

"Do you know what you are seeking?" asked the raftsman.

Yanni nodded nervously. "Three names."

The raftsman gave him a look that made Yanni's insides quiver.

"Then, child," he said with pity, "I wish you the best of luck."

He pushed off from the shore. Yanni had no idea where the raftsman was going – there was no sign of the waterfall that had brought them here, nor an exit that led out of the cavern – but the moment that Yanni blinked, he was gone. He was alone again, in the very depths of the Lower Kingdoms.

He turned and faced the door, his breath echoing off the cavern walls. Every detail was exactly as he remembered it. The chipped paint around the lock where Dad kept accidentally scraping it with his key; the dent near the bottom where Mum had bashed a chair against it once at a street party; the scorch mark at the top where they burned a cross above the door with a candle every year at Greek Easter. It was as if it had been cut from the real world and brought down here. It made Yanni ache with the pain of remembering. He had spent so long wanting to find a way back home, and here it was, right in front of him.

And that was when the thought struck him: what if all of this – the changeling, Lorde Renwin, Hallow Fall – was just a nightmare? A bad dream that he could wake from, simply by walking through that door?

He reached out and tested the handle. It wasn't locked. The handle even *felt* the way it used to.

Don't, said the voice in his head. *It's not safe.*

But Yanni had to. There was no other way to complete the challenge. And yet even so, his heart was singing for joy as he turned the handle and stepped inside, back over the threshold and into his old home.

It was exactly as Yanni remembered it. The close and cosy rooms that Mum and Dad had said were too small for them; the family photos above the TV; the comfy sofa they'd left behind. He looked behind him – but the front door was closed. Yanni couldn't remember shutting it. There was no sign of the cold and dismal cavern through the windows, either: it was his old street on a sunny summer's day, the pavements humming with warmth. It was as if he'd gone back in time; as if the challenge had never happened.

Yanni frowned. There was something different about the house, though – something he couldn't put his finger on. What had changed?

"*There* he is!"

Yanni spun round. There, smiling in the kitchen doorway, was Dad.

"Where have you been, mate? We've been waiting for hours!"

"For what?" asked Yanni.

Mum strolled out of the kitchen behind him. "Film night, dunderhead. It was your idea!" She started grabbing cushions off the sofa and chucking them on the floor. "Come on! Oven pizzas in five minutes."

Yanni stared around in amazement. They were having a film night. He couldn't remember the last time they'd done that. Mum and Dad looked more awake and happier than they had in months. It was all how it used to be, before everything changed, before...

Before what?

Yanni frowned. He couldn't remember. He'd been doing something important a few moments ago, but whenever he tried to think what it was, his thoughts muddied and slid between his fingers. Still – it didn't matter, did it? He was home. He never had to leave ever again or worry about a single thing or—

No.

The voice snapped inside his head like a finger click. Yanni shook himself. This wasn't right. He *knew* this wasn't right. But why?

"What's wrong, mate?" asked Dad. "Come on! It's film night!"

"Sit down, darling!" urged Mum, patting the cushions beside her.

Yanni stared at the cushions ... and something rose up inside him. A thread of truth. The cushions ... the ones from the old sofa … the sofa they left behind … when they moved to Fallow Hall … when they moved because of…

"Where's Ari?"

He looked at the photos lining the wall. *That* was what was missing. They were all of him. There wasn't a single photo of his sister.

His parents stared at him blankly.

"Ari," he repeated. "The baby. Where is she?"

Mum gave him the sweetest, most innocent smile he had ever seen. "There *is* no baby, sweetheart. You're our one and only boy."

Yanni felt a wave of horror. That wasn't true. He *knew* it wasn't true … but something was still blocking his thoughts, shifting between his ears like oil. He stepped back, away from them.

"N-no," he stammered. "You're wrong. I – I have to go…"

Mum suddenly howled with laughter and slapped her leg. "Your *face*! Oh, that was too good! We really got you!"

"Of *course* there's a baby!" chuckled Dad. "It's right there, mate!"

Dad pointed. Sure enough, there was a cot in the corner of the room. Yanni had no idea how he hadn't noticed it before. It was the largest cot he had ever seen:

a swaddling throne of soft white lace. Something inside it was puffing and deflating, taking short sharp gasps of breath.

"Come on, boy!" ordered Mum. "Sit down!"

Yanni startled with a jolt – he looked straight at her. "What did you just call me?"

The silence was chill. Mum and Dad stayed staring at him, their smiles bolted in place.

"You called me *boy*," said Yanni. "You never call me that. Say my name."

No one spoke. His parents stared at him for a moment longer – and then their smiles fell.

"This is what you wanted, isn't it?" said Dad. "You wanted us all to yourself. And now you have. You don't have to worry about anything else ever again."

Yanni froze – he'd suddenly realized that there was a sound hidden beneath the room, one that had been there the whole time. It was broken chimes, a half-step out from one another. He looked up – and the room had changed.

He was still in his old house. Mum and Dad were still sat on the floor in front of him.

Only … all the windows and mirrors were cracked.

And suddenly Yanni realized that the voice at the back of his head had been screaming the entire time.

GET OUT GET OUT GET OUT GET OUT GET OUT!

It all came back in a rush: Lorde Renwin, the Lower Kingdoms, the challenge to save Ari and Amy and Larry. Yanni grabbed the *mati* around his neck and held it tight, clinging to what he knew was true, pushing the poisonous oil out of his head, every single last drop of it.

"You're not real. You're a trap. You're something that Lorde Renwin made to try to stop me. That's why you don't know my name."

His parents stood up. The air between them suddenly shifted, smeared with oil.

"You really are being a silly billy today," chided Mum. It wasn't her voice any more; it was Lorde Renwin's. "Maybe you should take off that necklace and sit down, right now."

"That's right," said Dad in Lorde Renwin's voice, stepping towards him. "Give her the necklace, boy."

Yanni bolted past him, racing to the cot and grabbing the baby from inside the blankets.

"No, don't touch it!" screamed Mum.

Yanni picked up the baby – and it fell apart in his hands. It was just a heap of rotten mouldy rags, thick with flies, bursting out of the cot in a black swarming explosion…

And then it was all gone. The flies, the screams, the chimes. The room was quiet again.

Yanni turned around, heart pounding. He saw the truth of the room for what it really was: a pit of dark soil, lined with broken mirrors. His "parents" – two stick figures made of blackthorn logs – were collapsed on the floor. The front door was wide open. Yanni saw it wasn't really blue with gold numbers: that had been a trick, too.

Hidden beside it was another door made of sleek black wood, gleaming on the wall like wet tar. A stag's skull had been carved into the surface. In the centre was a golden keyhole; a needle of wind blew from within.

Lorde Renwin's stronghold.

Yanni stepped towards the door and ran his hands across it. The wood was cold to the touch. He steadied his breathing and turned the handle. Nothing – the door was locked. The golden keyhole was surrounded by ornate carvings: to Yanni, they looked like a circle that never quite met at the ends. He gazed around, but there was no sign of any key. How was he supposed to get inside? He couldn't break the door down – he had nothing that would let him prise it open, either. He had nothing left with him except…

He opened the backpack. There, at the very bottom, was the third and final object: the broken crown. Yanni held it up. The ring had snapped, its twisted ends were a mass of molten threads. A circle that never quite met.

Yanni held the crown with both hands and, with all his strength, heaved the ring apart. It was exhausting – almost impossible – but gradually, bit by bit, he straightened the metal crown into a line. It almost looked like a key. Then he turned back to the door and, with an uncertain hand, inserted one end into the golden lock.

There was a sharp click as the teeth bit against the tumblers inside: the grinding of an ancient mechanism.

Yanni closed his eyes, took a deep breath, and opened the stronghold door.

THE RECKONING

He FELT THE DOOR OPEN; A FROZEN WIND MET HIM head-on. When Yanni opened his eyes, he was inside Lorde Renwin's stronghold.

It took him a while to understand what he was looking at. It was a long corridor, unfurling into the darkness like a low moan. The air was freezing cold, blowing from somewhere deep, deep, deep within; it even carried flecks of snow with it. The gloom was lit throughout by shimmering gas lamps hanging from the ceiling. The walls were lined with shelves that stretched far into the blackness on either side.

This was it: this was where Lorde Renwin kept all the names he stole. Somewhere in this corridor, he would find Amy's and Ari's and Larry's names.

He turned to the nearest shelf, letting his eyes adjust to the gloom. Each one held a single row of small white stones. There were thousands of them, twinkling fondly in the lamplight. They almost looked like pearls. Yanni picked one up and held it close, studying it from all angles. Was *this* a name? It didn't look anything like he expected. In fact, it looked like...

Yanni felt a shudder of revulsion. It was a tooth.

He glanced down the corridor. There were thousands of teeth, laid out in rows like museum exhibits. That was what Lorde Renwin kept in his stronghold – *teeth*. But *why*?

And then a memory flashed through his mind: the faerie passing his hand over Amy's mouth when he took her name. The shudder convulsing through her body as he wrenched something out. He'd done it to Ari, too. And suddenly Lorde Renwin's words from Ari's bedroom came back to him.

How about a tooth, then? A single tooth. No one would miss a single tooth!

That wasn't all. Yanni held up his hand, studying the marks where Larry had bitten him at the graveyard ... and sure enough, there it was. A gap in the neat row of punctures. John had been missing a tooth, too.

Yanni's heart began to pound. That was it: the teeth *were* the names. A single tooth, taken from every one of Lorde Renwin's prisoners and bound with the stolen magic of their name. All Yanni had to do was find the right ones.

But which were the right ones?

Yanni gazed down the length of the corridor, and his heart sank. The rows of teeth stretched on for ever – there had to be thousands upon thousands of them. How would he know which ones belonged to Ari … to Amy … to Larry? There were no labels, no sense of any order. He studied the tooth in his hand. It looked like … well, like a tooth. There was nothing unique about it – no details, no defining features. It could have belonged to any person in the world. He picked up the next tooth, and it looked exactly the same as the first one.

He felt a pucker of dread inside him. Who knew how long this corridor went on for? How many more of Lorde Kenwin's traps were hidden down here in the dark? He'd never manage it – it was impossible.

No.

There it was again – the voice at the back of his head. Yanni couldn't help but feel like he recognized it somehow.

If you give up now, said the voice, *then you've doomed them all.*

Yanni swallowed. The voice was right. He was more frightened than he had ever been in his life. But he wasn't doing this for himself any more.

"For Ari. For Amy. For Larry."

He began. He worked his way down the corridor,

tooth by tooth, holding each one up and studying it by the light of the gas lamps. He felt every curve and chip and groove; he held each one against the marks on his palm to see if it matched the spot where Larry had bitten him. But it was like trying to match a photograph of a shoe to a drawing of a footprint. How could you ever recognize a person by their *tooth*? It was hopeless – completely, utterly hopeless. But still he kept going, deeper into the darkness.

The further he went inside the stronghold, the stranger the teeth became. These were not just human teeth; there were teeth of different creatures: teeth with holes and teeth with stains, teeth with chipped edges, sharp teeth and blunt teeth, teeth that were six inches long and had clusters of smaller teeth growing inside them. He found a tooth with a single word carved across its surface, written in a language that he couldn't understand. Deeper and deeper he searched, hour after hour, gas lamp by gas lamp, tooth after tooth, scrutinizing every millimetre of every single one of their surfaces, looking for something – *anything* – that he might recognize…

And then finally – just when Yanni had begun to feel that the corridor had no end, that he would be searching down here until the edge of eternity – he looked up, and saw that there was a person standing before him in the darkness.

Yanni screamed and jumped back. The other person – Yanni's exact double – jumped back, too. It took a heart-stopping moment for Yanni to realize that he was simply looking at his own reflection. The corridor had ended: the final wall was covered by a giant mirror, lit by the shuddering flicker of a gas lamp. A single crack split it in two from top to bottom. Yanni stared at it in confusion.

"But … this can't be the end. I haven't found the names!"

He looked at the shelf beside him. Sure enough, there was only one tooth left in the entire stronghold. He picked it up … and sank with despair. It was exactly the same as all the others. He had no idea whether it belonged to his sister, or to his cousin, or to the changeling, or to any one of the thousands of other people that Lorde Renwin had imprisoned. His only hope was to go right back to the beginning, and start all over again…

And Yanni understood, right there and then, that he was doomed. He would never find their names. The wager was lost.

He fell to his knees. He had failed. He was stuck in Hallow Fall for ever. He would never see his parents again. But that wasn't the worst part: the worst part was that he had failed the others. John, Ari, Amy, Larry, his parents, Yiayia and Pappou. The guilt and shame and misery welled inside him, smothering everything in sight. He wanted the Lower Kingdoms to collapse on top of him. He wanted to be buried under miles of darkness so that no one would ever see him again. He wanted to be alone, for ever.

That's what you always wanted, wasn't it? said the voice at the back of his head. *To be alone.*

Yanni didn't argue with the voice any more. It was the only thing he had left. Besides, it had always been right. It had told him not to go near the dolmen, not to trust Lorde Renwin, and Yanni had ignored it.

You never did listen to me, did you? You never wanted to hear what I had to say.

The voice had always tried to tell him the truth, and Yanni had never listened, not once.

Are you finally ready to listen?

Yanni stared at his reflection, and saw a small, scared, sad boy staring back at him. He clutched the *mati* around his neck and nodded. He wouldn't run away any more.

"Yes," said Yanni. "I'm ready."

The voice took a deep breath and began.

You've been selfish and unkind and spoiled. You didn't want to share your parents' love, and so you took it out on everyone around you. You took it out on your parents. You took it out on Ari. You took it out on Amy. You could have been a good son, but you weren't. You could have been a good brother, but you weren't. You could have been a good friend, but you weren't.

Yanni nodded as his tears fell. It was all true, all of it.

You weren't even good to yourself. You lied to your own heart. You told yourself you were angry when you were sad. Why did you do it?

"I was frightened."

And why were you frightened?

"I don't like change," Yanni whispered.

And with that, it was like a spell had been broken. The stronghold was silent. The voice inside his head gave a long, low sigh of satisfaction.

Right! Well, glad we finally cleared that up. Now – what do you want?

Yanni blinked. "What do you mean?"

I'm better at making decisions than you are. I can help you find a way out of here.

Yanni was baffled. He was *certain* he recognized the voice somehow. "Sorry – who are you?"

I'm your instinct, said the voice. *I've always been here – you just never listen to me. Now, how are you going to get out of here?*

"I don't know."

Stop lying. Try harder.

Yanni wanted to argue – but he was done arguing with himself. "Er…"

Look ahead, said the voice. *What do you see?*

Yanni looked. "A mirror."

And?

"Nothing."

Don't be thick.

Yanni frowned. His instinct was turning out to be a pain in the neck. He bit back a sarcastic retort and looked at the mirror again. It was hard to see himself properly with that great crack in the middle.

"A broken mirror."

And what does that mean?

He rummaged through his thoughts. "They've been everywhere. That was the very first thing that changed, when Lorde Renwin took Ari. All the mirrors cracked. The windows, too. Amy's glasses."

Very good. And what else do you see?

Yanni frowned. "I see me."

And?

He looked down. "And my *mati*."

And?

"Nothing."

Look closer.

Yanni gritted his teeth. He leaned forward, right up to the crack that seemed to split his reflection in two…

And then he saw it. A change so small, you might not notice it at all – especially down here in the dark.

But the moment he allowed himself to notice it, it was as clear as day.

His eyes had changed colour. There, right at their very edges, was the thinnest, finest ring of black.

Yanni staggered back in shock. "But ... *how?*"

How do you think?

Yanni stared at his reflection, clutching the *mati* in his fist ... and all the pieces of the jigsaw fell into place at the same time.

The mirrors. The signpost's warning. Lorde Renwin knowing everything that they'd done on their quest. John's words as he lay on the floor, using his final breaths to tell Yanni that it was *the very, very, very last one.*

He gazed at the tooth that he had just picked up in sheer amazement. He understood everything at once, like a landscape glimpsed in a lightning flash.

See? said the voice smugly. *You should try listening to me more often.*

Yanni was amazed. "So ... what do I do?"

You know what to do.

Yanni gulped. The voice was right. He had no idea if it would work, no idea if he could pull it off ... but it was his one, his only, his last and final hope.

He turned again to the mirror, facing the crack that split his reflection perfectly in half. The other Yanni stared back at him – and he saw now that *that* had changed, too. It was still scared, still small, still alone – but now it knew the truth.

With a hand that was suddenly very steady, Yanni placed his fingers either side of the crack.

Then, as easily as if turning the page of a book, he opened it.

THE LAST HAND

Yanni stepped through the crack in the mirror, back into the ballroom of Lorde Renwin's tower.

He had stepped out of one of the mirrors on the walls. Everything was as he had left it. Larry was still locked and whining in his gilded cage; Amy was perched on top of the throne in raven form; Ari sat imperiously in Lorde Renwin's lap. Only Lorde Renwin had noticed he was there, gazing at him with mild surprise.

"I'm back," said Yanni.

The others spun round. Larry gave a cry of delight; Amy flapped her wings, her beak still clamped shut under Lorde Renwin's spell. Ari gazed at him with the coldness of a sculpture. Yanni took a stride towards them, and the crack in the mirror closed itself behind him with a sound like splitting ice.

"What was it you told me?" said Yanni. "*Whenever*

you see a crack, you can always bet there's a faerie watching!
It took me ages to work out what you meant – but I get
it now."

He nodded to the shattered frames that lined every
wall of the ballroom.

"You've been using the windows and mirrors. That's
how you've been watching me, this whole time. It's how
you keep an eye on everything that goes on in Hallow
Fall. You watch through the gaps."

Lorde Renwin gave him an indulgent smile. "Then
how could I have known what happened in the Goblin
Keep? Or on the ghost ship? There were no mirrors there."

"You didn't need them," said Yanni. "You had Amy's
glasses."

He pointed to the glasses that still lay by her scattered
clothes. The white line of a crack in the lens gleamed in
the firelight.

"You've used them to watch us the whole time,"
said Yanni. "So long as Amy was wearing them, you
could see what we were doing through the crack. That's
why it took you so long to work out what drew the
statues away – you couldn't hear the voice, only see
what we were doing. That was why John thought he
could save us."

Lorde Renwin nodded, impressed. "Very good!
Anything else you've worked out, boy?"

332

Yanni nodded. "Yes. I know why you can't read my mind, the way you could read Amy's."

He held up the *mati* at his chest, its glass eye shining.

"It's my necklace – the one that Yiayia gave me to protect me from the evil eye. It blocks your magic."

Lorde Renwin's eyes sparkled. "*Very* good! Not bad at all, for a human…"

"But I'm *not* human, am I?"

Yanni swallowed. The truth had to come out.

"I'm part faerie now. The signpost warned me it would happen. John tried to warn me, too, but I didn't understand." He held out his hands to the room. "It's your tower. The longer you stay inside it, the more faerie you become. That's why my eyes have started changing – why I could open the crack in the mirror. Why I had the power to free the ghosts and use their necklace. I can use faerie magic now."

Lorde Renwin howled with pleasure, clapping his thin white hands. "Right on all counts! I have to say, I *never* thought you'd work it out…"

"Well, I did," said Yanni. "And now I'm back. None of your traps could stop me – none of your tricks were good enough. Maybe you're not as powerful as you think."

They faced each other in silence; the flames in the fireplace sparked. Lorde Renwin raised an eyebrow, clearly amused.

"Are you threatening me, boy? You think all of a sudden — now that you have a *shred* of faerie magic in your bloodstream — that you can challenge *me*, the most powerful faerie in all existence?"

The room began to swell around him. Lorde Renwin loomed forward on his throne, waves of stolen magic radiating from his skin and crackling in the air between them like gunpowder. The sound of untuned bells clamoured like a thunderstorm.

Yanni stood his ground, and calmly shook his head. "No — I've seen how many names you've stolen. You've got the power of thousands of faeries in your blood. I know I can't defeat you."

Lorde Renwin beamed, and the room shrank back to normal. "Correct again! So why don't we stop wasting time, and get straight to the matter at hand?" His eyes flashed with excitement. "The challenge, boy. Did you finish it, or not?"

Yanni held himself steady. He looked at Amy and Larry, staring back at him desperately. He looked at Ari, gazing at him with cold hate. They were all counting on him. From now on, he had to keep every single facet of his mind closed off from Lorde Renwin. He couldn't allow the faerie to see even a glimpse of the truth, not even for a moment.

"You said that I could bring back three names from

the stronghold," said Yanni. "Whichever ones I came back with, I could keep. Agreed?"

Lorde Renwin nodded impatiently. "Yes, yes! So tell me – which three did you bring back?"

Yanni took a deep breath. He had to be more careful than ever before. He had to get this right.

"I – I couldn't save all three," he said. "I only brought back two names."

Lorde Renwin's eyes widened with delight. "You mean ... you've already doomed one of them? Wonderful news!" He drummed his feet eagerly on the floor. "Tell me – which names did you bring back?"

Yanni looked at Ari, at Amy, at Larry. All their eyes were fixed on him. He swallowed.

"The first name I brought back," he said, "is my own."

There was a moment of pressed silence. Yanni glared at Lorde Renwin with hatred.

"That was another one of your tricks, wasn't it? You said I could keep any three names that I brought back – but that included mine. There was no way I could ever save all three of them and myself. You were always going to make me leave one behind. I could never win."

Lorde Renwin stared at him in amazement – and then clapped his hands once again.

"My word – you *have* learned a lot! You are part faerie, after all!" He sighed fondly. "I'm quite annoyed that you worked it out, to be honest. I was looking forward to that bit."

The faerie leaned closer with an evil grin.

"So, you have decided to save *yourself* first – which means that you have only one name remaining. One person to save. Oh, this is even better than I'd hoped! You've doomed *two* of them for all eternity!" He was bouncing on the throne with excitement. "Which one did you choose to save – your sister? The girl? The changeling? Tell me, tell me!"

Yanni stood very still, trying to stay calm. He couldn't reveal how frightened he was – how much rested on the next few moments going exactly as planned. A single bead of sweat ran down his forehead.

"Swear it again," he ordered. "Bind it with your word. Whoever it is whose name I brought back with me, I can keep them. No tricks. They belong to me and you can't take them back, not ever!"

Lorde Renwin stamped his feet in frustration. "For the last time, *yes*! Why must you keep stalling like this? You know how much I despise waiting! The name is yours – now which one is it?"

Yanni swallowed. It took every ounce of his strength to hide how much he was shaking. "Swear it on blackthorn."

Lorde Renwin roared with anger and leaped from his throne, holding his hands above his head. The air between his palms thickened and churned into the shape of a black log and instantly burst into green flames.

"*There!* Satisfied? Bound by eldritch magic, the most unbreakable of faerie laws! Now stop wasting my time, boy – it's over! Which name did you save?"

Yanni held out his closed fist. "What was it you said to me? It's not over until the last hand has been played…"

The faerie screamed with fury, and suddenly he was the size of the room itself, his whole body rippling with anger. He bore down over Yanni, the burning log still held high above him, his eyes roaring in the green flame.

"I WON'T STAND FOR IT, BOY! Don't you understand who you're dealing with? I am the most powerful, brilliant, beautiful faerie in all existence! You're lucky I'm not tearing you into pieces right now!" He seethed with hatred. "Mark my words – whoever you leave behind will be made to suffer for your impertinence, a thousand times over! Trapping them in that piano will be too good for them. I'll bind them in iron and fill their bones with oil! I'll hang them from the highest gibbet of the tower for the crows to feast on! I'll send them howling to the Lower Kingdoms and leave them there until the world is ash and the universe has rotted at its edges!"

He stamped his feet so hard the floorboards cracked beneath him.

"For the last time – *SHOW ME THE NAME*!"

Yanni took a deep breath, closed his eyes … and opened his hand. There, lying in the centre of his palm, was a single tooth.

"It's yours," said Yanni.

The entire room held still for a moment, like it had been captured inside a snow globe. Lorde Renwin stared at the tooth.

"It's your name," Yanni repeated. "The one you hid in the deepest part of your stronghold, so no one would ever find it. The one you hid so no one could ever take your powers from you."

Yanni gazed up at him.

"And you just gave it to me."

Lorde Renwin's face was a frozen mask of disbelief. The ballroom was silent. Nothing moved.

Then, very slowly, Yanni allowed the corners of his mouth to lift into a smile.

"I tricked you," he said.

The Eyes
Behind the Eyes

Lorde Renwin didn't move a millimetre as he gazed down at the tooth in Yanni's hand, still holding the blackthorn log high above his head.

Whoomph.

The log burst in his hands, and a fine cloud of ash settled over his shoulders. The faerie still didn't move – he stayed exactly where he was, holding empty air.

"You're bluffing," he said.

Yanni shook his head.

"No, I'm not. John told me all about it. He even told me where I'd find it in your stronghold: *the very, very, very last one.* It's why you're missing a tooth, too."

Lorde Renwin quickly closed his mouth. When he next spoke, his voice was soft and dangerous.

"Boy – you don't understand what you're doing. Give me back the tooth, and I will forget all about it."

But Yanni shook his head again. He stepped closer, the tooth held out in front of him.

"No. We just made a deal in blackthorn. You've given me your name. And you know what that means, don't you? It means I have total control over you now. It means all of the powers that you've stolen are mine."

Lorde Renwin sneered. "Ha! And what use is faerie magic in the hands of a human?"

"But I'm not human, am I?" said Yanni. "I'm part faerie now – thanks to you."

What little colour was left in Lorde Renwin's face drained away. He licked his lips; his eyelids flickered. Once more, a bright friendly smile appeared on his face.

"Well! There is no reason for us to be unpleasant to each other, is there?" He held out his hands. "You and I are both civilized beings! Let us make another deal – a fair one this time! I am *very* happy to give you back all three names that you asked for and let you go home, in exchange for—"

"No."

Yanni stepped further forward, the tooth still clutched in his hand. "No more deals. No more trickery. There is nothing you can offer me that will persuade me to give you back your powers."

Lorde Renwin nodded quickly, his eyes panicked.

"Nothing? Really? How about gold? Or eternal life? I can do that, you know!"

Yanni said nothing – he just kept moving towards him, brandishing the tooth. The faerie stumbled backwards and fell to the floor.

"You – you might have my magic, boy, but there is nothing you can do with it!" he cried. "You cannot possibly understand how to wield it!"

But that wasn't true. Yanni could feel the powers building inside him, the way you can feel a storm approaching. The floorboards were warping and creaking beneath his feet. The walls were bowing with every swell of his breath. Electricity was raking across the skin of his arms and legs, bristling and sparking off his hair. He knew, without needing to see them, that his eyes shone like torches. Words were appearing in his mouth automatically, thoughtlessly, straight from his gut.

"I know exactly what I'm doing with your magic," said Yanni. "I'm giving it back. Lorde Renwin – I return every ounce of the magic you stole from Hallow Fall. Release your prisoners and return their names."

Lorde Renwin gasped, and scrambled to the black piano that still stood in the corner of the room. "No! No, they're mine…"

"It was not a request," said Yanni. "Give them back."

The black piano exploded, scattering keys and

wires across the room. The air was instantly filled with groaning voices, spinning out of the ruins of the piano and circling into the air like a tornado. They were faeries – thousands of trapped faeries, released from centuries of torture and imprisonment. Lorde Renwin screamed and tried to hide from them, but they bore down on him from all sides, shrieking in revenge and pulling his hair and rending his clothes. Yanni kept a tight grip on the tooth as its magic pulsed through his bones.

"All your spells and enchantments are broken!" Yanni cried. "Release the changeling and return his name!"

"No!" Lorde Renwin shrieked.

The bars of the gilded cage burst apart, and Larry was flung squealing for joy across the ballroom. Right in front of his eyes, Yanni watched as the missing tooth grew back inside his mouth – and suddenly he'd transformed into a golden hawk, swooping up to the ceiling and joining the faeries and crying with a new freedom. Yanni kept going, the tooth now smoking and sizzling in his palm.

"Amy is no longer your servant! Remove the spell that binds her and return her name."

"Noooo!" wailed Lorde Renwin.

But it was no use. Amy was wrenched from the throne as if by a set of invisible hands. Her black feathers spread and transmogrified to fingers; her body twisted in the air like moulded dough. Her clothes and glasses twisted and danced around her in a double helix, until what landed on the floor was not a raven, but Amy – wonderful Amy, his cousin, his friend – her face alight with amazement.

"Yanni!" she screamed, her voice finally restored. *"You're flying!"*

It was true – Yanni was floating an inch off the floor, his whole body humming like a spun wheel as every drop of Lorde Renwin's stolen magic flowed through him and back to the creatures of Hallow Fall. The ballroom rang with the sound of fixed magic, *true* magic, the clamour of a thousand church bells chiming over and over. Yanni felt like a river had burst its banks and was surging through his veins, like he'd plugged himself into the mains. When he spoke, he spoke with a thousand voices at once.

"It is time – we are done. Your wager is finished. Return what you first stole from me."

Lorde Renwin grabbed Ari from the throne, clutching her tight. *"No! She's mine!"*

"She is not yours," said Yanni. "She was *never* yours."

He held up the *mati* with his free hand. It suddenly blazed with a beam so bright that the faerie shrieked and fell back, covering his eyes in agony.

"I know why this necklace blocks your power," said

Yanni. "It's because Yiayia gave it to me with love. And *you* – who know only falsehoods, who have bound yourself with lie upon lie – are powerless against that. No matter how much you tried to change Ari, no matter how much you took from her, her love for me is still inside her. No magic can ever destroy it."

He towered over Lorde Renwin like a thundercloud and, for the first time, the faerie looked terrified.

"I'll – I'll do anything! I'll turn back time. I'll make you king of the world! I'll bring back Gustiver."

"His name is John," said Yanni. "And this is for him."

He held out the tooth, the final shreds of Lorde Renwin's stolen magic trembling in his clenched fist.

"Now, for the last time – *give me back my sister*!"

Ari was torn from the faerie's hands and sent pinwheeling through the air towards him. She was changing back to her true form right in front of him – the smell of her, the feel of her, the weight of her body as she landed in Yanni's waiting arms. He watched in wonder as her one and only tooth grew back, and the brown returned to her eyes like oil drops in water, and her love for him exploded out in wave after wave after wave. She squealed with happiness and pulled his face to hers and bit him so savagely on the nose that it brought water streaming to his eyes, but it was the single best feeling Yanni had ever felt in his life.

And with that, the last of Lorde Renwin's stolen powers were returned. The last of the broken chimes rang out; Lorde Renwin's tooth stopped smouldering in his palm. Yanni felt its magic slip from his body like a sun passing below the horizon, and his toes gently touched the floor.

Lorde Renwin was slumped beside him, trembling. He pushed himself up with shaking hands ... and when he did, Yanni could see that all of his beauty was gone. His body was warping into monstrousness. He grabbed and clawed at his own face as it sagged and twisted, but there was nothing he could do to stop it. The last of his veils were falling away.

"Noooooo!" Lorde Renwin shrieked. *"No, no, no, no, no, no!"*

The room lurched beneath them, and Yanni gasped. The faerie wasn't the only thing that was falling apart. Right in front of their eyes, the walls were beginning to crumble. The tower was shaking, the floorboards bending and splitting. The mirrors were dropping to the floor and shattering, one by one.

"Y-Yanni! Look!" cried Amy, pointing out of the window in terror.

Yanni spun round. The purple sky was racing away from them, the treetops tumbling past the window. The stolen magic that had built the tower was draining out of it; now it was falling down, with them inside it. Yanni grabbed Amy's hand and clutched Ari tight to his chest.

"We have to get out of here! Now!"

They hurtled down the staircase as the steps cracked and split beneath them. It was like running down a gushing plughole: the tower was shrinking towards them as they tore down it, the banister twisting up to meet them as fast as they could sprint. Yanni reached the bottom and his foot sank into cold, wet soil. The once-beautiful hallway was the worst it had ever been. It was now just a swarming pit, a crater, a grave. The doorway at the end of the hall was little more than a dirt hole, a crawl space of light that was winking shut as the tower collapsed...

"Quick!" Yanni cried. "We have to—"

It was too late. There was a hammering above them – *bang, bang, BANG* – as something great and terrible stamped through every floor of the tower. The ceiling collapsed, and Lorde Renwin burst down into the hallway before them, blocking their escape. He roared with fury, with his *real* voice, the one that lurked beneath the layers...

"NO! You'll never leave! I'll never let you get home!"

The faerie was in his final form. His skin had fallen away like dry plaster, and what lay beneath it was vile beyond reckoning. His face was matted with filth and cobwebs: it was the face of a pike, a hagfish, a goblin shark, a creature living only in darkness with a slit mouth that reached his ears. And there they were: his eyes, his real eyes, glaring at Yanni with hate.

"You can try to run, but I will hunt you down! For as long as you live, for as long as your children's children's children shall live, I will never let you get away! I'll hide in the cracks and watch and wait until the day you finally rest and believe that all is well, and that is when I will come for you..."

Yanni stepped back, terrified. He had no more stolen powers – nothing left to fight against this monster...

And then he felt a hand take his. It was Amy, standing beside him – and when he looked down, Ari was clutching him, too, their love filling every part of him and making him stronger. And there in his head was a message planted deep inside him in a dream, burrowing up to the surface.

You kill a monster by saying its name.

He bound his arm with Amy's and held Ari tight, and the three of them stood against the creature, a gang of three.

"No," he said. "I know who you really are. I have your true name. And with its power, I banish you from Hallow Fall. I banish you from the Land of Fae. I banish you from the land of the living. Lorde Renwin, Pale Stranger, Riddle King, Prince of Two Faces, Sperrit Grey, Man Upstairs, Old Tom Tuttle, King of the Cats, Feond,

Oathbreaker, Night Marcher, Grand Prince Blackthorn, Tsar of Ravens, Stag Dancer, Chime Master, King of Thistles, Viscount of Lies, Lord of Misrule – I'm taking all your disguises. I'm sending you down to the Lower Kingdoms, where you belong."

"*NO!*" screamed the creature.

"Your real name is Hatred," said Yanni. "Get out and never come back."

The walls wrenched and shuddered; the floor behind the creature split like a crack in a mirror, widening into a yawning darkness. Yanni could finally see where the tops of the pillars in the Lower Kingdoms ended, and he watched as the floor of the hallway sank like sand through an hourglass.

"*NO!*"

The creature flung itself towards Yanni, its mouth wide open and its eyes wild and raging, and Yanni realized with horror that it was going to drag them all down to the Lower Kingdoms with it…

And then something flew over Yanni's shoulder with a great cry: a golden hawk, its wings outstretched, its talons clawing at the creature's eyes with all its strength. It took Yanni a moment to realize that it was Larry. He was saving him, fighting the creature with everything he had, driving it slowly backwards. The creature shrieked with agony as Larry clawed and slashed at its face, its cloven feet slipping and scrambling at the edges of the abyss…

"NOOOO!"

As the creature fell into the Lower Kingdoms, it seized Larry by the talons – and then they both were gone, plummeting into the blackness beneath the world. Yanni screamed.

"Larry, no!"

The roof above the staircase collapsed behind them; it was impossible to see anything in the clouds of dust that now filled the hallway. The tower was falling down around them. The doorway leading outside was shrinking and shrinking, barely a fading dart of light…

"Yanni, quick!" Amy screamed.

She grabbed his hand and scrambled along the wall as the pit in the floor widened still further, dragging him through the shrinking exit just as the last of the hallway sank into the depths…

And then they were outside, collapsing to the ground as the tower gave a final great groan and fell into the crater beside them. A mountain of dust filled the air, a great black cloud billowing from the earth and obscuring the moon. Yanni threw himself across Amy and Ari, shielding them with his own body, as the final pieces of the world fell apart around them and all of Hallow Fall was smothered in darkness.

LARRY

YANNI LAY STILL FOR AS LONG AS POSSIBLE. WHEN the sounds of the collapsing tower had finally faded away and the world was silent, he opened his eyes.

The three of them were lying on the rocky outcrop where the tower had stood. It was gone, for ever, collapsed into the fathomless gorge beside them. Amy looked up, blinking in disbelief behind the cracked lens of her glasses.

"Do – do you hear that?" she whispered.

The air rang with the sound of tiny bells – but now they were all in tune with one another, a perfect harmony. It was a beautiful sound. Lorde Renwin was gone; the magic had returned to Hallow Fall. The world was in kilter once more. They were safe, and alive, all of them...

Then it hit Yanni like a wall – the memory of Larry as a hawk, being dragged down into the Lower Kingdoms. He scrambled to his feet.

"Larry? *Larry?*"

But the changeling was nowhere to be seen. Yanni's eyes filled with tears. He knew where Larry was: he'd been sealed up inside the Lower Kingdoms with Lorde Renwin. The faerie child had saved Yanni's life twice … and now he was doomed for ever. It was the worst, most awful punishment imaginable.

"No … no, no, no, not Larry…"

"Child."

Yanni spun round. The voice had come from the place where the black tower once stood – now there was just a pile of rubble, stacked in a crumbling heap. There was no one there.

But the cracks between the bricks were glowing.

There were creatures crawling out from inside them: faeries, thousands of them. They had hidden inside the gaps of the collapsing tower for safety, and now they were slipping out one by one. They looked nothing like Lorde Renwin – and they looked nothing like the drawings in Amy's manual, either. They glowed like stars. Yanni had no idea which were men and which were women, which were young and which were old…

The tallest faerie at the front stepped forward, their face deathly serious, their raven-black eyes fixed on Yanni. Yanni gasped, clutching Amy and Ari close to him. "Get away! Get back!"

But the tall faerie kept walking forward, reaching out. Yanni suddenly understood what they wanted – he opened his palm, and sure enough there was Lorde Renwin's tooth. He flung it at the tall faerie.

"Here – take it!" he cried. "Its powers are gone. I used them to send Lorde Renwin to the Lower Kingdoms." His voice trembled. "Along with … along with…"

He could no longer hold the tears back. They poured out of him. The memory came again and again, never once changing, never once becoming less awful. Larry being dragged into the abyss. Yanni couldn't bear it; he had come so close to saving him, and now he was gone for ever…

The tall faerie stepped past the tooth, shaking their head. "No, child – we do not want *anything* from you."

The faerie crouched in front of him and held his face so, so gently.

"You have given us more than we can ever repay you. You have saved Hallow Fall. You've freed us from an eternity of torture." Their voice shook with emotion. "But more than that … you have brought my child back to me."

Yanni looked down … and cried out for joy. A child was strapped to the faerie's chest, wrapped in a binding of leaves. It was Larry – back in his faerie form, safe and well, clutching his parent so tightly he looked like he might explode.

"He's *alive*!" cried Yanni.

The tall faerie nodded. "All thanks to you. You fought for him – you fought for all of us. And for that, we can never thank you enough."

They held out their arms to the faeries that stood behind them: and as one, they bowed down. Yanni gazed at them in amazement.

"Name your price, and it is yours," said the tall faerie. "Anything you want, we can give to you."

Yanni glanced at Amy. He thought about all the things that he had ever wanted – all the things he'd ever dreamed about. But he only had to take one look at Amy's eyes to know that they were both thinking the same thing.

"We don't want anything," he said. "Just make sure that Lorde Renwin never comes back. Make sure he never steals another child from Fallow Hall, like he stole John. Take out all the poison that he put into Hallow Fall and make it beautiful again."

"And make peace with the goblins, too, while you're at it," Amy added. "They're all right, really."

The tall faerie looked at Yanni with surprise. "You don't want to go back to your old home, where you were happy?"

Yanni shook his head and held Ari tight. "No. I don't want you to change anything. I want things to be exactly how they were. Even the bad things. I want to change them myself."

The tall faerie smiled. "As you wish. But there is one thing we cannot do."

Yanni frowned. "What?"

The tall faerie held out their hands to the world around them. "We cannot make you remember any of this. When midnight comes, and All Hallows' Day arrives, you will forget everything about tonight." They gestured to Amy and Ari. "Your companions will forget faster than you will – after all, there is still some faerie magic in your blood. But sooner or later, you will forget, too."

Yanni's heart stung; he looked at Larry, at the face he had grown to know so well. Tiny, sad black eyes looked back at him. "But ... but if I forget everything, then that means I'll forget how to get back here."

The tall faerie nodded. "That is correct."

Yanni almost couldn't bring himself to say it. "But ... I'll forget *Larry*..."

The tall faerie laid a hand on his. "No. You learned to love him, and nothing loved is unlearned. He will never forget you – and you will never truly forget him. Your heart will remember him, long after your mind forgets."

Larry suddenly reached out and slowly – tightly – wrapped his fingers around Yanni's wrist. The changeling was making a shackle with his hand. Yanni understood at once. The golden chain that had once bound them together was gone – but there was another chain between them now, one that was made of an even stronger magic. A chain that they had forged themselves.

"And now you must go," said the tall faerie. "The wager you made with Lorde Renwin is complete. Time has returned to normal: All Hallows' Eve is nearly over."

Yanni gasped – the faerie was right. The moon was suddenly swooping down to the horizon; the sky was fading fast from purple to blue at its edges. The crack in the lens of Amy's glasses was slowly fixing itself.

"Yanni – the gateway!" Amy cried. "It's going to close!"

She grabbed his hand and tried to pull him towards the footbridge – but Yanni stayed where he was. He gazed at Larry, his eyes still full of tears. For the very first time in his life, he knew exactly how he felt. But he didn't have words to describe the feelings: the sadness and happiness all rolled into one, the weight of the love that held him down and lifted him up at the same time.

"Wait," he said. "There's something I need to know before I go."

The tall faerie's eyes flashed with urgency. "Child, you're running out of—"

"What's his name?"

He wiped his eyes, but it was no use. He felt like they would never be dry again. He pointed to the changeling.

"I – I'd like to know his real name, please, before I go," he whispered.

The tall faerie smiled at him. "You already know, child. It's Lari."

Yanni looked at the changeling – and laughed through his tears. He hadn't pulled the name from nothing – he had always known, deep down, what Lari's true name was. His bones had known the truth before he did.

Yanni wiped his eyes – it was time to go. He clutched Ari to his chest and squeezed Amy's hand.

"Goodbye – all of you!"

They raced over the footbridge together, back towards the path – and just as they reached the end, Yanni looked back one final time. There, across the vast divide, was Lari – the changeling he had learned to love – waving sadly over his parent's shoulder. Yanni stored the image in his heart, and turned away for the final time as they headed home.

They tore back towards the crossroads, where the signpost was waving its hat for joy.

"Well done, children! I knew you could do it!"

"Thank you for everything!" Amy cried as they skidded past.

They couldn't stop now – time was running out, second by second. They flew down the final path, back through the forest that had once seemed so frightening, back over the bridge just as the stone frog leaped into position on its toadstool...

"You'll never make it!" it grumbled. "That fireplace'll close any second..."

Yanni gasped, and he and Amy and Ari sprinted into the house, flying towards the fireplace as the final sound of bells began to chime...

Don't shut don't shut don't shut!

...and the three of them sailed through the wall and tumbled back into the world of Fallow Hall, back into his living room, as the faerie gateway sealed itself behind them with a *snap*.

Yanni and Amy lay gasping on the floor. They had made it – right before their very eyes, the last of the faerie's magic was draining from the room around them. The cracked family portraits were fixing themselves on the walls, one by one; the windows and mirrors were sealing along their fault lines, filling the room with the crack of glass unbreaking. The split in Amy's glasses fixed itself with a satisfying *click*.

"*Finally!*" she said. "That's been driving me nuts all night..."

Yanni gazed down at the baby in his arms. There

she was: Ari, his sister, finally here, finally back home, perfect and precious and fast asleep.

"She's sleeping!" Yanni laughed. "How could *anyone* sleep after…"

He trailed off – Amy's eyes were drifting shut. She slumped to one side, and was sound asleep on the floor in seconds, snoring loudly.

Yanni gawped. "Amy? What's happening? Are you…?"

Yanni's words drifted to silence in his mouth. Somewhere in the house, a clock was striking midnight – the chimes rang through the house, one after the other, swimming between his ears. He had a final moment to reflect on the fact that they didn't *own* a clock, before he found himself sinking to the floor beside his cousin, as if the carpet was the most comfortable bed in the world…

"Oh *no*."

Mum and Dad pulled into the driveway. Up ahead, the windows of the house gleamed with electric light.

"Why are they still up?" said Dad. "It's gone midnight!"

"They must have been worried sick," Mum groaned. "Oh, we should have been home *hours* ago…"

Dad shook his head. "It was no one's fault. We didn't know the car was going to break down in the middle of nowhere, with no reception…"

Mum unbuckled her seat belt. "I just hope nothing happened while we were out."

She ran inside the house.

"Yanni? Amy?"

Dad rushed in after her. "Is everything…"

Mum was standing in the living room, smiling. There, tucked up on the floor and fast asleep, were Yanni and Amy and Ari. Ari lay in Yanni's arms; Yanni and Amy were curled up together. A little gang of three.

"Look at that," marvelled Mum. "Look at how he's holding his sister. That's new, isn't it?"

"He's growing up," said Dad. "Almost makes you want another one, doesn't it?"

"Absolutely not," said Mum.

She leaned down to kiss her children. "My Ioannis. And my little Ariadne. You two are going to be best friends one day, aren't you?"

"That's right. They'll look after each other now. And we had a nice time tonight, didn't we?"

Mum smiled, her eyes shining. "We did."

They kissed, and there was a single spark of magic between them, a magic that they had made themselves and no one else knew but them.

"Right," Mum sighed, walking into the hallway. "They can't sleep down here; I'd better sort out a bed for Amy before…"

She trailed off. She was staring up at the ceiling, her brow furrowed.

"What's the matter?"

Mum looked at the ceiling for a moment longer … and then shook her head and turned away.

"I must be drunk," she muttered. "For a moment, I thought I saw footprints on the ceiling."

ALL HALLOWS' DAY

THE SKY HAD NEVER BEEN MORE BLUE.

Yanni opened his eyes and sat up. It was morning. He was back in his own bedroom, but he had no memory of being put there. Every part of him was aching.

The night came back to him in a sudden flash – Lorde Renwin, Hallow Fall, the challenges... The fear hit him cold and hard. Where was Ari – and Amy? Had they both been taken from him?

Then a sound drifted up from the kitchen: a baby laughing.

He threw himself out of bed and raced down the stairs. Mum and Dad were both there, dancing in the kitchen as they made breakfast. They looked different – younger, happier, full of life again. They were taking it in turns to hold Ari as she threw food around the room.

"*There* he is!" exclaimed Mum when she saw him. "We were wondering when you were finally going to—"

Yanni charged straight into her and hugged her tight, then did the same to Dad. He gently took his sister and bounced her up and down.

"There she is! There's Ari!" he cooed.

Mum and Dad stared at him in amazement. Ari was gnawing ferociously at his hand and dribbling all over him, but Yanni didn't mind.

"How was last night?" Yanni asked. "Did you have a nice time?"

"It was great!" said Mum. "Did you have fun with Amy?"

"You two must have had a great time!" said Dad. "She was still out cold when I dropped her back home this morning! Could barely talk straight…"

"She forgot her backpack," Mum sighed. "Yanni, would you mind…?"

"I'll drop it round later!" he promised. "I've got a few other things I want to do in the village first – after I've played with Ari for a bit."

He gave her another bounce. She gurgled, leaning back to study his face with her deep brown eyes.

"Ah-ih," she said.

Dad beamed. "Did you hear that? That was a word!"

Mum rolled her eyes. "It was a *sound*…"

"No child of mine makes *sounds*," said Dad. "She's a genius, that's what she is."

Sure enough, she did it again. "Ahhhhhhhhhhhh-ih."

Yanni smiled. "It's *Ari*! She's saying her name!"

Mum gave him a bear hug from behind, kissing his head. "You know, I don't think she is. I think she's saying *Yanni*."

Yanni gazed at his sister. He had no idea if Ari remembered anything that had happened the previous night – the tall faerie had said that she would forget everything. But he knew, deep down, that it didn't matter. Something had changed between them now: he could feel it. Ari had always loved him. But now, Yanni had learned to love her back.

"Ah-ih," she said. "Ah-ih, Ah-ih, Ah-ih."

Yanni strapped on Amy's backpack and walked out of the house. It was a glorious morning – there was a feeling in the air that hadn't been there the day before, as if everywhere was in colour for the very first time. The sky looked like a set of open hands, cupping the whole wide world. The cracks in the dirt lane had gone; the village sign almost sparkled in the sunlight. He glanced at the frog statue as he went past – and sure enough, its missing eye had been replaced. It even looked like it was smiling at him.

He strolled down the lane towards the village. He wasn't imagining it – Fallow Hall *felt* different. The grass in the fields seemed brighter; a gentle wind sang through the electricity pylons in the distance, sounding like tuned bells. Yanni knew why, of course. It was the faeries: they were returning Hallow Fall to the way it was before Lorde Renwin appeared. The way it should always have been.

He came to the crossroads. Sure enough, the signpost had changed as well. The old woman from the church stood on a ladder beside it in a pair of dungarees, holding a bucket of paint.

"Morning!" she sang, giving Yanni a wave. "Lovely day, isn't it? Who would have thought it – flowers in November!"

She swept her arm to the fields around them. Yanni gazed – and saw that they were filled with white petals, thousands of them, covering the grass on every side.

"I thought it was high time to give this old thing a lick of paint, too!" she said, patting the signpost. "Doesn't it look handsome?"

Yanni smiled. The signpost *did* look handsome – it was now painted a rich and vibrant green, its letters standing out in gold. Yanni could even have sworn it was preening.

"It needs a hat," he said.

"Pardon?" said the woman.

But Yanni was already strolling away, making a

mental note to bring a fresh hat down the next time he walked past.

He came to the village shop … and saw that it had changed, too. The bars had gone from the windows; the glass had been cleaned, and the old burglar alarms removed from around the door. The door was wide open, letting in fresh air for the first time in years. The shopkeeper sat behind the counter in a slightly cleaner vest, sunning himself in the heat through the windows. He saw Yanni and his face fell.

"*Hmph*. It's you," he said gruffly.

Yanni smiled. "Good morning. I was just wondering if…"

Before he could finish the sentence, the shopkeeper pushed something over the counter towards him – a bag of sweets.

"They're for you," the shopkeeper muttered, blushing. "An apology for yesterday. I can be a right miserable old git sometimes. I've had terrible back pains for years – yesterday was the worst it's ever been. But I woke up this morning and felt like a new man! Must be this weather." He heaved something else onto the counter. "And you can have that magazine you were looking at, too."

Yanni glanced at the counter – it wasn't the magazine. It was Amy's ORC'S QUEST manual, scuffed and worn from where it had been dropped on the path. Yanni had a feeling the faeries had something to do with this, too.

"Thank you!" Yanni beamed. "How much do I owe you?"

He reached into his pocket for some money, but the shopkeeper refused. "It's on the house!"

Yanni held up a pound coin and frowned. "But … but I need to give this to you."

"Why?"

Yanni opened his mouth to answer – and nothing came out.

It was the strangest thing. Five seconds ago, Yanni could have told the shopkeeper *exactly* why he had to give it to him. It was important – something to do with what had happened last night. But now, for the life of him, he couldn't remember. All his thoughts were fuzzing at the edges. Whenever he tried to put his finger on them, they slid from beneath him like wet soap.

"N-never mind," said Yanni, giving the shopkeeper a smile. "Have a nice day."

He stepped outside with the manual, still looking at the pound coin in confusion. He couldn't remember what he was supposed to do with it – he just knew that it was something important, something to do with a promise he had made.

Slowly, without really understanding what he was doing, he walked up to the nearest drain and dropped the coin between the bars. He felt better immediately – but he had no idea why. Still, it didn't matter. He had another stop to make before he went to Amy's.

The church looked nicer in the sunlight: even the graveyard was beautiful. Yanni made his way around the graves, searching until eventually he found what he was looking for. He laid down a garland of white flowers he had gathered on the way, and read the words on the memorial.

Here lies
JOHN GUSTIVER
23 June 1941 – 31 October 1953

And just beneath, as if they'd been freshly carved:

Never forgotten

Yanni swelled with happiness. It was the faeries again. They were putting the village to rights, making sure that John would never be forgotten for what he had done. But it also made Yanni feel sad, in a way he couldn't describe. Yanni would never be able to thank John for what he'd done; he would never be able to see him again, either.

And that made him think of Lari. Yanni would never see *him* again, too. It was on this spot, in another world, where he had first held Lari in his arms and learned to love him. Now he had no idea where the changeling was, or if he remembered him, or if he was even *thinking* of him…

He stopped, and looked down. Without realizing it, his left hand had wrapped around his right wrist.

And Yanni knew at once what it meant: it was a message from another world. Lari was right here beside him, and he was thinking about him, too. Yanni laughed, his eyes filling with tears once more. He opened his mouth to tell Lari that he missed him and he would never forget him and…

Nothing. All of a sudden – as if from nowhere – Yanni had completely forgotten what he was doing.

He looked around at the graveyard and the flowers … but it was no use. He couldn't remember why he'd come in here. He didn't even recognize the name on the memorial in front of him.

He shifted uneasily. This was getting really weird.

"I'd better get to Amy's," he said out loud, to no one. Then he marched down the road, feeling more and more puzzled with every step.

By the time he reached Amy's house in nearby Riddleton, the sun was high in the sky and it was so warm that he had to take off his jumper. He searched for his cousin's front door, and got a shock when he finally found it – it was blue, with gold numbers. He knocked on the door and Amy opened it, wearing a set of wizard pyjamas. She didn't recognize him at first.

"Yanni? It's … you!"

"Sleep well?"

It took Amy a long time to work out how to answer this question.

"Yes? I think? I don't know. Er … it's been a weird morning." She suddenly turned bright red. "Look, I'm sorry about last night. I didn't mean to upset you with the whole ORC'S QUEST thing. I just thought it'd be fun. If I'd known you were going to storm upstairs and not come back down again, I'd never have suggested we play it."

Yanni frowned with confusion. What was Amy talking about? She was acting like she barely knew him – as if none of their adventures last night had happened.

Then, in a single moment, he understood. Amy *had* forgotten everything. She'd remembered nothing after Yanni stormed upstairs. Everything they'd learned about each other – everything they'd been through – had been lost, just as the faeries said it would.

But then Yanni saw that it wasn't quite true. Amy had *changed* since yesterday; she wasn't the awkward, nervous girl who had first arrived at his house. She stood taller, prouder – she was confident. Her mind might have forgotten what happened in Hallow Fall, but her heart hadn't.

And besides – that meant Yanni had a second chance. A chance to put everything right.

"No – *I'm* sorry," he said. "I was a complete idiot. I can be like that sometimes." He held up her backpack and manual. "I brought your stuff back – ORC'S QUEST, too. How about we have another try tonight? You can teach me how to play properly. I thought we could run a lunchtime club at school, once term starts again."

Amy beamed. "Omigod, that'd be amazing! We could make our own plaque, with our own insignia—"

"And get some rings made," said Yanni. "And you should invite Chloe, too. I know you two haven't been talking lately, but I have a feeling she'll have changed her mind since last night. I think a lot of things have changed around here recently."

Amy shrugged. "Meh – if Chloe wants to be friends with Cecile, that's up to her. I can't help it if she—" She stopped. "Wait – how do you know about me and Chloe?"

Yanni sighed. He couldn't hide it from her any more. He *had* to tell Amy the truth – about Lorde Renwin, and their adventures in Hallow Fall, and her being turned into a raven, and the two of them almost being killed a dozen times over. Perhaps then it would all come back to her. He opened his mouth to tell her...

And nothing came out.

He frowned. It was the strangest feeling. He *had* been about to tell Amy something important – something *really* important – but all of a sudden, he couldn't remember what it was. It was all gone in an instant: the shifting sands of a dreamworld, thrown to the wind.

"Er … I'm not sure," he said. "Maybe you told me and forgot?"

Amy nodded frantically. "Yes, that must be it!"

"Of course!"

"That makes so much sense!"

"It does!"

"Glad we straightened that out!"

"Yes!" said Yanni, relieved. "Well … see you later!"

He walked away quickly, not entirely sure why he felt so strange. The answer to everything felt so close, just out of his reach – but it didn't matter. He could hear a voice at the back of his head, telling him that he and Amy had been through a lot together, more than they would ever know, and that was all that mattered. Yanni had decided to start listening to that voice a lot more now.

He walked back home in the glowing sunshine of an autumn day, and came to the dolmen, surrounded by a sea of flowers. Mum and Dad were right – Fallow Hall *was* beautiful. Yanni felt like he was suddenly aware of the beauty of the world for the very first time. He knew why it was happening: he was changing. And even though change could sometimes be frightening and sad and difficult, what came out the other side was always better for going through it. Yanni didn't feel lost any more. In fact, he felt more Yanni than he'd ever felt in his life. He didn't quite know who Yanni was yet, but he was looking forward to finding out.

He decided that he would gather some more flowers, as many as he could, and put them in his room when he got home. Then he'd help Mum and Dad play with Ari for a while, and phone Yiayia and Pappou and tell them that he loved them. Then he would head back to Amy's and the two of them would get to know one another properly for the first time. He was looking forward to that.

Yanni stepped into the field, and caught first sight of his house over the far hedge, his new home, and he found to his surprise that he'd begun to love it.

ACKNOWLEDGEMENTS

The Chime Seekers was written entirely in lockdowns. I started it in April 2020, when everyone in Britain had just been ordered to stay at home, and sent the final draft a year later in April 2021, just as the third lockdown was ending. I imagine some of the strangeness of that time has found its way into this book. Frankly, there were points where I'd have gladly crawled through a fireplace just for a change of scenery. For that reason, I'd like to start by thanking my girlfriend, Helen – Helen, I love you, and being locked up with you was absolutely brilliant.

It takes a village to write a book about a tooth-stealing faerie, and there's no way I could have done it without a team of lovely people around me. First off, I'd like to thank everyone at Walker Books – Rebecca Oram, Laurissa Jones, John Moore and everyone in between – but particular thanks must go to my editors, Megan Middleton and Denise Johnstone-Burt, for being so supportive and patient, and never once complaining about me wearing my pyjamas on Zoom. Huge thanks to David Dean for producing, once again, such a jaw-dropping cover – I'll never forget how it felt to see Gustiver for the first time!

I'm also very lucky to have a team of genius publishing types around me: massive thanks to my agent Claire Wilson, you big legend you, and to all the Juvenile Literary Society (SkunkPirates4evaaa), and to the numerous authors I know who've been so kind and made me laugh so much over the last few years. Particular thanks to Katya Balen for her constant Whatsapp support, almost dying of frostbite with me on a park bench during a blizzard, and for reading this book when it was twice as long as the Apostle Paul's Epistles.

There were lots of people who gave me their time and insight for nothing, for which I am enormously grateful. First off, Darren Chetty, who was so incredibly generous when I started piecing this book together, and who I still very much owe a coffee. Sorry, Darren, a pandemic got in the way – here's the offer repeated for posterity in full typeset. Big thanks also to Julien Godfrey, to whom this book is dedicated – thanks for being a fantastic friend to me for twenty years, and for all your tireless support, and for contributing pages of poorly translated French which were all deleted in Draft Two. You are Dungeon Master to my heart.

It was really important to me to get Yanni's Greek heritage right, and I was overwhelmed by the generous and enthusiastic support I received from so many lovely people. Thanks to: George Nianias, for solving approximately 8,745 plot points in a single two-minute conversation; Alexandra Roumbas Goldstein, for her amazingly detailed feedback; Zoe Antoniades, for her time and brilliant suggestions (read her Cally & Jimmy books – they're a hoot!); Veronica Smith; Annalise Davis; and Eleni and Efthymis Porfyridou, a mother-son feedback team. Ευχαριστώ παιδιά!

Last of all, I'd like to thank Wolf Ces, who I used to teach back when I was a teacher. About four years ago, he wrote a story in which an evil music teacher stole children and imprisoned them between the keys of a piano (his eventual punishment was, brilliantly, to continue being a teacher). It was such a fantastically creepy idea that I never forgot it – when I started writing this book, I just knew I had to include it. Thank you for agreeing to let me use it, Wolf – I have a feeling we'll be hearing more from you one day.

"An enthralling, Narnia-flavoured novel."
Guardian

When evacuee Col's childhood imaginary friends come to
life, he discovers a world where myths and legends are real.
Together with his guardians – a six-foot tiger, a badger in a
waistcoat and a miniature knight – Col must race to Blitz-
bombed London to save his sister. But soon Col is pursued
by the terrifying Midwinter King, who is determined to
bring an eternal darkness down over everything.

ROSS MONTGOMERY started writing stories as a teenager, when he should have been doing homework, and continued doing so at university. His debut novel, *Alex, the Dog and the Unopenable Door*, was nominated for the Costa Children's Book of the Year and the Branford Boase Award. It was also selected as one of the *Sunday Times'* "Top 100 Modern Children's Classics". His books have also been nominated for the CILIP Carnegie Award, while his picture book *Space Tortoise* was nominated for the Kate Greenaway Award and included in the *Guardian's* Best New Children's Books of 2018. *The Midnight Guardians*, Ross's first fiction novel with Walker Books, was selected as a Waterstones Children's Book of the Month and has garnered huge praise. He lives in London with his girlfriend and their cat, Fun Bobby.

#TheChimeSeekers
@mossmontmomery
@WalkerBooksUK